BRAINWASHED

RAMDYAL BHOLA

BALBOA.PRESS
A DIVISION OF HAY HOUSE

Balboa Press books may be ordered through booksellers or by contacting:

Balboa Press
A Division of Hay House
1663 Liberty Drive
Bloomington, IN 47403
www.balboapress.com.au
AU TFN: 1 800 844 925 (Toll Free inside Australia)
AU Local: 0283 107 086 (+61 2 8310 7086 from outside Australia)

Because of the dynamic nature of the Internet, any web addresses or links contained in this book may have changed since publication and may no longer be valid. The views expressed in this work are solely those of the author and do not necessarily reflect the views of the publisher, and the publisher hereby disclaims any responsibility for them.

The author of this book does not dispense medical advice or prescribe the use of any technique as a form of treatment for physical, emotional, or medical problems without the advice of a physician, either directly or indirectly. The intent of the author is only to offer information of a general nature to help you in your quest for emotional and spiritual well-being. In the event you use any of the information in this book for yourself, which is your constitutional right, the author and the publisher assume no responsibility for your actions.

Print information available on the last page.

ISBN: 978-1-5043-2335-2 (sc)
ISBN: 978-1-5043-2334-5 (e)

Balboa Press rev. date: 11/13/2020

I dedicate this book to my late parents, Dhanpatia and Ramnauth Bhola, and my late wife, Debra Joy Bhola, who always wanted to be a writer, but her life was cut short before she could realise that dream. Also, to my children, Nalini, Ahsha, and Ramil, and my grandchildren, Abigael, Oliver, Morrison, and Max. I hope they will find it interesting and informative.

CONTENTS

ACKNOWLEDGEMENTS

A special thanks to those friends and family members—especially my wife, Debbi—who thought my story was interesting enough and encouraged me to record it in the form of a book. Now that I am retired, I have had the time to devote to this task.

The editing, formatting, and insertion of photographs were done by Yvonne Sneddon, to whom I am grateful.

Special thanks to my son, Ramil Bhola, for his artistic creation of the front and back covers.

Thank you to all my teachers who taught and moulded me to realise my ambition, and to all the people who have been part of my life and my experiences.

Lastly, I would like to thank everyone at Balboa Press for helping to prepare my book for publication.

INTRODUCTION

Wherever I go and whenever I meet new people, they always seem curious to know where I came from, especially because I look Indian but do not have an Indian accent. They find it difficult to place my accent, as it is virtually no accent. I like to think of myself as a curious mixture of West Indian, English, and Australian, since I spent the first eighteen years of my life in Guyana, the next eleven in England, and the last forty-five in Australia.

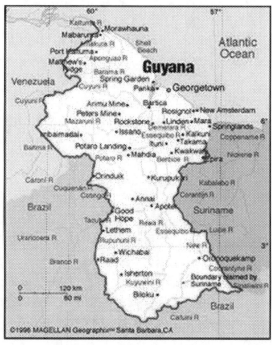

Map of Guyana

Guyana is in South America. As a former British colony, it has close ties and a common language with the British West Indian islands of Jamaica, Barbados, and Trinidad. There is free trade and a shared culture between them. It has very little to do with the other South American countries, which are all Spanish speaking—except for Brazil, where Portuguese is spoken. Cricket fans would realise this, as the West Indian team always has some Guyanese players in it. My primary and secondary schooling was in Guyana.

To attend university and especially medical school, I had to go overseas, as Guyana had no university at the time. My secondary school principal, Basil Beharry, encouraged my father to send me to London to attend college, as he thought I would have a better chance of getting the grades required for medical school if I did my advanced-level general certificate of education in the UK. He facilitated my entrance to the City of Westminster College in London, which I attended for two years and got the required grades to gain entrance to the University of Newcastle upon Tyne. There I gained my MBBS degree before going on to post-graduate education, acquiring a diploma in obstetrics and gynaecology and membership in the College of General Practitioners.

In 1975, I emigrated to Australia with my first wife (Moira) and daughter (Nalini). I have lived in South Australia ever since. I never thought my life was that interesting, but when I told friends of my experiences in the different countries I've lived in, many of them thought I should write a book. After hearing it so many times, I began to believe that maybe my life is interesting enough to be recorded, if only for my children and grandchildren.

I wish such records were kept by my forefathers, who were taken from India by the British six generations ago, in the late nineteenth century, to work in the sugar and rice plantations (more on this later). People, especially of Indian origin, always ask me where in India I came from and are always disappointed and amazed that I don't know. I regret that I don't have the answer to such questions. The truth is, I have never been told by my parents or grandparents and was never curious enough to ask them.

So, this book, although not a chronological record of my life history, may shed some light on the influences of the various cultures I have lived in and offer an explanation as to why I am the person I am. In writing it,

I tried to record instances and experiences that will not only be interesting and humorous for the reader but also demonstrate the influences of the different cultures on me as a person.

I have included many photographs to complement the prose and hope the reader finds these interesting. Where there are several people in photographs, their names are written from left to right.

CHAPTER 1

SOWING THE SEEDS

"Come hay, bai, si down and meh go teach yu fi say de alphabet and count, cause yuh gonna be a dacta."

These were the words uttered to me in Creole by Paa (my father) when I was about four years old. I was born on April 16, 1946. He was, at the time, working as a manufacturing jeweller, a trade he learnt by apprenticeship. His workshop was underneath our wooden house, which was built on stilts. He made silver and gold jewellery using raw materials mined in British Guiana, as my country was named at the time. It was the only British colony on the mainland of South America. It changed its name to Guyana when it gained independence in 1964 and later became a republic.

I had to sit down beside him as he worked, and for about two hours each day he would get me to repeat the alphabet from A to Z and to count, initially, from one to ten and later to one hundred. He progressed to teaching me small words and then sentences. I also learnt nursery rhymes and songs like "Baa Baa Black Sheep" and "Twinkle, Twinkle, Little Star."

In mathematics, I learnt to do simple addition, subtraction, multiplication, and division. Each day, he would reinforce the message that "Yuh ga fi to do dis, bai, cause one day you gonna be a dacta."

Medicine and law were the two most prestigious professions in Guyana. It was my father's dream to have a doctor and a lawyer in the family. He himself left school at age twelve, so he only had a primary school education. My mother, in fact, never went to school. They were married when he was just sixteen and she was only fourteen. This was not unusual at the time, and of course it was an arranged marriage, as was the custom among my people.

In the absence of sex education and contraception, they started having a family, and in fact had a total of eleven pregnancies, with nine surviving children. I was number eight in this line-up. There were six daughters and three sons. Large families were the order of the day.

Because we were a relatively poor family, my older sisters left school early to help with chores and look after the younger siblings. My father selected my eldest brother to be the lawyer and me to be the doctor. He named me Ramdyal after the district doctor at the time. I was lucky to be lower down the order, as he became better off financially as time went on and could afford to educate me. Only boys were educated, as girls were expected to learn to be good wives and cooks so they could marry well and be looked after by their husbands.

We had to leave home to attend high school. My eldest brother went to the capital, Georgetown, and lived with a family friend. He absolutely hated it and soon refused to go back. He changed direction and became a primary school teacher by apprenticeship in our village school.

One day when I was around five years old, I was ill with a cough and fever, so my mother put a white flag in a bottle and placed it by the roadside. This was a signal to the district doctor, Dr. Ramdyal, to call in as he did his twice-weekly trips along the country road in his black Humber car. His chauffeur doubled as his dispenser. In the boot was a supply of medications.

The doctor asked me what was my name, and I replied, "Dr. Ramdyal."
He said, "No, that's my name. What's yours?"
I repeated with all seriousness, "Dr. Ramdyal."
He smiled and said he hoped one day I would realise that dream.
News of this went around the village, and everywhere I went, people would ask me "What's your name?" just to hear me say "Dr. Ramdyal," and then they would laugh. To them it was amusing, but I was deadly serious.

Paa—Ramnauth Bhola

I started primary school at age six and was soon promoted to grade two, as I had already covered grade one's work with my paa. I was a conscientious student, always striving for the top marks and invariably succeeding. I was particularly proud to present my end-of-term reports to my dad, as he would say, "Well done, bai, yu now one step closa to be a dacta." I skipped one more grade and was in the same class as my older sister, much to her disgust.

Whenever Paa had friends over for food and rum, of which he drank copious amounts, he would call me over and proudly announce to them that "dis a me son—he topped his class again and gonna be a dacta, you know." This did not embarrass me; it made me feel good. I always wanted him to be proud of me.

One day, Paa returned from one of his regular trips to New Amsterdam, the capital of our county of Berbice, carrying a pink sheet of paper in his hand. He had given up being a manufacturing jeweller by then and was running a taxi service along the single coast road to and from the city of

New Amsterdam. He waved the pink paper at me and said, "Meh now gat permit fi you to be a dacta from de govment." He then filed it on his punch file, as was his custom, along with other important documents.

I, of course, believed him and was very happy and encouraged by it. I later found out that the pink paper was only a car insurance certificate. It was his way of providing more encouragement to me.

At age twelve (1958), I, too, had to leave my parents' home. I went to live with an older married sister whose house was about two kilometres from Berbice High School, where I was to spend the next five years. I continued to study hard and was always top of the class. Whenever I presented my report to Paa, he would not only praise me but would boast to his rum buddies, "Ramdy [as the family called me] top de class again. He is gonna be a dacta, you know." This kept my interest alive and made me feel good. It spurred me on to work hard at my studies, and there was no doubt in my mind that I would achieve that dream in time. I never ever wanted to be anything else, and as time went on, others began to believe in my dream.

I named this book *Brainwashed* because my father did such a good job of convincing me, virtually from birth, to be a doctor, and I never ever wavered from this goal. Many students have difficulty deciding what vocation to follow, considering the wide choices available. I was fortunate not to have this problem.

CHAPTER 2

VILLAGE LIFE

Guyana (formerly British Guiana) is situated between two and eight degrees north of the equator, so the climate is tropical. It is on the mainland of South America bordered by Surinam on the east, the Atlantic Ocean on the north, Venezuela on the west, and Brazil on the south. It has three counties: Berbice, Demerara, and the largest, Essequibo. The main rivers are Corentyne, Berbice, Demerara, and Essequibo, which are all very large, with wide mouths opening to the Atlantic Ocean. Ferries are required to cross these rivers. There are also creeks that are larger than the main rivers in many countries of the world. These are named Canje, Abary, Mahaicony, and Mahaica.

When I lived there, the main industries were sugar, rice, bauxite, hardwoods like greenheart, and some gold and diamond deposits. The population was about 750,000. Now there are as many Guyanese outside the country as there are in the country. At the time, the population consisted of native Amerindians (5 per cent), Indians (50 per cent), Africans (30 per cent), Chinese (5 per cent), Europeans (2 per cent), and people of mixed races.

The Africans had been taken from West Africa as slaves. After the abolition of slavery in 1834, they were no longer keen to work in the plantations and sought government jobs. The British had to find people to work in the rice and sugar plantations, so they took the Chinese there in 1834. They found it too hot and humid, so they became merchants and opened Chinese laundries and restaurants. Some Portuguese arrived in 1835. The British scratched their heads and thought, *What shall we do now?*

In 1938, they decided to take Indians from India, most of whom had no idea they would never see India again. I met one man who said he was playing on the beach when he was twelve years old. He was approached by some British sailors who enticed him aboard their ship for a joyride, promising to bring him back ashore. That was the last he saw of India and his family. This is an example of a stolen generation.

Most of the Indians, however, went voluntarily to seek a better life and to earn a decent living. Many were indentured labourers on five-year contracts who expected to return to India later, but most never did. They and their children had numbers tattooed on their forearms. The first *Jahaj* (Hindi word for *ship*) with these indentured labourers was called *Hesperus*. The Indians proved to be very successful at farming and are still the main farmers today.

The main religions in Guyana are Hinduism and all denominations of Christianity. There are a small number of Muslims and other religious groups. When I was growing up, many of the schools were run by the Christian churches, so children were mainly exposed to Christianity and not as much to the other religions.

The capital, Georgetown, is situated at the mouth of the Demerara River, and the second largest city is New Amsterdam, situated at the mouth of the Berbice River. When I was growing up, most of the population lived in the cities and in villages along the coast. A single road wound its way along the coast through tropical vegetation, and the houses were built on both sides of it. They were generally made of wood and built on stilts to allow for ventilation and avoid flooding, as most of this land was at or below sea level. Further inland was the swampy zone and beyond that the mountainous zone. I was told that St. George's Cathedral was the largest free-standing wooden building in the Southern Hemisphere.

Landmark buildings in Georgetown, Guyana

Strict Discipline

The tide was coming in. I was about six years old. It was quite exciting for my friends and me to see the muddy water rising in the trenches that led from the sea, about a kilometre away, past the mangrove bushes. The terrain was flat and was at or just above sea level. The water overflowed the banks of the trenches and covered the salt bushes behind the houses. It even filled the trenches along the road and accumulated in low-lying areas between the houses, most of which had access bridges over the trenches. Some of these were made from the trunks of coconut trees.

This was too good an opportunity to miss. My friends and I decided to go bathing in the muddy waters in the main trench. Our feet sank in the mud up to our knees, yet this did not keep us from having fun. After several hours of swimming, I decided it was time to go home, covered from head to toe in muddy water. There I was greeted by Paa, who asked me where I had been.

When I told him, he got a pair of *chimtas* (tongs) from his workshop and whacked me on the legs several times, hard enough to leave wheals, as he warned me, "Don't let me catch you doing that again. It's dangerous." This was only one of two times in my life that my father disciplined me using violence.

The second time, when I was eight, my friends and I were about a kilometre from home climbing small coconut trees and picking green coconuts for drinking. As I looked ahead along the path, I noticed Paa in the distance on his way home after working in the rice fields. I hoped he hadn't noticed me, as I knew that if he did, I would be in serious trouble. I hid behind some bushes keeping very quiet.

As he arrived where he thought he had spotted me, he called my name. When I did not answer, he walked on, saying, "You have to come home sometime."

After several hours, I decided to return home around dinner time, hoping that he would have forgotten by then. No such luck. He got his leather belt and whacked me with it on the buttocks several times, as he warned me, "Don't let me catch you so far away from home again."

Both these punishments I thought were grossly unfair, as I was expected to go with my slightly older siblings to catch crabs, fish, and shrimps for dinner—dragging a small seine while neck deep in the muddy waters in those same trenches. Also, it was quite acceptable for me to bathe in the freshwater portion of those same trenches, which were infested with small alligators, before going to school. It was a lot of fun swinging from the coconut branches and dropping into the water. Besides, I was often sent by my mother to collect dried coconuts that had fallen from those same trees where my father caught me. She used them to make coconut oil.

Maa—Dhanpatia (Elsie) Bhola

Interestingly, my mother and grandmother never ever chastised or punished me in any way. My mother was a gentle soul who hardly raised her voice. Even though she was illiterate, she could count money accurately, and one had no chance of cheating her.

Storytelling

A favourite evening pastime of myself, my siblings, and the neighbour children was to gather around my nani (my mother's mother), who, despite then being in her late fifties, always seemed so much older. She had been living with us since before I was born, after she lost her husband.

After dusk, as there was no electricity, we relied on kerosene lamps or moonlight to provide some light. Nani would sit in her hammock slung between two posts under the house, and we all sat on empty rice bags spread around her as she told us stories. We called these *nancies*. We didn't care that the same stories were repeated several nights each week. We never seemed to get tired of them. Some even involved singing, and we always joined in the choruses.

It was especially thrilling to hear her ghost stories when we would all try to get as close to her as we could. After hearing such stories, we were afraid of the dark. We were each allowed to request our favourite stories in turn. She loved it when I told her stories I read in books, like "Jason and the Argonauts" from Greek mythology. She would remember these and then add them to her repertoire. On evenings when we did not have storytelling, we would play hide and seek, skipping, hopscotch, or rounders.

My Nani—Latchmin

A Visit to the Doctor

My nani was a diabetic who had diabetic peripheral neuropathy (as I now realise). She had no feeling in her feet. She had a chronic diabetic ulcer under the ball of her right big toe, which was missing due to gangrene. She cleaned the ulcer with Dettol and redressed it daily.

To control her sugar, she had no medications, but avoided sugar in her tea and drank the juice obtained by boiling leaves from the neem tree, which was quite bitter. She also ate fried karela or bitter melon, which I now know is helpful in lowering blood sugar and is currently recommended by Ayurvedic practitioners, usually in combination with Diabecon (Gymnema Sylvestre).

The lack of sensation in her feet was so absolute that when she was asleep at night, rats would feed on the dead skin on her feet, and she would not know about it until she noticed blood on the sheets the next morning. This rat attack was witnessed on a few occasions. It made control of her ulcer more difficult.

One day, because the ulcer was getting bigger and obviously not showing any signs of healing, she asked me to accompany her to see a doctor in New Amsterdam, thirty-two miles away, a journey that took about three hours by bus. I was about seven years old at the time. The reason the journey was so slow was because people could stop the bus anywhere along the road. They could carry with them any cargo—for example, baskets of provisions for the market, bits of firewood, and bags of rice, apart from suitcases and handbags.

There was a cargo cage on top of the roof, which was accessed by climbing a fixed ladder at the back of the bus. These buses were built by local carpenters on truck chassis. They only ran every three hours or so, negotiating their way along the narrow road, taking care to avoid wandering cows, donkeys, goats, pigs, ducks, chickens, and the odd drunk. They had to be watchful of the people drying their rice and copra on part of the road. Of course, there were no fences to keep animals off the road.

On arriving in New Amsterdam, we walked several blocks to Dr. Searwar's office and sat at the end of the queue on the benches along the walls of the waiting room. The room had no character, just stark light blue walls. There were no posters, notices, or magazines, and people just stared at each other.

Drying rice on the main road

No appointments were offered or made to see the doctor. You simply took a seat and shuffled along the bench in an orderly fashion as each patient was called into the doctor's consulting room. After what seemed like an eternity (about three hours), it was our turn to be seen. Nani got up to go into the consulting room, and so did I. The doctor asked if I wanted to wait outside, to which I promptly replied, "No, I am going to be a doctor," and so I was allowed in. No way was I going to miss this opportunity to see exactly what a doctor did.

After establishing that Nani was worried about the ulcer on her foot, he asked her to lie on the couch and proceeded to debride the ulcer, cutting off chunks of dead skin with his scalpel. He did not use any local anaesthetic. Of course, this was understandable, as she had no feeling. It was certainly fascinating to a wide-eyed seven-year-old would-be doctor.

He then dressed the wound, presumably with antibiotic powder and a gauze dressing. Nani then asked the doctor how much she had to pay, to which he replied, "How much can you afford?"

She said, "Not much," and gave him thirty Guyanese dollars. He seemed happy with that. All doctors practiced like that and charged patients whatever they could afford. Those who did not have any money paid the doctor in kind—say, by giving him some eggs, a few pounds of rice, a chook, or some vegetables.

People generally expected to be treated and cured at their first visit to the doctor. They often travelled from afar and did not expect to have to return. Consequently, doctors usually dispensed their own drugs and would give enough to hopefully cure the condition, and they often used single injections of long-acting antibiotics. I had personal experience of that on one occasion and did not appreciate it. Patients felt if they were given an injection they were treated properly—a bit like France, where suppositories were regarded as superior to tablets.

The Coconut Tree

The coconut tree was perhaps the most useful tree to the locals. The trunks of the felled trees were used to make bridges over the trenches. The kids used the trunk of the live trees as cricket wickets. The branches were used to thatch the roofs of houses, and for craftwork—for example, weaving baskets, fans, and hats. The vanes of the leaves were also used to make brooms. The green coconuts provided a refreshing drink and soft jelly to eat. Kids used the very young coconuts as cricket balls and sawn-off branches as cricket bats or wickets. Proper bats and balls were not readily available or affordable, but this did not stop kids from improvising and enjoying the national game.

The dried coconuts were the most versatile, providing very sweet water for drinking and a kernel that was used to make coconut oil, soap, confectionery, cosmetics, and as a cooking ingredient in various dishes. Coconut oil was used for cooking, as massage oil, and as lubrication for machinery and hinges. Some even used it as hair oil and as a sex lubricant.

The shell was used to make buttons and other souvenirs, as well as fuel for cooking. The husk was used to make a smoky fire to ward off mosquitoes, especially at dusk, when they were most prevalent. The fibre from the husks was also used to stuff pillows and mattresses, as well as to keep potted soil from drying out. I became quite skilled at all these activities.

The coconuts were usually gathered by climbing the trees or using a bamboo, to which was attached a curved grass knife. If a coconut tree was too tall, two bamboos were joined end to end to reach the coconuts. Dried coconuts sometimes fell off the trees and could be gathered on the ground. I could dislodge dried coconuts from the trees by hurling a piece of wood at the bunch.

As a child, I could climb coconut trees of moderate height, but I lost this skill after spending years in England and later Australia. I remember one time while helping my mother to gather coconuts, we couldn't find many but noticed that one very tall tree had four bunches of dried coconuts. Of course, this was so because no one could reach them, and the tree was too tall for bamboo rods. So, trying to be a hero, I decided to climb the tree. I got halfway up and the tree started swaying in the breeze. I panicked, and my legs went to jelly. They started shaking uncontrollably. I humbly accepted defeat and came down empty-handed.

When I took my wife, Debbi, to Guyana in 1986, she did not believe I used to be able to climb coconut trees—so while she was in my mother's house, I went into the backyard and picked some water coconuts for her. When I showed them to her, she was annoyed that I did not call her to take some photographs of me climbing the coconut tree. She calmed down when she realised that the tree in question was only eight feet tall, and I did not have to climb it to pick the coconuts!

A typical coconut tree plantation

Fishing

Fishing to provide food for the family was another activity children were expected to do. Apart from crabbing and using a seine to trawl the trenches and ponds, we also used a cast-net (a net with lead weights attached to its perimeter and a drawstring) to trap fishes under it when it was cast in a trench or pond. I recall getting up at four in the morning to travel nine miles to the beach with my mother and friends to catch shrimps by trawling a seine on the ocean floor. We caught more shrimps in ten minutes than we needed.

My nani had a homemade fishing rod made from bamboo, a string, and a cork from a wine bottle as the floater. With this she would go fishing, after getting me to gather some earthworms from the garden as bait. She chopped these up in small pieces to thread onto her hook.

Family and friends fishing with a seine

I accompanied her, carrying a can for the catch. We would walk a long way looking for suitable ponds that might have fish in them. I walked barefooted, as we had no shoes as children, but Nani had a pair of yachting shoes with the toes of the right one cut out to avoid pressure on her diabetic ulcer.

Hassa is an interesting freshwater fish that is regarded as a delicacy by the Guyanese. I can recall two interesting reactions to this fish, which has horny scales. The first was an English soldier who reported that he was given two curried baby crocodiles for dinner, and the second was in a letter written by my wife, Debbi, to her friends in Australia, in which she said she was given a fish that was like an armadillo. This fish has a coat of armour instead of a skin. The flesh is a light pink and sweet.

The fish lives in what looks like a bird's nest floating on the water. To catch it, one must approach the nest quietly and, with hands positioned as if catching a cricket ball, create small ripples. This is interpreted as the presence of a small fish, and as the hassa comes out to investigate, it is grabbed. After that, the roe is harvested, and this fried is better than caviar. Any fish that was excess to the family's needs could be sold or given to the neighbours.

Later, in Australia, I bought some salad servers in Tasmania that were called *hassa hands*. They were made of Huon pine, a rare and expensive wood found in Tasmania. The servers when used are held like we held our hands to catch this fish. I suspect this fish gave the servers their name.

Hassa fish

Childhood Chores

Children were expected to do chores, especially after school, at weekends, and during school holidays. This included fetching drinking water by buckets from an artesian well five hundred metres from home and filling an empty oil drum, which was cleaned and coated with tar to prevent rusting. We had no running water so relied on rainwater and water from this well. Of course, that meant no flushable toilets or inside showers with hot and cold running water. We had to use long-drop latrines positioned in the backyard. Bathing was done in a bathroom enclosure using a bucket of water and a pail. Also, there was no toilet paper, so one had to wash oneself after doing number two, again using a bucket and pail.

A long-drop latrine

There was no electricity or gas, so lighting was by kerosene lamps, and cooking was done on a clay fireside using dried wood, which we gathered from wooded areas a kilometre from home. We tied the wood in bundles and carried these on our heads. Because of the lack of lighting, most activities were done between dawn and dusk. People got up early, having been awakened by donkeys braying or roosters crowing at around four in the morning. It was not unusual to hear Indian music blaring from the radio as early as five o'clock as housewives cooked roti and dal for breakfast. Most people were in bed by nine at night.

One of my sisters' jobs was to sweep under the house (which was on stilts) and the yards using brooms made from the vanes of coconut branches. The dirt was clay, which set like concrete, and my sisters kept the surface refreshed weekly by using a slurry of clay mixed with cow down (daub). I quite liked helping with this task. It was like playing with mud and somewhat therapeutic.

One of my chores was to cultivate, plant, and water the vegetable patch in the backyard. I grew tomatoes, okras, eggplants, snake, and same beans and shallots. I also accompanied my mother to gather coconuts to make oil for cooking. We fetched the coconuts in bags on our heads. If we had too many, we borrowed the neighbour's donkey and cart to fetch them.

We first removed the kernel from the coconuts using a special tool called a grater, then washed the grated kernels or pulp with water, releasing the milk. After straining the pulp, the liquid was then boiled in large wok-like cast iron pots called *karahis* until the water evaporated, leaving an oily residue. This was allowed to cool and then strained to provide pure coconut oil. This was then bottled for future use.

We were expected to help with rice cultivation. I became adept at growing rice either by sowing the seeds in dry ploughed fields or by transplanting young shoots from nurseries to the fields, which were covered by water. During the growing period, we made sure there was enough water in the fields by directing it from nearby irrigation trenches. We also removed any weeds.

When the paddy was ripe, the water was drained, and the fields were allowed to dry out. At harvest time, we cut the paddy by hand using a curved grass knife and packed it in bundles, which were then transported by cart and oxen or tractors. These bundles were scattered around a central post around which the oxen were tied. They went around and around trampling the paddy to separate the grains from the straw. The straw was then removed with a pitchfork and the paddy bagged.

My task was to sit on a seat at the top of the central pole and, with a whip in hand, drive the oxen around the pole. My sister used to cut rice for other people for a fee and would take me to help her bundle it. I was paid pocket money for my effort, as much as fifty Guyanese cents per day, equivalent to twenty Australian cents at the time.

A typical rice field during growing season

A typical rice field ready for harvest

When it was time to make a chicken curry, my mother would ask me to go and catch a fowl from the backyard pen and kill it. I could catch the fowl but could not bring myself to cut its head off with a knife. I would get my friend Kenneth from next door to do the honours, as he liked doing it. He took great pleasure in cutting the head off and then letting go of the fowl; the body would run around aimlessly until it bled to death. My sister was scared of the headless fowl and thought it was chasing her, so she would run and hide, much to everyone's amusement.

Folklore

Like many older cultures, especially in underdeveloped countries, Guyana had its fair share of folklore, and as children we were brought up to believe in these tales. Many symptoms, like tummy aches, headaches, and depression, were attributed to possession by evil spirits, so the sufferer was taken to the local *pandit* (Hindu priest) to ceremoniously drive out such spirits. The patient invariably improved, which I now suspect was due to faith healing or the passage of time.

Another belief was that someone—because of spite, jealousy, or as payback—could cast a spell on you or look at you with "bad eye" and make you ill. This was a bit like "pointing the bone" in Aboriginal society. This too required a holy person's intervention for treatment. Some believe this could be prevented by placing a red or black dot on the forehead, using a paint called Sindoor, which was sold in small tins like shoe polish.

During a visit to Guyana in 1986, my mother was concerned about a bad eye being cast on my eleven-month-old son because he was a fair-skinned, chubby, good-looking healthy baby. She promptly placed a black dot on his forehead before we could show him to the villagers.

Old wrinkly ladies were feared by children because they might be an *ol Higue* or a *fire-rass* who could hurt you. An ol Higue after dark could peel off her skin and suck your blood, somewhat like a vampire, leaving you weak and exhausted. A fire-rass, on the other hand, was also active at night, and could hurt you by blowing fire from her mouth.

There were a couple of old neighbours in the village who fit the bill as far as I was concerned, and whenever I saw them, even in broad daylight, I would cross to the other side of the road, leaving adequate distance between them and me. My older sister took delight in hearing me scream by pretending to be one of these ladies, as she opened her mouth wide and threatened to eat me. I would have been about three or four years old at the time.

One dark night at about eleven thirty, my older brother and I were walking home from our rice factory after being relieved from security duties by our parents. This was a frequent occurrence, as my father used to take bags of rice to sell to the Rice Marketing Board in Springlands with his truck during the day. Because of his habit of stopping at every rum shop on the way back home, he seldom returned before eleven o'clock at night, often drunk.

That night, on our way home, we noticed a flashing light in the distance in the coconut grove and immediately assumed it was a fire-rass. We were both so scared that we ran home so fast that I think Cathy Freeman (four-hundred-metre Olympic gold medallist) would have had a hard time keeping up with us. In retrospect, I now think it was someone with a gas lamp looking for fallen coconuts, and the light effect was created as that individual walked past the tree trunks.

Jumbies was the name given to spirits of the dead. We feared the dark because they were thought to lurk in dark places and would hurt us. We always wanted someone, preferably an adult, to accompany us when going into the dark.

Customs and Ceremonies

Whereas most of the people of African descent were Christians, the Indians were predominantly Hindus. There was practically no integration between the two races and certainly no intermarriage. The Hindu customs and beliefs were taken from India and kept largely preserved and unchanged to this day, even though my Indian friends tell me that things have changed in India at a very rapid pace over the years.

The Indian dishes were North Indian in style, and most of the meals, whether breakfast, lunch, or dinner, were various forms of curries. These were freshly cooked every day, as we had no refrigeration. Cooking was the responsibility of the mothers and daughters. Home-grown vegetables and self-caught fish were mainly used and were either fried with onions, garlic, chillies, spices, and coconut oil, or curried with enough sauce to go with rice.

Dal was always available and a good filler, especially when a large family had to be fed (in the absence of contraception, it was common for couples to have six to ten children). Chicken and lamb or goat were reserved for special occasions. Beef or pork were generally not used by the Indians because the cow was sacred, and pigs were reared and consumed by only the lower castes.

Root vegetables (cassava, sweet potatoes and eddoes), breadfruit, and plantains were also available and popular. These were boiled and then fried with chillies and onions like *gado* in South East Asia. A coconut soup (*metagee*) was made utilising these vegetables plus or minus meats, fish, or crabs. I suspect this was more of an African dish and was adopted by the Indians. Some other African dishes were garlic pork (pork cooked with garlic, vinegar, and black pepper), *souce* (a cold dish made with pork steeped in lime juice and layers of cucumber, tomatoes, and onions), *akee* (a vegetable) with salted fish, and pepperpot (meat in a cassava extract called *casreep*).

It is a shame that our forefathers did not try very hard to preserve and promote the Indian customs or language with us. English was taught in schools, but Hindi was not taught or spoken at home. We spoke Creole, which is a dialect of the English language, somewhat similar to pidgin English. It is only a spoken and not a written language.

The Hindu religious ceremonies (jandhi, pooja, and jag), prayers, and marriage ceremonies were conducted by the pandits in Hindi and were not well explained to or understood by us. Thus we lost not only interest but also the ability to speak or write Hindi. One evening, I accompanied my sister to Hindi classes at the temple, and the teacher, not appreciating that it was my first night there, asked me to say the Hindi alphabet. When I couldn't, he gave me several lashes on my palms. That was the end of my Hindi lessons.

As children, we went along to religious ceremonies because our parents expected it but were bored, especially with the jags, which can go on for three to seven days. The pandit read from the Bhagavad Gita and the Ramayana and tried to explain the lessons to be learnt from the stories contained in those religious books. We the children were more interested in, and looked forward to, the food and Indian sweets after the ceremonies.

Indian weddings were always enjoyable. We as children loved all the food and to have lots of relatives around. The match was generally arranged between the parents, taking into consideration the family's standing in society and the candidate's character, prospects, looks, and education. It was not unusual for the prospective bride and groom to have only seen each other once or twice before the wedding. Such weddings were generally arranged after puberty, from age fourteen onwards, when children started to have sexual feelings. Parenthood followed soon after.

I had sisters-in-law who were fourteen and sixteen years old. My mother married my father when she was fourteen and he was sixteen. All my siblings had arranged marriages. I was not only the exception but also the only one who got divorced! The situation has now changed in that even though parents can make suggestions, children have the final say in whom they marry and when.

The wedding ceremony usually took place at the girl's house on Sunday, but close family would gather for a week or two beforehand at both parents' houses. Everyone in the village would be invited by word of mouth. The celebrations started on Friday night with a religious ceremony followed by music, eating, and dancing. This night is referred to as the *matikore*. The highlight was music by tassa drums.

On Saturday, there was another religious ceremony, followed by music and dancing, and the food preparations were started. The men generally did the cooking in large cast iron pots suspended over firepits in the ground, while the women helped with the preparations, such as peeling potatoes and pumpkins and rolling puri rotis for deep frying. Meanwhile the prospective bride and groom were rubbed down with a turmeric paste to make the skin fairer.

The wedding ceremony on Sunday was followed by a feast, which was normally vegetarian and served on lotus or banana leaves. People ate by hand (no cutlery available), and the leaves were buried in the ground afterwards (no washing up and environmentally friendly).

On Sunday morning, the groom and his male companions travelled to the bride's house for the wedding ceremony and celebrations, after which she accompanied the groom back to his parents' house. They spent the night together, and the marriage was expected to be consummated. I am told that it was customary for the aunties to inspect the bedsheets for evidence of consummation the next morning.

On Monday, after bathing and a small ceremony, the bride returned to her parents, where she stayed for a few weeks before returning to her husband. Meat was consumed on this day.

Cooking for the masses in large iron pots over firepits

Ramdyal Bhola

Childhood Entertainment

With no televisions, computers, iPads, phones, board games, Legos, or plastic toys, we had to improvise and make our own entertainment. There was an AM/FM radio, but that was used for the news, death notices, and Indian music. We had no swimming pools, basketball or netball courts, gymnasiums, or volleyball or tennis courts. There was a cricket ground, but we had no bats or balls. Only the adult team had cricket gear. We played cricket, using bats made from pieces of wood or coconut branches, and for balls we used rocks and small coconuts. Occasionally we were given a bumper ball.

We also played rounders using a bumper ball. We created marbles using rocks or seeds that we smoothed out by rubbing them on concrete. Hopscotch and skipping rope were also popular. We made spinning tops from palm seeds, and slingshots or catapults from wood and the rubber from old inner tyre tubes.

Making kites at Easter time was also a popular activity. This skill was demonstrated to my children later in Australia, who laughed at me when I said I would make a much better kite for them than the one they had bought in the shop. They were quite impressed when my large homemade kite not only flew but sang in the air. My son still remembers being impressed when my sister added an extra piece of cloth to the tail of my kite to stop it spinning around and around.

Apart from sports and helping with chores, we swam in alligator-infested trenches and went in search of fruits to eat on trees belonging to anyone. Popular fruits were mangoes, bananas, guavas, guineps, byres, pomegranates, coconuts, sapodillas, jamoons, and paw paws. We often raided fruit trees at nights. Fruits were our snack when we got hungry, as there were no biscuits or other snacks in the cupboards to be had in between meals. If we did not like the meal that was prepared, we went without.

We often covered many miles during the day. We walked barefooted, as we had no shoes. I had my first pair of yachting shoes to play school cricket when I was eight and my first pair of black leather shoes at age eleven, to go on a school trip to see Princess Margaret in the city of Georgetown. That was my first trip to the city. We gathered on the boundary line of Bourda cricket ground and watched her as she travelled around the ground in an open-top vehicle. Later, we were taken to the botanic gardens. My second school trip to the city later was to see the epic film *Ben Hur*, starring Charlton Heston.

24

Boys did not wear underpants until adolescence and were not given long pants until about age sixteen. The short pants and long trousers were mostly made to measure by local tailors using khaki material. Being tropical, there was no need for long-sleeved shirts, so we wore mostly locally tailored short-sleeved cotton shirts. Kids generally had no more than about five outfits.

Our hair was cut by one of the neighbours. Brylcreem or coconut oil was applied daily after washing, depending on whether one needed to have a wave in the front or not. I always had a wave, as I wanted to look like Elvis Presley.

My Father: A Self-Made Man

I had a lot of admiration for my father, who was a very hard-working self-made man. He was ambitious and always looked for ways of improving his situation to provide adequately for his family. He started out in life no better than his fellow villagers, but with his hard work and entrepreneurship, we eventually became perhaps the most well-to-do family in the village. He always set himself an agenda that most people would consider impossible, but he never failed to complete it.

When at age sixteen he married my mother, he was working as a woodcutter—gathering dried wood from the nearby swamp and transporting it sixteen miles by donkey-drawn cart to sell to a rice factory for a few dollars. The wood was used to fire their boilers to produce steam for parboiled rice. I am told he also used to cut sugar cane for a wage, using a cutlass or machete at a sugar cane plantation sixteen miles from our village.

By the time I came along, he had learnt a trade and become a manufacturing jeweller. He did some really intricate work with basic tools using gold and silver produced in Guyana. He made custom jewellery but also spec jewellery, which he sold to people in neighbouring villages. He made jewellery for my mother, some of which was later given to my wife, Debbi, and is still in my daughter Ahsha's possession. This trade earned him the nickname of "goldsmith," by which he was known by many for a long time.

His own mother died after having four boys long before I was born, and my grandfather later married another lady who became a grandmother to us as we were growing up. My nani (mother's mother) also lost her partner before I was born, and she moved in to live with us. Three of my grandparents were already dead when I came along. My paternal grandfather and his new lady proceeded to have three more sons and a daughter. All these uncles and aunt were close to us and treated us very well.

**Our family home in Number 47 Village (above)
and our village road (below)**

It was customary for married children to live with parents and other siblings in the same house until they could afford a house of their own, which might be years later. My father, however, was impatient and found a way to buy the family home and help his siblings move out. This all occurred long before I was born.

My parents eventually had nine children, me being number eight. We were all born at home with an attending midwife. In fact, after marriage, my sisters also came to the family home to have their children. I have vivid memories of when my younger sister was born. I was six years old, and no one told me I was going to have another brother or sister. I did not notice anything different about my mother, as I was accustomed to women wearing loose clothing.

One day, I noticed the midwife had arrived, and soon after that there was the sound of a baby crying upstairs. That was the arrival of my younger sister, the last in our family of nine—six girls and three boys.

My father then gave up his trade and bought a motor car, which he used to provide a taxi service carrying passengers between the villages and to the cities. It was customary to fetch as many passengers as one could fit in the car, some sitting on others' laps. Seat belts were never heard of in those days. and for air conditioning, the windows were left open. This occupation probably was more lucrative than making jewellery, so he went through several cars over many years.

We were not given pocket money, and if we wanted a few cents to buy lollies, we had to ask. I quickly worked out a way of getting money from my dad, by approaching him when he was in a hurry. He would stop to grab something to eat while his passengers waited in his car, on his way to the city. I would lie to him, saying I need money to buy slate pencils, but I would use it to buy lollies instead. He was too much in a hurry to question why I needed new pencils every few days!

His next venture was to open a rum shop, providing a venue for the men in the village to gather and drink rum. He befriended Mr. Da Costa, an older experienced rum shop owner, whose wife was the district postmistress. He learnt to blend his own brand of rum using high wine (90 to 100 proof) and marinated fruits. This way, he could offer a good rum cheaper and still make a good profit. It was fascinating for me to see him using a hydrometer to check the specific gravity of his brew, bearing in mind he left school at the age of twelve years.

One day coming back from school, I noticed a large tank in our front yard and a large hole being dug next to it. My father was at it again. His plans were never communicated to us children, and we only found out what he was up to at the same time as the other villagers. He was having a Texaco petrol station built. This was eventually completed, and we children took turns with our mother to man the station and sell oil and petrol, plus accessories. We had to manually pump the petrol into the tanks of the cars and trucks, as the pumps were not electrically operated. I even learnt to fix punctured tyres and vulcanise (seal) holes in the inner tubes.

Not content with his achievements so far, or the rate of progress, he decided to borrow from others and take money from my brother (by then a teacher) to build a rice factory to convert paddy to rice for the local farmers for a fee. He even provided transport by his truck and storage for the farmers' paddy, making sure they used his factory.

He did a lot of the work himself assisted by my mother, volunteering friends, and us kids. I learnt how to make concrete using bricks (kilned by my father), sand from the beach, and cement. We created vast expanses of concrete on which the boiled paddy was dried to make parboiled rice. He installed many of the machines he needed himself.

Spreading rice to dry on concrete slabs

Our rice factory with rice mounds under cover on the concrete slab we laid

He often had aching, tired muscles, and sometimes at the end of the day he would get me to walk all over his back, with him lying face down. This was supposed to provide deep-tissue massage. It took a lot of effort to maintain my balance, since I was only about eight years old.

At about age twelve, I decided to attempt to drive our Kramer tractor, which was parked on the grounds of the rice mill. It did not require an ignition key. I just jumped on board and started it. As I put it into gear, it started to move. I panicked and did not know how to stop it. I could not steer it properly, so it ended up in a ditch, where the tractor stalled and the engine stopped. The next morning, my father was cross and wondered who did that. I kept very quiet and have never owned up to it until now.

My father was a generous man to his friends and relatives, and he was well respected by all. His one fault was that he liked his rum too much and often came home drunk late at nights. He could become argumentative and belligerent when under the influence. He was a strong strapping man, and I saw him get the better of three or four opponents. Once he was going up the stairs to his room in a hotel in Georgetown when he was accosted by five knife-wielding young pickpocket. He smashed the first two and threw the third against the fourth, knocking them both to the floor. On seeing that, the fifth one fled!

Unfortunately, his lifestyle probably caught up with him, and he developed heart failure, maybe due to alcoholic cardiomyopathy. He passed away when he was fifty-four years old. At the time, I was in my second year of medicine at the University of Newcastle upon Tyne in the UK. I was not told of his death immediately and only learnt about it through a letter sent to me by a sister three months later, in which she said, "I am wondering how you are coping, now that we have lost our father." That was news to me.

I collected my mail at the hall of residence and was reading this letter on the bus one Saturday morning on my way to do some extra studies in the anatomy lab at the medical school. The family had made the decision not to tell me earlier, fearing that it might affect my studies. I didn't understand that, as I had to know sometime, and I still had four years to go in my medical course. I couldn't concentrate on my studies, so with tears in my eyes, I took the next bus home. The only person I told was my Sierra Leonean friend Llewelyn Jarrett, who went out and bought me a sympathy card. A few weeks later, it was my twenty-first birthday, and again, the only person who knew was Llewelyn. He bought me my only gift, a shirt.

My father's will is worth mentioning at this stage. Boys were expected to look after their wives, whereas girls were expected to marry well and be looked after by their husbands. Under this system, boys inherited the parents' assets, and girls missed out. My second brother was a liability to my father, and instead of helping him, this brother stole from him and fought with him. He too drank too much rum, which was his undoing in the end. My father left nothing to him and only one hundred dollars to each sister—except the youngest sister, who was still at home.

The house and some land were left to my eldest brother, as his money helped my father built his assets. The rest of the estate—consisting of the rice factory, house blocks, rice fields, and coconut plantations—were left equally to my eldest brother, mother, youngest sister, and myself. I was also given a block of land along the road on which I was expected to put a branch medical practice to look after the villagers once I returned home as a qualified doctor.

My second brother was very unhappy about the terms of the will, so he started fighting with the rest of the family. To settle this dispute, while I was home on holiday, I called a family meeting. I offered my share of the estate to my second brother and suggested he buy the others out at ten thousand dollars each. This was accepted and suited the others, as my mother was ready for retirement. I started giving her a monthly allowance, which was a decision I made once I was qualified. My older brother and youngest sister were planning to go to America and Canada, which they eventually did.

My second brother promptly took my block of land and built his house on it. I did not bother to take issue with that, as I had my profession and was not planning to return to live in Guyana. I learnt recently that he only paid the others eight thousand dollars in total, and my eldest brother took five thousand and split the remainder between my mother and younger sister.

I got my drive, entrepreneurship, and ambition to succeed from my father, who was an ambitious self-made man.

CHAPTER 3

MY SECOND PARENTS

At the age of twelve (1958), I had to leave my parents' home and go to live with my sister and her family so that I could attend Berbice High School in New Amsterdam. This was only thirty-two miles from my parents' home, but public transport was such that commuting daily was not an option. The school was a mile from my sister's house, so I rode a push bike (which was donated by my older brother) to and from school.

Gem and Ivan

My sister Gem and brother-in-law Ivan lived in a wooden house with the lounge and bedrooms upstairs, kitchen downstairs, and bathroom and long-drop latrine in the backyard. There was also a grocery store downstairs, which they ran as their business. Ivan's father and I helped in the shop during busy times, usually Thursday to Saturday. I also chopped firewood for cooking and fetched water to top up the rainwater drums from the artesian well across the road. I used to love using a bucket of water directly from the well to bathe, as it was warmer than water from the drums. I also grew a kitchen garden.

Gem and Ivan's house

Ivan rode his bike, which had a large tray over the small front wheel, to deliver grocery orders to customers' homes and fetch bulk foods from the wholesalers in New Amsterdam. I remember him often arriving home all sweaty and hot, having ridden his bike laden with bags of sugar, flour, split peas, salt, and sundry other items in the hot afternoon sun.

When I joined the family, they had three daughters, and while I was living with them, they had a son and two more daughters. These children grew up to be my little sisters and brother, and although I was in fact their uncle, that relationship remains to this day. Furthermore, Ivan and Gem acted and behaved like my second parents.

I never paid boarding fees, but whenever I went home to visit my parents for the weekend or school holidays, they always sent me back on the bus with a bag of rice from our factory and wood for fuel, plus any other foodstuffs they could spare. Gem cooked for me and washed my clothes. Sometimes when she got too busy with the shop, she employed a domestic called Eunice to help with the chores. Eunice was part of the family and was overjoyed to see me when I visited her later as a qualified doctor.

Ivan took Sundays off and liked to go to the movies. He would take me along for company, and to ride the bicycle, with him sitting on the crossbar. He paid for my tickets. His favourite movies were Westerns with stars like Audie Murphy and John Wayne. He also liked horror movies like *House of Horror* with Vincent Price and *Brides of Dracula*. We had to travel back in the dark, as there were not many street lights. It was spooky, as we had to pass a mental asylum and a graveyard. I couldn't pedal my bike home any faster after a horror movie!

The family belonged to the Arya Samaj religion and took their religion seriously, going to church regularly and doing hawans (religious ceremonies) often. Ivan was a vegetarian and lived on dal, rice, rotis, and vegetables. He was an avid reader of religious and philosophical books.

Often, when I had finished my homework and the shop was quiet, I found Ivan sitting in his hammock. I would sit beside him as he explained to me some of what he had learnt from his reading. To this day, I remember him telling me that God was omnipotent (all-powerful), omniscient (all-knowing), and omnipresent (all-present). I think he loved this expression. He often engaged in discussions and debates with certain customers who would stay for hours discussing politics, world affairs, and religion. I learnt a lot listening to them.

He was a gentle man who made quite an impression on my wife, Debbi, when she met him later. They had many conversations, and she regarded him as one of my more intelligent relatives. He challenged her at times, like when he said to her, "On Indian custom, wherever the man goes the woman must follow." This was in response to her refusing to consider moving to Canada so I could be nearer my relatives. To this she simply replied, "I am not Indian." Debbi believed my calm nature and philosophical attitude to life's challenges was partly due to Ivan's influence.

The skills I learnt helping in the shop came in handy when Debbi later ran a health food shop in Port Augusta. The staff were quite impressed by how quickly I could weigh and bag spices and grains. When my patients saw me helping there, they asked the staff if I owned the shop, to which they took great delight in saying, "No, he is just the parcel boy." This was because I would drop parcels at the railway depot and to couriers for outback customers on my way back to work for the afternoon session.

In high school, I made sure I studied hard and remained in the top grades. I took great pride in being top of the class and being able to show my reports to my father so he could brag to his drinking mates. Despite studying hard and helping in the shop, I found time to play cricket and volleyball at school and at weekends. I was not distracted by girls and was in fact too shy to mix with them. One pretty classmate took a fancy to me and started sending me love letters through a friend of mine. I did not know how to handle these and felt very uncomfortable. I did not reply but threw each letter, torn in small pieces, into the Canje creek on my way to school.

I carried a heavy workload, as I was doing ten subjects, the maximum allowed by the University of London at the Ordinary Level General Certificate of Education. Most students did less, with a maximum of eight. The teachers usually suggest which subjects each student should sit in the examination, as they had a good idea of whether a student was likely to pass a subject or not. My teachers and the principal thought I could handle all ten subjects, even though I had dropped two subjects one year earlier and would have to catch up.

I discussed it with my father, who said that if they thought I could do it I should attempt it. If successful, it would be a great achievement for me and a feather in the school's cap. It had never been attempted before. It created a lot of extra work for me, and I was only averaging about five hours sleep per night, with all the homework I had to get through.

I was studying using a kerosene lamp for light and had to cope with being pestered by mosquitoes and flying beetles, which were attracted by the light. I collected hundreds of beetles and dropped them in buckets of water to drown them. When I passed all ten subjects with good grades, the school was given a half day off to celebrate, and the news went around the community quite quickly.

One day, none of us did our French homework, and we were marched to the principal's office to be disciplined. We were each asked in turn our reason for not doing our homework. Most of the class had no excuse. I said I ran out of time. He proceeded to line us up with our hands outstretched and gave each of us two lashes with his cane. He sympathised with me, as he understood I had a very heavy workload, but he could not make an exception, so he reluctantly also caned me.

The principal knew my ambition was to be a doctor, and he felt that to get the required grades at advanced-level GCE, I needed to go to England. He summoned my father to suggest this, and my father agreed. Arrangements were made for me to go to London, and with the principal's help, I was accepted to the City of Westminster College. He in fact wrote my application and gave me a glowing reference.

Unfortunately, my father was hit on his head in a fight and suffered a fractured skull. His recovery was slow, and as he was my financial support, I could not go until I was sure he would be okay. He eventually improved enough, and arrangements were made for me to go to London, by which time I was already six weeks late for college. Before I left home, the principal invited me to dinner and tried to hook me up with his daughter, much to my father's chagrin.

CHAPTER 4

THE BIG SMOKE: FROM GUYANA TO LONDON

There was much excitement as I prepared to fly to London. My brother went and booked my fare with British West Indian Airways (BWIA). It cost six hundred Guyanese dollars, which seemed like a lot of money then. A tailor-made suit was ordered, which was so bad that I had to get rid of it soon after arriving in London. Just as inappropriate was an overcoat bought in Georgetown, which was unflattering and met a similar fate. I guess one could not expect a good selection of winter clothes in tropical Guyana.

My farewell at Timehri Airport, Georgetown—Rita, Ramesh, Ram, Darsan, Betty, Gem, and Doreen

I had dropped a large piece of wood on my right big toe while helping my father prepare the ground to lay some concrete a few weeks before I was due to fly out. It was not healing, probably because it was fractured, so I had to wear a pair of sandals with the bandaged toe exposed to travel to London, and I placed my shoes in the large heavy suitcase that had been bought for me. This was a challenge, as London was already cold when I arrived in September of 1964. It was six weeks before I could tolerate shoes.

A busload of relatives accompanied me to Georgetown, a journey that took all day. They took food and drums, making music and general merriment. Everybody was excited that I was going to England to become a doctor. Little did they, or I for that matter, know what hurdles awaited me.

We had to overnight at friends' homes in Georgetown, and then we proceeded to the airport the next day for a mid-afternoon flight. I knew that my parents, especially my father, were worried that I might be distracted by getting involved with girls and get married before finishing my studies. He particularly did not want me to be entangled with a white girl. I felt the need to promise him not to get married before completing my studies, and certainly not to a white girl. It was a rather tearful speech and, as you will find out later in this book, I broke both promises. They were having a few rums, and my brother Darsan insisted that I have a beer with him, even though I did not drink at that stage. I obliged but hated every mouthful of it.

My first passport photo

I said my goodbyes and boarded the plane. As I waved to my folks from the top of the steps, it suddenly dawned on me what I was about to do. I sat in my seat and could see them through the window, but they could not see me. I was suddenly overcome with sadness and realised I was going a long way and did not know when I would see them again. I started crying, and felt sure my folks were doing the same. This feeling lasted until I reached Port of Spain in Trinidad, where we had a six-hour in-transit stop. I took the opportunity of doing a sightseeing trip by bus to the city.

When I reboarded the plane, a young Trinidadian girl sat beside me. Like me, it was her first trip away from home and first time on a plane. We chatted all the way to London, stopping en route in Jamaica, Barbados, Antigua, and Bermuda. With so many stops, the journey seemed to take forever.

My friends who were at Heathrow Airport to meet me were looking on rather horrified as I removed six pieces of luggage from the carousel, thinking their car was not big enough. They were relieved when they found out that I was just being a gentleman, helping my Trinidadian friend, and only had two pieces that belonged to me.

Adjusting to Life in London

I still remember clearly being struck by how cold it was as I stepped out of the plane. I stood for what seemed like a minute in shock, thinking this was like being in a refrigerator. How on earth was I going to survive? It was not even winter yet, but only early autumn! After immigration and customs, I said goodbye to my Trinidadian friend and was met by Edna and Paul, who I eventually called my third parents.

Edna and Paul, together with their eight-year-old daughter, Anita, and their six-year-old son, Stanley, had been visiting their relatives in Guyana earlier that year, and I had been summoned by my father to come to the village from school so I could meet them. My father invited them for lunch. Paul had a brother who lived in our village. Another of Paul's brothers married my first cousin, so we were distant relatives by marriage. I was fascinated to hear these two little brown kids speaking with a broad London Cockney accent, so I kept asking them questions to hear them speak. Paul and Edna kindly offered to meet me in London when I eventually arrived. This was what my father was hoping for.

Edna and Paul in 1964—my third parents

It was late afternoon and already dark when we travelled from Heathrow to Upper Tooting, where Edna and Paul lived. I was quite in awe of the bright lights, the tall buildings, the busy traffic, and the crowds. My head felt like it was on a swizzle stick as I took in the sights. It was like being in a wonderland and was in direct contrast to my little village in Guyana.

We eventually arrived at their house, which was a terraced brick house at number one, Holderness Road, Upper Tooting. The curvature of the attached terraced houses as they followed the bends in the streets fascinated me. I wondered why the streets weren't straightened out before the houses were built to make building easier. It was an amazing sight to see rows and rows of these houses with chimneys on the roofs spouting black smoke, creating an eerie dull atmosphere, with the sun nowhere to be seen.

The house had four levels. On level one was the lounge with its coal-fired fireplace, master bedroom, dine-in kitchen, and a laundry with a second toilet. The laundry had direct access from the outside. There was a small backyard that had a shed and rotary clothesline. The second storey, or rather the mezzanine floor, had Anita's bedroom and the main bathroom. The next level had Stanley's bedroom and a larger bedsitter, which I occupied. The attic housed another bedsitter rented to Edna's uncle Charles.

The room I had was normally rented as a bedsitter, but fortunately for me, it was vacant at the time. It had two single beds, a table, a gas cooker, a wardrobe, and a gas fire, but no fridge. The sink was just outside the door in the corridor. I stayed there for the weekend while being assessed by Paul and Edna to see if I was a suitable tenant. They then said to me that they could help me find digs, as bedsitters were called, or I could stay in the room I had for a rental of three pounds fifty per week. This also covered gas and electricity. I was happy and relieved with this offer, as I knew absolutely no one else, except for a cousin in a nearby suburb, two aunties, and a family from my village in North London.

I was responsible for my own laundry, food, cleaning, and ironing, and I could only take a bath twice per week to save water and gas. I could have a dicky bird bath daily. This was something I was not used to but had to come to terms with. I was also allowed to watch television (black and white) in their lounge, provided I watched what they wanted to watch.

Cooking and washing clothes by hand were challenging initially, as in Guyana boys did not do such chores, which were left to the mothers and sisters. I did not even know how to boil an egg or make a cup of tea! My favourite food became frozen fish fingers, carrots, and potatoes, all cooked in the same frying pan with some tomato ketchup. Yuck! These were bought from the corner store on my way home and were simple to cook. For dessert, I discovered jelly and instant whip, which I could place outside on the window sill to set, as the outside temperature was not much warmer than inside a fridge.

Uncle Charles was a good cook and, realising my limitations, would on average once a week knock on my door when he heard me arriving home and present me with a large plate of metagee (coconut soup with chicken and root vegetables). This was accepted gratefully and thoroughly enjoyed.

The following Monday, it was time to visit the City of Westminster College, as I was already six weeks late. The term was half gone. Edna accompanied me and showed me how to travel by Tube (underground train) and surface train. We met the principal, who understood why I was late and gave me my book list. I was expected to start the following day, so Edna took me to the bookstore on our way home.

I was in a class of sixteen international students. They were from India, Nigeria, Hong Kong, Israel, South Africa, Guyana, and the UK. We were all aspiring to go to medical school and become doctors. The subjects we were taught were the three required at advanced-level general certificate of education for entrance to medical school: physics, chemistry, and zoology.

On my first day at college, I became quite concerned, as two of my three lecturers spoke English with very thick accents—one Cockney and the other Russian. I was only picking up about every fifth word and wondered how the hell was I going to cope with the work. I not only had to keep up with my current work but also catch up with lessons I had missed for half a term. Fortunately, as the weeks progressed, I began to understand them better.

At the end of the term, I was surprised that I came seventh in my overall class marks. That gave me hope. The second term I was more settled and came second. By the end of the third term, I was top of the class, and I stayed there for the rest of the two-year course. I also did a course in the use of English, which was required of foreign students by certain provincial universities. That was easy for me, coming from an English-speaking country.

I studied very hard and helped at home with the chores and shopping. I even cut the lawn and washed the car. I entertained the kids at parties. Slowly, I became part of the family, and Anita and Stanley were like my little sister and brother.

After the first year, Edna and Paul offered to cook for me for an extra one pound fifty per week. This was an offer I could not refuse. It included breakfast and dinner during the week, as I had lunch at college, and three meals at weekends. They took me to visit friends, to the beach at weekends in the summer, and occasionally to a ballroom dance. Some friends thought I was their eldest son.

Paul started to drop me off at college, as it was on his way to work in a jewellery store in the Strand. He would drop me off on Westminster Bridge, and I would walk from there past the Houses of Parliament and Westminster Abbey to the college.

I had never used a knife and fork to eat before, as in Guyana we ate using our fingers. Paul taught me the correct way to hold and use them. I also decided "when in Rome, do as the Romans do," so I started eating anything that the family was having, including beef and pork. When my family heard this, they were surprised, as it was not our custom to eat such meats. This was because the cow was regarded as sacred, and only low-class people used pork. It was interesting that after being exposed to it, I stared eating ham, tongue, liver, kidneys, beef and pork sausages, roast pork, and beef with Yorkshire pudding. I began to enjoy them all.

Edna got me to stop wearing bathers as underpants and to go to Marks and Spencer and buy some white Y-fronts. She taught me to use the coin-operated machines at the local laundromat. She and Paul suggested I enrol with a GP and a dentist and have regular check-ups. I ended up with eleven amalgam fillings! Not surprising, as I never had regular check-ups in Guyana.

I even went and had some ballroom dance lessons and appreciated non-Indian music from their collection. There were many lessons in etiquette and behaviour that I picked up from Paul and Edna. In fact, my wife, Debbi, said after she met Paul that I was more like him than my own people, especially my respect for others and particularly women. My command of spoken English improved by living with this family.

I couldn't afford records but wanted music of my own, so I bought a reel-to-reel tape recorder and proceeded to tape most of their records. The collection included Frank Sinatra, Bing Crosby, Max Bygraves, Jim Reeves, Johnny Mathis, and Gene Pitney.

Christmastime was particularly enjoyable, especially if there was snow on the ground. On my first Christmas morning, I was awakened by two excited children, Anita and Stanley, telling me it was snowing outside. It was magical to witness snow falling for the first time. These soft white flakes gently descending from the sky and landing on the trees or the ground made me feel I was in some sort of fairyland. It was great to see all the houses and the stores with Christmas decorations and to have carol singers calling from door to door. We drank sweet sherry at breakfast while presents were exchanged. This was followed by a sumptuous lunch of turkey, ham, roast vegetables, and Xmas pudding with brandy sauce.

I made regular visits to my cousin and aunt in London, enjoying Guyanese food with them. I also did a lot of sightseeing. A visiting uncle and aunt took me to the theatre on two occasions to see *Charlie Girl* and *The Black and White Minstrels*, both long-running shows in London's West End.

My closest friends at college were a South African and another Guyanese. We often played cricket at weekends and occasionally went swimming in some rather cold outdoor pools. I liked visiting the Guyanese, who lived in digs in the nearby suburb of Balham, because he gave me tinned peaches with Carnation evaporated milk. Sometimes we had corned beef sandwiches.

I applied to every medical school I could in England and Scotland and obtained interviews at several. The London schools at Guys and St. Thomas were a revelation. At the interviews, I was asked questions like, "Do you follow the arts, and which one do you prefer?" I had only recently been introduced to the theatre but had never been to the opera, or even an art exhibition or gallery. All I could boast was going to movies. This did not go down well with them, and they soon lost interest in me. Apparently, I was not cultured enough!

Newcastle upon Tyne, on the other hand, was a breath of fresh air. At the interview with the readers (next in line for professorships) in physiology and anatomy, I felt relaxed and at home discussing my country, cricket, and why I wanted to do medicine. They were interested in my plans after graduation. I said I would return to my country as a specialist, as Guyana had a shortage of specialists. I was offered a place providing I obtained an average of Cs in my subjects at the advanced-level GCE examination. It was the only offer I received, probably because I had it as my first choice. I liked Newcastle because it provided a campus atmosphere with all the faculties together.

When the A-level results came out, I went with my two closest classmates to the college office to get them. I was very happy with my results, but I could not express my jubilation, as one friend failed all three subjects and the other only passed one. I had two As, one B, and a grade 1 on a special paper in chemistry.

My friends decided we should go out and celebrate or drown our sorrows over lunch. I knew then that I had satisfied the requirements for Newcastle University. Only two of the sixteen students in our class were accepted into medical school. The others had to change courses.

Even though my folks were sending me what money they could afford, it was not enough to meet my expenses, so I worked during the Christmas holidays. The first Christmas I worked in the post office carrying bags of mail from delivery vans to the sorters. This meant going from the cold to the heat all night long. I did twelve-hour night shifts with an hour meal break at midnight. For my troubles, I received nine pounds fifty pence per week.

The next Christmas holidays, I worked in a mail-order warehouse. We had to report to the department store at seven thirty in the morning and were then transported by bus to the warehouse. My job was to gather products requested by the store, which were then transported by truck so mail orders could be filled and sent to customers. All day I was climbing up and down ladders in the cold warehouse. It was winter, but there was no central heating. The best part of the day was morning teatime, when we were offered tea with fresh warm toast smeared with real butter.

Between finishing college and starting university, I had a three-months break, so I applied for and got a full-time permanent job as a legal clerk in the public trustee's office. I omitted to tell them about my university admission, as I was desperate to have a job. I did very well, writing simple legal letters acknowledging correspondence without giving any advice. These letters were then signed by the lawyer before they were posted. I also had to retrieve and return files to the archive.

I must have impressed them, as they told me that I had the potential to be a good lawyer and that they were prepared to sponsor and pay for me to study law part-time. One month before I was due to start university, I had to confess that I had been accepted into medicine and would be leaving. They were happy for me and wished me well in my studies. I moved to Newcastle in September of 1966. Edna and Paul sold their house soon after that and bought a bungalow in Wickford in Essex.

CHAPTER 5

UNIVERSITY LIFE (1966-1971)

At Newcastle, the medical degree was a very intensive five-year course with very little time off and lots of contact hours—forty per week. We only had one long summer break at the end of the first year and only two weeks each at Easter and Christmas. I thought it would be best for me to live in a hall of residence instead of digs so I could have the cleaning and cooking done for me. I only had to wash and iron my own clothes, for which a coin-operated laundry was provided.

Eustace Percy Hall of Residence was for male students only. It was an old converted army barracks set in an open field about five miles from the university and town centre. Most of us used the public buses to and from university, as we could not afford cars. It accommodated about three hundred and fifty students and a few prefects. The manager's residence was on-site also.

There was a large kitchen and dining room, a TV room, a library, and a games room with dartboards and table tennis tables. The student rooms were arranged along corridors on both sides of two long central walkways. It was a sprawling single-storey building. Each student's room had a single bed, a desk and chair, a coffee table, a hand basin, a wardrobe, and a lounge chair in addition to a mirror. A kettle, a few crockeries, glasses, and cutlery were provided. The cleaners cleaned the rooms and changed the beds once per week. Each corridor had a shared bathroom and toilet block.

We were given breakfast and dinner seven days per week, and lunches on weekends. The meals were generous, and we could have seconds. Lunch and dinner were three-course meals, which we appreciated, being growing boys. The office sorted our mail and we each had a pigeonhole for it.

Ram with Llewelyn in Jesmondene Park

Life in the hall of residence was comfortable and conducive to studying. It was easy to make friends, and for breaks from studying, we would visit each other, share a cup of coffee, or listen to music and chat. Sometimes we played in the games room. Jesmondene Park was within walking distance and was a pleasant place to spend some time on weekends.

After a year, a new hall was built within walking distance of the medical school and the main teaching hospital—the Royal Victoria Infirmary (RVI). The new hall had separate multistorey buildings for male and female students. This replaced some of the older student residences. My new room had the same facilities but was more modern. This site was near St. James's Park, the home of the Newcastle United soccer team.

I played cricket with the medical school team against some of the local teams. Unfortunately, we spent more time waiting for the rain to stop than playing cricket. I also played table tennis and became good enough to

the course more interesting and relevant. In the third and fourth years, we were allowed on the wards in the mornings for tutorials by registrars and consultants, in our small groups, often around patients. We were taught to take medical histories and to examine patients with various medical problems. Sometimes we had to research certain topics and do presentations to the group.

We had lectures in the afternoon. It was hard to stay awake, especially if a lecturer had a monotonous voice. I took copious notes to stay alert. With practice, I got so good I could take down a lecture word for word, and that's without shorthand training!

The fifth year was a clinical rotation through the various wards, and sometimes we would be the only student attached to the unit. We followed the interns and learned from them. We attended ward rounds with the consultant or senior registrar and presented patients who were admitted. When the intern took holiday, the student acted as intern. This was very good experience and prepared us for our turn as interns. We could attend and assist at surgical operations and do certain procedures. After the final examination, we attained the MBBS (bachelor of medicine and bachelor of surgery) degree and provisional registration with the medical board. We could then become interns.

I was very lucky to secure an internship with both the medical and surgical units of my choice, much to the envy of some of my colleagues. I had been the final-year student attached to these same units. The intern year was perhaps the most important year. It was the year when all the theoretical knowledge could be put into practice and became relevant. It was the year we were given autonomy in decision-making and obtained a lot of supervision and guidance. It was only after the end of the intern year that one felt confident enough to treat patients. Full registration with the medical board was then granted, if favourable reports were received from the supervising consultants.

The life of an intern in those days was a hard one. We worked twelve days in every fourteen, including every second night, averaging one hundred and eighty hours per fortnight. We were not paid overtime. I took home ninety-one pounds per month.

One shift I used to dread was the one starting at seven thirty on Friday morning and ending on Monday afternoon at five thirty, especially when our unit was on intake, meaning we admitted all emergency patients to our unit. I got no sleep for days. A bed was provided in the doctor's residence, but I seldom had time to use it. I would fall asleep in the lounge chair as soon as I got home at the end of that shift, while my wife was still talking to me and cooking dinner.

My graduation photo

Interns were not regarded as ordinary humans. No other groups would tolerate such abuse. Thank heavens they are treated much better these days. The one bonus was that a lot of experience was crammed into one year. We were allowed a two-week holiday every six months.

Working as a Nurse

At the end of the first year, my tutor, Professor Eric Blair, who incidentally was one of the interviewers who accepted me into the medical course through his contacts, got me a job as a nurse's assistant at a nursing home (Wooley Sanatorium) in a small town in Northumberland. It was so-called because it had initially been a tuberculosis hospital when TB was rife. In fact, there were still a few TB sufferers there in isolation. I was grateful for this job, as I not only got paid but was also provided with accommodation and all meals free of charge. This allowed me to save some money, and I had enough time to study and to keep fit by going for jogs along the country roads. I also made some good friends.

Some weekends, I was invited to spend time with Professor Blair and his family. They had a rather grand home in the posh suburb of Ponteland. It had a tennis court and a large paddock at the rear of the house. His wife, Dorothy, came from a well-off coal-mining family. They were quite surprised with my aptitude at tennis, considering had I never played it before and had to be taught the rules.

Dorothy still mentions this in Christmas cards. She has always corresponded with Debbi and I over the years, even after Eric passed away. We visited them during trips to the UK. He was always interested in what we were doing. I remember once, at dinner at their house, Debbi being taken aback when he referred to her as a colonial!

At the nursing home, I looked after the patients' needs. My duties included bathing and dressing them, changing beds, attending to pressure areas each night, and feeding some of them. Shower time was like a conveyor belt. The patients were wheeled in one after the other. My job was to wash them using a hose with a shower end and a large sponge of the type I later used to wash my cars. I had to wear Wellington boots to avoid getting my feet wet. The wheelchairs were commodes with an open seat that allowed access to patients' private areas without them having to stand up. The shower was an open one that allowed easy access. Another nurse did the drying. It was a bit like a car wash. This experience made me appreciate what nurses do.

Once, much later, while I was working at Port Augusta Hospital, an indigenous patient was admitted to the medical ward. She was filthy and smelly, with maggots in a wound on her leg. I asked a nurse to clean her up a bit so that I could examine her.

The nurse was reluctant and responded, "You high and mighty doctors don't know what it is like to be a nurse."

I said, "And you, nurse, do not realise that I worked as a nurse before I became a doctor."

She simply stared at me.

A Major Hurdle

My father's death in 1967 was a major setback for me, as he was my main financial support. I wrote a letter to my family offering to give up my medical course and return home to run the rice factory. My mother could not run it, and my second brother was hopeless. My eldest brother was a schoolteacher.

The reason I was given for them not telling me about my father's prolonged illness and eventual death was that they did not want me to worry, as it might affect my studies! The family had a discussion in Guyana and advised me that they wanted me to finish my studies and that they would work the factory and support me as best as they could. This gave me added determination to finish my studies and fulfil my father's wishes.

I knew it was going to be difficult for my folks to support me, so I wrote to the Guyana High Commission in London explaining my problem and requesting some support in the form of a loan or a scholarship. In exchange, I offered to sign a contract to return to Guyana on completion of my studies and work in the Georgetown public hospital for a period of five years. My request was denied.

When I eventually graduated, within a week, I received a letter of congratulations from them and an offer of a job at the above hospital. You can understand my surprise and annoyance. I immediately wrote a lengthy abusive letter pointing out their short-sightedness and cheek.

I next decided to apply to the British army, navy, and air force for sponsorship and expressed a willingness to serve after qualification. Somehow, before I got around to making these applications, my tutor, Professor Blair, got wind of my situation, and I was summoned to his office. I explained my predicament, and he told me not to commit to the armed forces but to leave it for a few days, and he would see what he could do. I saw him a few days later, and he said he managed to get the university to waive all my tuition fees and to grant me a bursary of sixty-five pounds per term.

This money had been left by a benefactor to the university to help students in financial stress. There was no compulsion to repay it, and there was no interest charged, but it was appreciated if such loans were repaid in due course so that other students could benefit. This was such a relief and help to me that I repaid it with interest once I graduated and started to earn a salary. I remain forever grateful to the University of Newcastle, Professor Blair, and the British people for such generosity.

Trip to Guyana in 1968

Over the years, correspondence with my folks was by mail, and letters were exchanged on average once per month. Various siblings wrote to me in turn. My father only wrote a couple of letters in the early years. My mother was illiterate and told my sisters what to say to me, and they would write it and post it on her behalf. They also read every letter I sent to her. I longed so much to see them again and shed tears every time a letter arrived, but I could not afford the airfare to go home.

In 1968, an opportunity to visit them came up. The National Union of Students, of which I was a member, chartered a plane to fly students to visit relatives in the West Indies, including Guyana. It was a one-off trip, and the fare was only one hundred pounds. This I could afford, so I booked and went home for four weeks.

On arrival at Timeri Airport in Guyana, I was greeted by several carloads of my relatives. I remember how dark they all seemed to me. I had become fairer living in cold dull England. We were excited to see each other. It was such a wonderful emotional reunion.

I spent the time visiting everybody and eating and drinking a lot. I gained several kilos. My mother was so proud that she wanted me to visit everyone! Of course, my father was no longer there, as he passed away in 1967. During my time in the village, I took the opportunity of visiting his grave and placing a wreath of flowers there in the presence of my mother and other relatives.

A few of the villagers recalled teasing me when at age four I called myself Dr. Ramdyal. Now they accepted that the dream was about to become reality.

Every morning at six o'clock, I saw my mother praying in the backyard as she faced the rising sun. She had some flowers and a brass goblet of water, which she poured slowly onto the ground in front of her. My sister told me that she had prayed for my success every day since I left home. I was not aware of this.

I'd had a crush on a girl when I was at Berbice High School. She was quite stunning, with sparkling mischievous eyes, and was two years my junior. I visited her now at her parents' home and was welcomed by her and her mother, who gave me some refreshments. They invited me to a barbecue, but I had to return home, so I declined the offer. I often wondered whether my attendance would have altered the course of my history. I later found out she had an illegitimate child and promptly lost interest, so that was the end of that.

Ram laying a wreath on his father's grave

When it was time to leave, a busload of my relatives, armed with food (dhal-puri, chicken curry and rice) and drums accompanied me to the airport. I was sad to leave but happy to have visited, and I knew that I had to return to finish my studies.

Just before boarding the bus, I realised I had not said goodbye to my nani. She was not by the bus. I went looking for her and found her upstairs. I asked her why she was not downstairs to say goodbye, and she said, "Me too upset bai, me na think meh go see you again."

I responded saying, "Of course I will see you again. I will be back in a few years."

I genuinely believed that, but she was right. She died from a heart attack a few years later and was not there when I visited in 1972. She was one of my favourite persons. We had a special bond.

My First Serious Romance

I was dating a classmate for a little while until one day, a dental student friend told me that there was a Guyanese girl in the first year of dentistry. There were no other Guyanese students at Newcastle University as far as I knew. I asked him to find out her name. When he later told me that her surname was Ferdinand, I became curious, as I'd had a classmate, Mary Rose, at Berbice High School by that name. Her father was a GP in New Amsterdam and in fact treated my father before he died.

In the first year, dental students had lectures in anatomy and physiology at the medical school, so one day I stood by the stairs as they came down after the lecture and tried to spot the Guyanese. I picked the right one and asked if she was Miss Ferdinand. She answered in the affirmative, and then I said, "But you are not Mary Rose."

She replied, "No, that is my sister. My name is Moira, her younger sister. And who are you?"

"Ramdyal Bhola. I was in the same class as Mary Rose at Berbice High School," I responded.

She then commented, "I remember you. At the end of each term, Mary Rose would come home in tears and throw her books on the table, saying, 'That Bhola boy, he beat me again, and I tried so hard.'"

We got on well and arranged to catch up later. The friendship grew. We started meeting for lunches in the medical school canteen, usually a sausage and baked beans on toast for one pound sterling. We also played table tennis in the games room next to the canteen. We started studying in the library together in the evenings and later visited each other in our respective halls of residence. We accompanied each other to the annual residence balls and later to parties.

The friendship grew, and we decided to go together during the next university holidays to London, where we stayed at her sister's house. We also spent a few days over Christmas with Edna and Paul in Essex. I was later told by Edna that her daughter, Anita, was not happy when I took Moira to their house, as she had a crush on me and expected in time to marry me! This was a surprise to me, as I regarded her as my little sister.

Moira had a boyfriend in London from her college days who she gave the flick, and he was not happy either. We made further trips to London and Essex during subsequent holidays, and our relationship grew stronger and stronger. I eventually took her to an upmarket Indian restaurant and proposed to her with a ring I obtained from Paul for six pounds. He was a jeweller. She accepted, and we became engaged. No engagement or dinner party with friends, as we could not afford that.

My Elective in New York 1969

At the end of the third year of the medical course, we could do an elective for three months anywhere in the world. I chose New York and was accepted by the Morisania City Hospital in the Bronx. Moira decided to travel with me to New York to stay with friends of her parents in Brooklyn and do a side trip to see her family in Guyana for a few weeks.

On arrival in New York, we stayed the first night in a hotel and made our way by subway the next morning to her friends'. There we stayed together for a couple of days before she left for Guyana. One afternoon after lunch, we decided to go for a walk. As we walked along the street, we came across several groups of men staring at us. We felt so uncomfortable and threatened that we hastened back to the house. We learnt from our friends that we went the wrong way and ended up in a very unsafe area of Brooklyn.

The friends kindly drove me to the Bronx. When we arrived at the hospital, we were greeted at the reception desk by a rather good-looking young African American girl. By the way she looked at me, my friends thought she had tickets on me! I was given a room in the doctor's residence, which was across the courtyard from the nurse's residence.

The hospital was housed in a three-storey old brick building. It was staffed by interns and residents from the nearby Montefiore medical school and teaching hospital. There were other overseas medical students besides me. One was a classmate from Newcastle, and there were two girls from Glasgow University.

We met the director of medicine the first morning, and he explained what we would be doing. We were given free accommodation and vouchers for meals in the hospital canteen. Even though we had no responsibility, we were given a small salary. This was a very welcome and much appreciated gesture by four impoverished medical students who had no money after paying the airfare. It allowed us to do some travelling and sight-seeing during the weekends, visiting places like Greenwich Village, Times Square, the Empire State Building, and Central Park, where I saw a free rendition of Shakespeare's *Twelfth Night*.

We were attached to the interns and observed what they did. We attended ward rounds and tutorials by the registrars and consultants, and case presentations and discussions in the lecture theatre. We could chat with and examine patients on the wards and visit the emergency department. That was an eye-opener. I had never seen so many patients with gunshot and knife wounds in one place. The ambulance officers were fully armed and would not attend emergencies in apartment blocks without a police escort.

I walked onto the medical ward one day, and a patient greeted me with a smile and said, "Good to see you again, Frank, how are you? Good to have a drink with you yesterday."

I was taken aback because I had never seen him before and did not know what he was talking about. I simply said, "Yes, it was," and kept walking. The patient seemed happy with my answer.

The intern who was on the ward observed what happened and came up to me and said, "You handled that well." He explained that this patient was suffering from Korsakoff's psychosis as result of alcoholic brain damage, and fabrication was part of the presentation. To him, his fabrication was reality. If I had not gone along with his story, he would have become irritable, argumentative, and even aggressive. This skill came in handy when I had to deal with dementia patients later in my practice.

I visited Moira's friends in Brooklyn some weekends and was fed and taken sight-seeing. We went on the Staten Island Ferry to Coney Island and drove across the Brooklyn Bridge. Once they took me to a barbecue at some friends' place in New Jersey.

One hot evening, I went with the intern in his Ford Mustang for a swim at Far Rockaway Beach on Long Island. I had never seen such huge waves before. I had great fun bodysurfing and being out of control in these powerful waves. Having no fear, I was lucky to come out alive! It was a welcome diversion, as New York was very hot and humid in the summer.

The medical students were treated to dinner at a posh restaurant by the deputy director of medicine after a day of sight-seeing. It was the first time I saw a Diner's Card being used to pay a bill, and I wondered what this plastic card was all about and how it worked. The director had us over to his house on Long Island for a barbecue one Sunday. We had to make our own way there and back by train, which was an adventure.

Walking along the street just around the corner from the hospital, I noticed an advertisement in the window of a restaurant saying "staff wanted." I saw this as an opportunity to earn some money on the side, so I went in to make some enquires. The manager asked me what hours I could work and could I start straightaway. He offered five dollars per hour cash and one meal per shift. I could have anything to eat during my fifteen-minute break. I was also allowed to keep any tips. My job was to clear and wipe tables, and take dishes to the people stacking the industrial dishwashing machines. I was given an apron and started immediately.

I did eight-hour shifts from four p.m. to midnight every night, which meant I had to leave the hospital one hour early, but no one noticed. I was getting paid from two sources and doing very well. I saved several hundred dollars, which was earmarked for a trip to Montreal at the end of my attachment to visit Moira's brother and family. He was studying agriculture at the Macdonald campus of McGill University

While Moira was in Guyana, we wrote each other every couple of days. The letters were delivered to her dad's surgery, and because of their frequent arrival, he called me "a writing fool." Amazing what one does when in love!

Moira returned to New York after a month and immediately put a stop to my part-time job. We started spending weekends together at the friends' house or in my room at the hospital. She found a part-time job as a dental assistant with a local dentist. At the house, I was given a bed on the ground floor, and Moira's was on the third floor. Of course, I was sneaking up to her room at night—and when the old lady, Mom Jule, realised this, she was not impressed. She was very much old school and felt a duty to look after Moira's interest on behalf of her parents. She decided it was time we got married.

My First Marriage—1969

Mom Jule was determined that we were getting married, and that was that. There was to be no discussion or argument. Even though we were engaged we had no immediate plans to marry. She was such a huge, domineering, and somewhat scary personality that we were no match for her. She arranged to have the ceremony at her minister's house. I had to get my medical registrar to arrange the blood tests required to rule out sexually transmitted diseases for Moira and myself. We got the permit from the government office to get married on presentation of our blood test results.

The wedding reception was to be at Mom Jule's house, with a rent-a-crowd consisting mainly of her immediate family. A photographer friend was to take the photos and prepare an album. I was freaking out about the cost, as I felt we did not have enough money to pay for everything, considering we wanted to leave some for our bus trip to Montreal. We communicated this to Mom Jule, who simply said, "Don't worry about it. Go to the liquor store and get some drinks."

Moira and I made our way down the street discussing what was happening. We decided that we did not want to get married at this stage. We returned home to be greeted with "Where are the drinks?" We said we were not ready to get married. To this, with wide-open eyes and a stern scary face, she replied, "Nonsense. Just go and get the drinks. Everyone has been invited."

With our tails between our legs, we did as we were ordered to do. We bought two inexpensive wedding rings from a local jeweller, and with the help of Mom Jule's daughter-in-law, Moira acquired a wedding dress from a second-hand store. It was a beautiful dress and only required dry cleaning. It fit her so well that one of the guests thought she looked like Princess Grace of Monaco!

Ram and Moira's wedding day 1969

The wedding ceremony was a simple one at the minister's house, with Mom Jule as the witness. She was going to make absolutely sure we were married. This occurred in the late morning, and the reception followed that evening. It was quite an enjoyable affair with food, drinks, music, and dancing. There were about twenty of us altogether.

The next day, we asked Mom Jule what we owed her. She said, "Nothing. It's my wedding present to you." We breathed a sigh of relief and thanked her.

The next day, we went to collect the photos, which were in a beautiful album. When we offered payment, the photographer said that no payment was necessary, as it was his wedding gift to us. We estimated the whole wedding cost us only about four hundred dollars.

I had finished my hospital attachment, and Moira had given notice of termination to the local dentist. We took off by Greyhound coach for Montreal, a journey that took twelve hours. We were met by her brother and his wife, with whom we spent our two-week honeymoon before returning to the UK.

Settling into Married Life

I was a fourth-year medical student, and Moira was a second-year dental student. Our families were not happy about the marriage. My folks did not like the fact that Moira was not Indian. Her mother was from Scotland, and her father was a mixture of African, Portuguese, and French. He graduated in medicine from Howard University in the USA. They met in Glasgow, where he was practising medicine before returning to Guyana. It was the requirement that all non-British medical graduates spend twelve months practising in the UK before being allowed to work in Guyana. Further complicating matters was that Moira's family were Catholics, while I was born a Hindu.

Moira's parents were worried that she might not finish her course and might become pregnant. They withdrew all contact and financial support. Fortunately, she received a grant from the UK government, as she had dual citizenship. She took a part-time job in a wet fish shop. We managed quite well financially, as it was cheaper for us to live together than in two halls of residence.

We decided to find a flat after spending a few weeks living with friends. Applying for flats gave me my first experience of racial discrimination in England. I arranged to inspect a flat, and when the landlady saw I was Indian, she said she was sorry, but the flat was taken. Next day, the flat was advertised again.

With the next flat, I sent Moira to inspect it, and we were immediately accepted. It was a two-bedroom unit on the ground floor, with the landlady living upstairs. She had her own entrance. We had a small lounge, a small kitchen, and a bathroom. There was no heating and cooling. The winters were very cold, and often there was ice on the inside of the bathroom window. We bought a kerosene heater for the lounge, which made the entire flat smell of kerosene fumes.

We used public buses to get around. Moira prepared our food in the evenings, and we met at university for lunches as before. We went to the library to study at night to avoid distractions and to be warm. We used laundromats, as we had no washing machine.

The landlady was very friendly. I weeded the garden for her, for which she was grateful, as she was a widow. She remained a friend for a long time after we vacated the flat. We even caught up with her later in life in Australia, where she had relatives in Brisbane and Adelaide.

Our social life was confined to Friday and Saturday nights. We were often invited to parties by my friend Llewelyn. His group of Sierra Leonean friends threw some great parties. It was from them that I learnt to dance to Motown and Black American music. The popular singers included Otis Reading, Wilson Picket, James Brown, Desmond Dekker, Chuck Berry, Aretha Franklin, and the Supremes. At other parties thrown by English friends, we listened to the Beatles, Elvis, the Rolling Stones, and other English groups. My fondness for reggae and disco in general came later in the seventies and eighties. I learnt to dance to that style of music from Moira, her sister Mary Rose, and friends. Bob Marley and more so Jimmy Cliff became my favourite singers.

Moira and I took our studies seriously and were progressing well. I completed my fourth and fifth (final) years. After passing the final examination, I was ready to start my internship. I had to spend a lot of time working and studying at the hospital in those years, and Moira would often spend nights at the hospital, as I was provided accommodation. This allowed us some time together.

I took some driving lessons when I was in my final year and obtained my driving licence. I then became impatient to have a car, even though we couldn't afford one. We scraped some money together and borrowed some from Llewelyn to buy a second-hand Morris 1100 from a shonky car dealer for two hundred and fifty pounds. During the subsequent six months, we had so many problems with it always breaking down that we spent another two hundred dollars keeping it on the road. The dealer did not want to know us. I pestered him so much that in the end, he tried to avoid me.

One day, he was in his office and told his receptionist to tell me he was not in. I barged into his office and threatened to take him to consumer affairs for not honouring the three-month warranty. He agreed to take the car back and refund me two hundred pounds. I accepted the deal and was able to repay Llewelyn the loan. That was a bad experience, so I decided I would not have another car unless I could afford a new one.

I promised myself that when I qualified and started to earn a salary, I would reward myself with a new car. The car dealership I went to had a rather nice Audi sedan that took my fancy, but my heart sank when I found out it was 2,400 pounds. This was three times what I could afford! Interestingly, I owned several Audis later in Australia.

My absolute dream car was a 4.2-litre Jaguar sedan owned by a vascular surgeon who had a large private practice. Even other consultants could not afford that, but I set myself a dream that one day, I would own one of those—maybe when I was forty. This dream came true for me later in Australia.

For the moment, I settled for a Volkswagen Beetle priced at 725 pounds. I organised with the dealer that I could only buy it if I passed my final examination. We did all the paperwork, including a car loan. The excitement on passing my final examination in June 1971 and obtaining the bachelor of medicine and bachelor of surgery degree (MBBS) was indescribable. How proud would my father have been if he was alive! I certainly would have flown him and my mother to the UK for the graduation.

Moira and I went to pick up the car that very afternoon. After collecting it, we took it home to park it in the garage, that we rented from the landlady for an extra pound per week. We took the bus to the university, where we were invited to have celebratory drinks by the Medical Defence Union insurance company. So happy were we that we drank too much and stayed out too late. The buses had stopped running, and we could not afford taxis, so we walked the three miles to our home, arriving at three in the morning.

The very next day, we decided that I would give Moira some driving practice, as she'd had some lessons at the driving school by then. Not paying attention, I reversed the car out of the garage with the passenger door open. There was an almighty crash, and we thought we had done some serious damage. The door could not be closed completely, so we quietly tied it and drove the car back into the garage. That was the end of the first lesson! What a great lesson: never take off with the doors open!

We took the car to the dealership the next day and were relieved to find out that the door had merely come off the hinges, and there was no damage. What a huge relief that was. Thank heavens the Volkswagen Beetle was such a robust, well-made car.

CHAPTER 6

POST-GRADUATE STUDIES

I was told the best time to sit the ECFMG (Education Certificate for Foreign Medical Graduates) examination was soon after sitting our final examination, while I still had a lot of information stored in my head. This certificate was required if I wanted to practice in the United States. Not knowing what the future held, I applied to sit this examination and had to go to Edinburgh to do this. It was a multiple-choice medical examination, with an additional assessment for proficiency in English. The latter contained simple questions like *a chair is something to eat, sit on, write with, drive* etc. Of course, I passed this part with a perfect score. I also passed the medical part.

As I went through the various faculties during my medical course, I tried to decide which one to specialise in so I could return to my country as a specialist. There was a need for specialists in Guyana. I enjoyed paediatrics, obstetrics, and gynaecology. I eventually decided on obstetrics and gynaecology. I was accepted into the training course at the teaching hospital after completing six months as a medical intern at Newcastle General Hospital, followed by six months as a surgical intern at the Royal Victoria Infirmary.

Working as a senior house officer, I was still the first on call and had a heavy roster commitment, like that of an intern. During the first year, I did six months on the gynaecology ward at the Royal Victoria Infirmary and six months in the obstetric unit at Princess Mary Maternity Hospital.

Moira became unexpectedly pregnant during this time, and when she was ten weeks pregnant, I contracted rubella or German measles and gave it to her. I was not really sick and only had a few spots, but I was not allowed to be on the gynaecology unit for a couple of weeks. Moira's blood tests showed a grossly elevated antibody titre, and when the test was repeated a week later, it was even higher. This meant she had current infection.

By that time, she was already twelve weeks pregnant. We discussed it with her obstetrician and were given the statistics that there was a one in five chance of the baby having a very serious complication, such as cerebral palsy, a congenital heart defect, or deafness. We had to make the decision whether to have a termination or not.

Moira was in her fourth year of her dental course, so she would have had to defer if we had the baby. It was a difficult decision, and I left it to her. She found it impossible to make the decision and asked me to do it. I wavered for a week and then decided on termination. By now, she was sixteen weeks, and a hysterotomy had to be done. It was a little boy. I don't think Moira ever got over the loss of this baby and may have unjustifiably held me responsible for the decision.

I completed the year, gaining valuable experience in antenatal care, delivering babies, and dealing with complications requiring suturing, use of forceps and ventouse (suction), evacuation of retained placentas, and assisting at Caesarean sections. I sat and passed the Diploma of the Royal College of Obstetricians and Gynaecologists in 1973 (DObst.RCOG) and was told by one of our professors, who was an examiner, that my score was among the top five in the country. He was disappointed when he later heard that I was switching to general practice.

At this point in time, my relatives in Guyana were busy escaping from racial discrimination and oppression. They were going mainly to the United States and Canada. I had to decide whether to return to Guyana or stay in the UK. I was a naturalised British subject by then. Of course, the third option was to follow them to North America, as many of my classmates were doing. The attraction was money, as American doctors were paid a lot better than UK doctors.

At the time, there was a constant flow of UK and Canadian doctors to the United States and Indian doctors to the UK. Some UK doctors moved to Canada also. I decided we should visit Guyana to see our relatives and check out the situation.

In 1972, we travelled to Guyana. Interestingly, when we landed in transit in Port of Spain, Trinidad, we were surprised to be greeted by Moira's parents and younger sister. They were as excited to see us as we were to see them. They behaved as if nothing had happened, despite no communication with us for several years. We travelled together to Guyana.

I hadn't told my folks I was coming and wanted it to be a surprise. Unfortunately, someone from my village spotted us on the ferry and alerted my folks in the village that I was on my way. We stayed overnight with Moira's parents and visited my village the next day. It was great to see them all, but I was sad that my nani (maternal grandmother) was no longer there.

While in Guyana, we made two trips into the interior with Moira's parents. They had a property in a place called Sans Souci, which was along the Canje River. They had a house and several acres of rice fields. We spent a few nights there. It was accessible by unsealed road, so we drove there in their old Morris Minor station wagon. On our way there, the car radiator sprung a leak, and we had to return to New Amsterdam, topping it up every few miles. After it was repaired by a local mechanic, we continued our journey.

The second trip was much longer. We travelled by launch (long motorised pontoon) to a place called Kwakwani. An American-owned bauxite mining company was there, and Moira's father was the doctor who looked after the staff and managers. The workers were locals, but the managers were Americans. Moira's parents were given a house in the managers' compound, and we were allowed to enjoy the swimming pool on-site.

On Sunday morning, there was a lavish barbeque brunch with drinks around the pool. It was very relaxed and enjoyable—a great lifestyle. I was able to accompany my father-in-law on his ward rounds at the local hospital.

One night, they had a party and invited a few friends. We had some food, including local fish. Before the dancing started, I felt very unwell with a severe headache, vomiting, abdominal cramps, and diarrhoea. I did not know what was going on and received no assessment or treatment from Dr. Ferdinand.

I thought I was going to die and stayed in the bedroom. I could hear loud music by the West Indian group called the Merrymen, and everyone dancing and laughing. No one paid me any attention except for Moira asking once if I was okay. I did not want to miss out and tried to leave the room only to rush back to bed, as I was about to pass out. I think one family friend was glad I was sick, as he took the opportunity of dancing with Moira all night! Was I jealous? What do you think?

I believe my illness was due to an allergic reaction to the reef fish. I have had two further episodes of a similar reaction later in Bali and on Dunk Island on the Barrier Reef. I think, in retrospect, it was ciguatera fish poisoning.

We travelled back by small plane, a trip I did not enjoy. It was my first time on a small plane flight, and I felt very sick as the plane bounced about throughout the one-hour flight to Georgetown.

During that visit to Guyana I took the opportunity to visit and to speak to several doctors, including an obstetrician in Georgetown. They all were very disillusioned with the health system in Guyana, which was not a priority on the government's agenda. They couldn't get drugs and had no blood transfusion service. The doctors had the knowledge and the experience but not the facilities to treat patients well. Every one of them advised me not to return to practice, as they themselves were trying to leave. That convinced me that we should remain in the UK. Several of my relatives had already left the country.

Kaieteur Falls

My one regret is that, despite going back to Guyana several times, I never visited the Kaieteur Waterfall on the Potaro River, which is a branch of the Essequibo River and is situated in Kaieteur National Park. This waterfall is world-famous for having the largest single drop in the world—741 feet. This is five times higher than Niagara Falls in the USA/Canada and twice the height of Victoria falls in Zambia/Zimbabwe. It is one of the tourist attractions in Guyana.

On our return to the UK, I decided to switch to general practice and enrolled in the vocational training course for general practice. I could cut the course to two years instead of three, as my year in obstetrics and gynaecology was recognised as suitable training. I had to do six months of paediatrics, six months of general medicine, and a year in general practice, spread between two teaching group practices. I also had to attend tutorials at the university for a half day each week.

The reason for the switch from obstetrics and gynaecology to general practice was the recognition that it took years to achieve consultant status, with years in waiting as a registrar. It was a bottleneck, and one only got promoted when someone moved up the ladder or died. Besides, I was not research-oriented and preferred to spend my time treating clinical conditions, so I would end up not in a teaching hospital with the support of junior trainees but in a smaller country town, where I would be on call twenty-four hours a day. Also, general practitioners were paid better than registrars.

I was eager to get on and establish some sort of foundation for family life. We decided to buy a house and found a two-bedroom one that was very compact and something we could afford. We signed the contract subject to bank finance.

One of my colleagues was trying to sell his house in the same locality to buy a bigger one for his expanding family. He pressured me to buy his and cancel my contract on the other one. It meant a further seven hundred pounds of debt, which was going to be a strain. He made it easier for us and agreed for us to pay this difference to him in instalments as we could afford it, so we agreed to proceed. We told the previous vendor we couldn't get bank finance, which was not true.

In order to meet our financial commitments, I started working for the emergency locum service on my nights off, doing a six-hour shift. They provided a car, a driver, and an emergency drug kit. I was earning more from this job than my regular one.

One night, they needed someone to suture an episiotomy wound in a small hospital where the delivery was done by a midwife and could not find anybody. I was asked to do it because of my obstetrics experience, even though I was not on call. I obliged.

I also took my two weeks holiday each year to do a locum in Sunderland. I had to man a general practice while the husband and wife owners (both GPs) took a caravanning holiday to Europe. I did this for two years. It was great in that the very efficient receptionist moved into their house, to which the surgery was attached, and not only guided me but also provided morning and afternoon tea, plus a cooked three-course lunch every day.

For my paediatric attachment, I was placed at the Sunderland Children's Hospital under the watchful eye of a very experienced but strict and demanding old-school paediatrician named Dr. Heycock. He was a short stocky man who, befittingly for a paediatrician, had six children. Sunderland was about a forty-five minute drive from Newcastle. There were two senior house officers. We were the most junior doctors in the hospital and were expected to work every day. We were also on call alternate nights and weekends. We admitted emergency patients and those arranged by the consultants through their outpatient clinics. We initiated their treatments.

I had to be on the ward an hour before the consultant arrived for his ward rounds, as I was expected to know what was happening with every patient and had to check the urine of every child every day, including microscopy. Every child had to be in bed, and no parents could be present during ward rounds.

My consultant was a good teacher, and I learnt a lot during the six months I was there. He gave clear instructions and reasons for his decisions, quoting relevant statistics. He had personal experience raising his own kids. I had to visit the maternity unit at the General Hospital and check every newborn baby.

We were looked after very well, with cooked lunches and dinners and all-milk coffees. I had a room, and Moira came to stay on weekends when I was on call. She also brought some home-made food.

My next attachment was at Bensham General Hospital as a senior house officer for six months, gaining valuable experience in general medicine. Bensham was across the Tyne River from Newcastle. The Tyne Bridge across the river was an older and smaller version of the Sydney Harbour Bridge. I am led to believe it was designed and built by the same people. The arrangement was very similar to the Sunderland Children's Hospital, in that my on-call hours were the same, duties were similar, and meals and accommodation were provided, but the patients were adults. Again, it was hard work but a good experience.

Three things come to mind as I recall my time there. The first was being offered a "chip butty" by a nurse for a midnight snack. I did not believe that two slices of bread with potato chips for filling would taste good and laughed at the idea. With encouragement, I finally decided to try it, and to my surprise liked it.

The second was when a patient decided to have a cardiac arrest while we were about to discuss his case during a ward round. The consultant stepped out of the way and said to me, "Do something!" I started CPR, and the nurse summoned reinforcements. The consultant remained an observer. He did not know what to do! It has been a long time since he did emergency medicine. The patient survived.

The third memorable event was when I admitted a middle-aged lady who was pale, sweaty, and very breathless. She was in terminal cardiac failure, and after working on her for hours doing everything I could think of and giving her large doses of drugs, I gave her up for dead and went to bed. I told the nurses that I did not think she would make it, and I expected a call to say she had passed away. No such call came.

In the morning, I was curious to know how she was and went to the ward—to find her sitting up having a cup of tea and a light breakfast. She was smiling, had no breathlessness, and was joking with the nurses and other patients. It was wonderful to see, and it was the sort of result that made me feel happy to be a doctor. She simply said, "Thank you, doctor, for saving my life."

By this time, Moira was in her final year of dentistry, and she eventually graduated with a bachelor of dentistry (BDS) degree. We had her younger sister and one of my nieces, whom we had sponsored from Guyana, living with us and attending college. Moira became pregnant soon after.

I spent the next six months working in a group practice in Newcastle under the supervision of a senior GP, Tony Ashcroft. My classmate and friend, Keith, was already a junior partner in this practice. There I gained valuable experience and knowledge.

Around this time, our daughter, Nalini, was born by Caesarean section on September 26, 1974, at Princess Mary Maternity Hospital. Fathers were not allowed in the operating theatre at that time, so I had to wait in the doctor's lounge while she was being delivered. I waited anxiously for word from theatre as I paced up and down and drank many cups of coffee. No one rang me, so after an hour, I feared the worse and decided to ring the operating theatre. I was relieved to hear that all was well, and the baby was in an incubator in the nursery, as she needed some oxygen. Moira was in recovery. I was able to visit the nursery and see Nalini.

After a suitable period, Moira started working part-time in a dental practice to consolidate her skills, and I looked after the baby during those evenings.

Ram with baby Nalini

The final six months of my course was spent in a group practice in the small town of Blyth, half an hour's drive from Newcastle, under the supervision of a delightful GP called Harry Madgwick. I settled into this practice so well that I was offered the opportunity to replace a senior colleague who was retiring. I declined, as I was not sure where we should settle. While on call for this practice overnight and weekends, I stayed at the local hospital. I passed the examination and obtained membership of the Royal College of General Practitioners (MRCGP) in June of 1975.

Living in our house at number 7, Chelton Close, Wideopen, Northumberland, was enjoyable. It was a comfortable home and, being on a cul-de-sac, was very quiet. There were only eleven houses on the street, and we soon got to know the neighbours very well. We had a small backyard with a lawn area and a small kitchen garden. I took great pride in growing some vegetables like carrots, beans, Brussels sprouts, corn, and tomatoes. In the flower beds, I grew roses bordered by crocuses and tulips.

The best time in the street was New Year's Eve when we had a progressive party starting at house number one at five in the evening and then worked our way up the street, eating and drinking at each house. We always skipped our turn because they all wanted to end up at our house last, as we had the best party music to dance the night away, invariably finishing around dawn.

While we were living there, Moira's parents and sister Donna decided to visit us. For some strange reason, they flew to Ireland and then on to Prestwick airport in Ayr, Scotland. We had to drive from Newcastle to pick them up, a journey that took about six hours. Before that, I had to sell my Volkswagen Beetle and acquire a bigger car, an Austin Maxi, so we could all fit.

While they were with us, we heard that Moira's sister Mary Rose was arriving at Southampton by ship. They wanted to meet her. We drove all night along the M6 motorway, arriving at seven in the morning. After meeting her, we drove to London, but she had too much luggage, so she had to make her own way there.

We went to stay in Southgate in a house owned by another of Moira's sisters, Lily. The house was in a poor state, as it had been vacant for some time. There was dust everywhere, and we had to dodge cobwebs hanging from the ceiling. Moira and her mother wanted to start cleaning. This was after a long tiresome journey. We'd travelled along the M3 motorway and then the North Circular around London. The traffic was such that it took us three hours to travel about five miles. We arrived at the house at ten at night. We were exhausted.

I got so fed up that I decided to bundle everyone back in the car and drive a further four and a half hours back to Newcastle. We left Mary Rose in London. We arrived back home at about four in the morning, exactly twenty-seven hours after we had left for Southampton. I drove most of the way, about seventeen hours total.

I was working very long hours, so Moira's father had a word of advice for me. He said that I should not forget that I had a young wife who needed more of my time.

CHAPTER 7

THE GREAT DILEMMA

I was a bit disillusioned with British general practice at the time. I did not like the absence of hospital attachment and hence the lack of opportunity to treat medical conditions that I was quite capable of handling. There were also requests for an excessive number of house calls and repeat prescriptions, which were not screened at all and hence not an effective use of a doctor's time or in fact good medicine. The five-minute appointment system gave inadequate time to deal with patients' problems properly. Too many patients were in for bogus sickness certificates.

For one mad moment, I thought I might like to be farther down south nearer to London and my friends in Essex, so I started applying for jobs in those areas. I went for an interview in the Isle of Sheppey, and after seeing the poky little group practice and being treated to a typical stuffy English lunch, I was told they ran a three-minute appointment system! I said I couldn't justify seeing patients every three minutes and was promptly told that was non-negotiable. I offered my apology, and Moira and I made a hasty retreat to London.

We then started thinking that we went to the UK for an education, and having done that, there was no real reason to remain there, especially as the weather was crap. It was not an option to return to Guyana, so we started considering going to some other country where English was spoken and our qualifications were recognised. The obvious choices were the United States or Canada. These had the added advantage of being near to our relatives, many of whom had left Guyana and settled there. Better remuneration would have been an added bonus.

The one concern was what to do with Moira's sister and my niece. We discussed this with them, and Donna decided to move to London to work, while Devika decided to study nursing. I managed to help Devika get into the training course at the Royal Victoria Infirmary and to live in the nurses' residence.

I did not like the American health system with its high rate of litigation, so the choice was Canada, even though I did not like the thought of six months of winter each year. There was a shortage of GP/anaesthetists in Canada, and many positions were advertised in the *British Medical Journal*. I started applying for jobs and received an offer for a GP position in Halifax, Nova Scotia. I then thought that was a bit too isolated and far from my relatives in Toronto. I applied and got offered one of the four resident training positions in the department of anaesthesiology at the University of Saskatoon in Saskatchewan. The idea was to become a GP/anaesthetist.

I wanted a permanent resident visa for Canada but was only offered a student visa, as Canada felt it was over-doctored at the time. This meant that after finishing anaesthetic training, I would have to leave the country and reapply for residency, but without any guarantee it would be granted. I was disappointed and not prepared to go on that basis.

The head of the department in Saskatoon rang me to find out where I was, as I was four weeks late in starting the course, and the other three residents were having to do extra work, including after-hours calls. I explained my predicament, and he said he would see what influence he could bring to bear on the immigration department. He rang again two days later and said he was unsuccessful, so I asked him to offer the position to someone else.

By this time, itchy feet had well and truly set in, so we started to look at other options. We decided to try for Australia, as a few of my classmates were also considering it. It was English-speaking, our qualifications were recognised, and it had an abundance of sunshine. We were told it was a great country by our previous landlady, who had visited several times, as she had relatives there. I had also worked with an Australian senior registrar in the obstetric unit.

The one big disadvantage was that Australia was such a long way from any of my relatives, and they were not happy with this idea. We decided to go for twelve months and see what it was like. We could always return to the UK if it did not work out, as we were both British citizens.

I started applying for GP positions in Australia and visited the Australian Embassy office in Leeds. There I was met by some very friendly staff who said we would have no problems getting permanent resident visas, as Australia was looking for doctors, especially British-trained ones. Australia had a reputation of having a white Australia policy at the time, so I asked if I would be accepted. They laughed and said that it was only the reputation abroad, but once in the country, I would find that I would be given a fair go and not be likely to experience any racial discrimination. One staff member even said that she had an Indian GP in Australia who was very good and whom she liked.

By this time, I had already received communication from several practices in Australia and was interested in one in a place called Port Augusta in South Australia. I tried to get some information on Port Augusta from the staff at the embassy, but neither of them knew anything. I decided to look it up in a book. There were two sentences about Port Augusta, saying it was a coastal town in South Australia at the top of the Spencer Gulf. It was the gateway to the north and west of the country, and the main employers were the Commonwealth Railways and the Electricity Trust of South Australia.

I asked if they had a picture of a typical coastal town and was shown a poster of Coolangatta on the Gold Coast. This was a poster promoting tourism, but I thought, *Wow! That would do me!*

Port Augusta

Coolangatta Beach

Apart from thinking Port Augusta would be like Coolangatta, I was impressed by a letter from one of the doctors in Port Augusta, who expounded on the virtues of the city but conveniently ignored the drawbacks. He mentioned that Port Augusta was only a three-hour drive from the city of Adelaide and even closer to the wine-producing areas of the Clare and Barossa valleys. He gave details of the practice and the local hospital. So it was not surprising that Port Augusta was chosen above the offers from Naracoorte in South Australia, Bunbury in Western Australia, and Roseberry in Tasmania.

The embassy staff asked, "How soon can you go?" They could have all the paperwork done, including medicals, in two weeks! I did not even have to have a job lined up. Furthermore, they would pay our fares to Australia, and we only had to pay fifty pounds in total. Things were all moving so fast that it was making me nervous. I also felt I was being ungrateful to England, after all the help I was given. We decided we would go to Australia, but not before going to see our relatives in Guyana.

For many months before that, we had been trying to get a visitor's visa for my mother to visit England, to see where I had spent the previous eleven years. The application was knocked back, and an appeal to the Home Secretary was also unsuccessful, so we appealed to the Ombudsman. He could not understand why it was denied in the first place and ordered a visa to be granted to my mother and younger sister forthwith. My mother, being illiterate, needed my sister as her travel companion. The department thought I was trying to get my mother to live permanently in the UK, ignoring the fact that we were trying to go to Australia.

Even though the Ombudsman directed that visas be granted, the staff at the British High Commission in Georgetown were still trying to give us a hard time when we went to collect the visas. However, they eventually granted them.

After visiting Guyana, we brought my mother and sister back to the UK. We showed them around, and they were able to see all our relatives and where we lived. They then travelled to Toronto, where my sister was due to get married.

We sold our house, our car, and most of our furniture as we prepared for the move to Australia. The total sum of money we had to take to Australia was two thousand Australian dollars. Some of our possessions were freighted to Australia and took twelve weeks to arrive. We left Heathrow on September 2, 1975, arriving in Adelaide two days later after a lengthy, slow, and tiring trip via Bahrain, Bangkok, Singapore, Sydney, and Melbourne. I still remember the impression of wide-open spaces, sunburnt grass, and sunshine as we touched down in Sydney. This was in such contrast to the lush greenery of the English countryside.

CHAPTER 8

PORT AUGUSTA: A SOLID TOWN

On arrival at Adelaide airport, I looked for P. C., the Indian partner in the practice, who I was told would be meeting me. I had no description of him, and he had none of me, and certainly no photographs. His senior partner had asked him how would he recognise me, and he said that wouldn't be hard, as there would not be too many professional-looking Indians travelling with a wife and an eleven-month-old baby. It was true, as we recognised each other instantly.

After greeting each other, we collected our bags and went to the Travel Lodge on South Terrace, where he checked us in. We were allowed some time to rest and freshen up, and we had a room-service lunch. P. C. had made a booking in the restaurant for dinner at seven thirty. Unfortunately, we were so tired that we fell asleep—and woke up at nine thirty! I went and found P. C. and apologised. We decided to change it to another room-service meal. We tried to sleep that night, but our daughter's body clock was out of whack. She was wide awake all night, so we had little sleep.

The next morning, P. C. and I went to the medical registration board to complete my registration papers to practice in South Australia. There I received an apology that my diploma in obstetrics was no longer recognised as a specialist degree. Apparently, the diploma in child health was a specialist degree, however. This was a surprise to me, as I did not consider myself a specialist.

After checking out of the hotel, we had a quick drive through the city centre, and then P. C. picked up his new Jaguar Saloon, in which we set off to Port Augusta. I was in the front passenger seat. The car had to be run in, so we could not go faster than ninety kilometres per hour. The sun was in my eyes, and I pulled the sun visor down. It came off in my hand! You can imagine the embarrassment I felt as I apologised. P. C. was gracious and said, "Don't worry, I will get it fixed."

We travelled through Port Wakefield, Snowtown, Crystal Brook, and Port Pirie on our way. It was a long trip, and I remember asking myself, *Where on earth were we going?* As we travelled north, the trees became fewer and smaller until there were only short shrubs in the red dirt. Some peculiar large dry balls of twigs were rolling across the road at frequent intervals, and every now and again in the dry paddocks there was a small whirlwind carrying with it red dust in the air. I sought some explanation, and P. C. told me about salt bushes and tumbleweeds.

The road we were travelling on was called Highway One, and it went along the low mountain range, which I understood was the Flinders Ranges, named after the English explorer Matthew Flinders. The Spencer Gulf was now visible. I could see no sandy beaches or palm trees, and I then realised that I might have been conned. Where I was going was no Coolangatta!

A few years later, I was curious to see what Coolangatta was like and went for a visit. It lived up to all my expectations, and I bought two timeshare units there in a resort called Beach House right on the beachfront. My family and I have been holidaying there once or twice a year for over thirty years. Coolangatta had been beckoning to me since I was in England!

We arrived in Port Augusta and were taken to a house in an area called Augusta Park. It was a house owned by the South Australian Housing Trust, and it was rented for us at $29 per week. We had three bedrooms, a lounge/dining, bathroom, and kitchen. The front and back lawns were largely three-leaf clover. There was no garage. It had no air-conditioning. Two of the doctors' wives had put in some basic second-hand furniture and a cot, in addition to a few groceries.

That evening, we were invited to Dr. P. C.'s house for a rather sumptuous Indian banquet to meet all the doctors and their wives. Our daughter was still out of sorts and cried all evening. The doctors and their partners were all very friendly and welcoming. The practice set-up was explained to me, in addition to my terms of employment. I was expected to start work in two days.

Port Augusta

The next morning, one of the doctors introduced me to a local car dealer, who lent me a Holden Kingswood to use until I decided which car to buy. I had to learn to use a column gear change, which I was not familiar with. We decided to explore the town and get some groceries.

Port Augusta is situated at the top of the Spencer Gulf. It was once a thriving port for exporting grains, wool, etc. It lends itself to water activities like sailing, fishing, crabbing, swimming, canoeing, water-skiing, jet-skiing, and beach picnics. It had a population of around 12,000 at the time. Two thirds were born and raised in Port Augusta and were referred to as the locals. Others were professionals who came to town to work. They were the teachers, nurses, doctors, lawyers, policemen, bank clerks, and businesspeople. In addition, about 7 percent were Aboriginals who either lived in the town or in the Davenport Aboriginal Reserve just on the outskirts.

Port Augusta was in two parts: Port Augusta West and Port Augusta East, separated by the Spencer Gulf. There was a new bridge over the gulf, but the old bridge was still there and served as a walking bridge and a fishing platform for the locals.

Port Augusta was the big smoke for the smaller nearby towns of Stirling North, Quorn, Wilmington, Hawker, and the more distant townships of Leigh Creek, Cooberpedy, Andamooka, Roxby Downs, Maree, Glendambo, Kimba, and Woomera. It was also the city for the outlying farms and sheep/cattle stations. The Royal Flying Doctor's base was also there.

The main employers were the Commonwealth Railways, which had its workshops there, and the Electricity Trust of South Australia. The coal-fired power stations generated electricity for most of South Australia and Victoria. Other significant employers were the Port Augusta gaol and the

Port Augusta hospital, in addition to motels, hotels, petrol stations, and other tourist-related industries.

The climate was semi-desert and arid, boasting very hot summers (40°C) but mild winters. Spring and autumn were the better seasons. The houses needed air-conditioning and not heating, which was the opposite to those in the UK. It was hard to keep plants alive, and it was advisable to use native plants, which were hardy and needed less water to survive. Lawns needed frequent watering to keep them alive, quite unlike the UK. I had to learn to use a lawnmower from the local equipment hire place. I soon learnt that geraniums grew well from cuttings and only need frequent watering to survive. I developed a garden of geraniums from clippings from one of the other doctors.

There was a knock on the front door on our second night in Port Augusta. I opened the door to find a smiling gentleman standing there. He was a friendly sort and said, "Hi, I am Chris. I hear you are from the West Indies."

I said, "Yes, I am."

He then said, "You must play cricket then."

I answered in the affirmative, and he invited me to practice with his club, which was called Centrals, even though the cricket club was called Stirling North Cricket Club. I did take up his offer and played for the club for several years. They were impressed by my batting and not my bowling, so I was picked as a batsman and batted up the order. I was not used as a bowler. In contrast, I was a bowler in the university team and batted lower down the order. At high school, I was a batsman. Nowadays, I would be an all-rounder, which did not exist in those days. However, toward the end of my career, when playing for the C grade, I was allowed to bat and bowl.

The soil was red sand with little nutrition. Very soon, I witnessed dust storms the likes of which I had never seen before. It was heartbreaking to clean the porch and windows, and then a dust storm would arrive and undo all my good work so that I had to start all over again. This was particularly annoying in my second house, where I had installed an outdoor swimming pool. The dust storm was particularly bad, as across the road was a public park with a few pieces of play equipment standing on red sand. There was no grass or trees. The visibility during a storm was two metres. That's worse than the snowstorms and fog I witnessed in the UK.

The town had a main street running through it, and it was the main shopping area. There were a few satellite shopping complexes elsewhere. We made our way to the biggest supermarket in town—called Jack's Supermarket, named after its owner, "Jack the Price-Slasher," who owned two other supermarkets in town.

As we wandered the aisles looking for items, we must have looked lost to the manager, who was observing us from the mezzanine level. She concluded that I must be the new doctor in town and came down to see if she could be of help to us. We were grateful for this and soon were directed to where we could find the items on our list. We thought, *What a wonderful and helpful lady!* We learnt afterwards she was anxious to meet me as I was the doctor she was advised to see by her previous doctor, whom I was replacing.

We were later invited to her house for a barbecue and became good friends—a friendship that is still ongoing. As the family doctor, I delivered three of her grandchildren, one of whom had congenital dislocation of the hip. That was the first case that I personally picked up at birth.

My neighbours were interesting in that on one side, I had the local police superintendent, who was a rather unfriendly and somewhat sarcastic individual. He apparently did not like doctors, especially brown ones. His only saving grace was his eighteen-year-old daughter, who loved to wash her car on the front lawn in her bikini, hoping she would be noticed, and no doubt admired!

As I was mowing my lawn one weekend, a voice from across the opposite fence asked if would like a beer. It was my other neighbour. He was a friendly ocker type with a ruddy-complexioned, weather-beaten, alcoholic face. I accepted his beer and had a chat. He then invited us over for a barbecue, and we became good friends with him and his family. His mother taught me to play some card games, such as canasta. This family was a true example of the local Port Augusta people. From them, I learnt many slang words.

Konanda Medical Clinic

I turned up to work on the following Monday and was allowed to sit in with one of the other doctors to learn the ropes, after having been introduced to the staff and given a tour of the practice. It was a group practice in an old converted house, with an extension added on to the side.

I had never given anaesthetics, so my Irish partner spent three months training me, and I became so competent and confident that I gave anaesthetics even for ear, nose, and throat surgery, babies, and caesarean sections. I also learned to do tonsillectomies, appendicectomies, circumcisions, vasectomies, and wedge resections for ingrown toenails, and continued the skills I had in gynaecological surgery. I was competent to do tubal ligations, dilation and curettage, termination of pregnancies, instrumental deliveries, and removal of retained placentas.

We had our own operating theatre lists two mornings per week and grouped ourselves into two teams. Our practice was a teaching practice, so we had students from Adelaide medical schools and overseas. One day, I gave an anaesthetic for a patient, then turned and did the operation on the next patient. This left the student perplexed, so he had to ask the question whether I was an anaesthetist or a surgeon. This took me by surprise. I said, "Neither. I am a country doctor." Of course, he was not used to seeing this, as it would never occur in the city hospitals, where there is specialisation and in fact super-specialisation.

I recall a funny incident when one day one of our senior partners was using the newly acquired diathermy machine and accidentally set alight the pubic hair of a female patient. He panicked and called for the fire extinguisher!

It was an equal partnership, in that we shared the net income after expenses equally, regardless of how much work each partner did. This in fact led to problems, as I will explain later. Management was largely left to our Indian partner, from whom I learnt a lot about practice management. This became very useful when I managed my own practice later.

There were some tensions early in the practice, partly because I attracted the younger women and their young families, especially the pregnant ones who had once attended the other doctors in the practice. There were two other single-doctor practices in town, but we were self-sufficient and gave no cooperation to them at that stage. The tension was such that I was interrogated by my partners after accompanying one of those doctors to a Rotary dinner meeting. They feared the doctor was trying to poach me.

Our senior partner was a Rotarian, and he used to leave patients in his waiting room in the evenings while he attended the Rotary dinners once a week. The patients were so used to waiting that the ladies brought their knitting and flasks of tea, while the men brought their books. It was an enjoyable practice, and we took up to nine weeks' holidays and a week's study leave each year. This allowed us to travel overseas regularly.

A doctor who lived and worked in the neighbouring town of Whyalla, which was known as the Steel City, heard about me coming to Port Augusta and became very excited. He thought with a name like Bhola, I probably was from the Punjab area of India and might be able to speak Punjabi. For months, he looked forward to having someone he could converse with in his native language. He made a special effort to visit me in Port Augusta and was absolutely deflated when he found out that I was from South America and did not speak a word of Punjabi.

Dental Practice

Moira wanted to retain her skills as a dentist, so we approached the only dental practice in town and asked if they would consider giving her some part-time work. This was done over dinner at the senior partner's house. They decided they could not offer her work, as there was only enough work for the two of them.

It was a big mistake! Moira decided to set up her own practice, and as it so happened, premises that housed the part-time Flying Doctors became available. The Royal Flying Doctor Service decided that their doctors had to give up general practice and become full-time Flying Doctors. We set up the practice, and Moira, being such a competent dentist, attracted most of the patients belonging to one of the other dentists. He had to leave town.

We juggled our time to look after our daughter. We had her attending day care in the mornings, and I picked her up at midday. The housekeeper did her work in the mornings and babysat our daughter in the early afternoon until one of us got home.

Cars

I initially bought a Holden Kingswood, as I felt obliged to do so, having been allowed to use one free of charge for three months by the dealer. However, I did not like it. Moira had a Ford Escort.

After nine months, I realised I could fulfil my ambition to own a Jaguar. This was possible because I could lease one, so long as I could make the monthly lease payments. Besides, lease payments were tax deductable. My partners, who all had Jaguars, thought I was a bit precocious and was copying them, but they did not realise that I'd had that ambition since I was at medical school.

Our cars were damaged by hailstones, as we had no carport or garage. I had never witnessed anything like it before. On a hot sunny summer's day, the weather suddenly changed, as a heavy cloud moved over and hailstones the size of golf balls came crashing down. I had to run for cover. Some people ended up with black eyes and bruises. Our cars were pitted all over. Fortunately, the windscreens and windows were intact. They were repaired by covering the tops with vinyl.

That was it! I decided it was time and ordered the Jaguar and a Toyota Crown for Moira. The choice of colour for the Jaguar was limited. None were in stock, but three were on a ship from the UK. I discounted the blue and maroon ones, as my partners had those colours, and settled for the yellow one, sight unseen. I am told that my partners had a Jaguar brought to them from Adelaide by the dealer, and they took it for a test drive along the highway to Whyalla. To test the brakes, one of the doctors slammed them at high speed and wrote off all four tyres! They had to be rescued, and the car towed away.

Yellow Jaguar car in the driveway of Stirling North House

When I went to pick up my car, I had a couple of friends with me. I was shocked to see the bright canary-yellow car with red leather seats. It took me by surprise, and I spent the next half hour pondering whether I wanted it or not. In the end, the more I looked at it, the more it grew on me, and I thought that even though it was a bold statement, I would have it. As I drove off along the narrow lane, it was so quiet that I could not hear the engine. Thinking I had stalled it, I pressed the accelerator, and the car took off, throwing all of us back against our seats.

Everyone in Port Augusta soon knew to whom the yellow Jag belonged. I was no longer incognito. I remained a Jag man and later had a further three Jags interspersed with two Mazda RX7s. Later, I had a Mercedes wagon, an Audi A4, a Holden Caprice, an HSV Holden Avalanche, and an Audi Allroad Wagon. At present, I have an Audi TT and a Subaru Outback. Interestingly, the Holden HSV Avalanche attracted the most attention of all, and the TT the most admiration.

The Audi TT ... my indulgence

Some Early Holidays

Surfers Paradise

I woke up in the morning, looked out across the garden from the hotel balcony, and appreciated the sight of palm trees and hibiscus shrubs with their bright red flowers around the swimming pool. The weather was warm, even at eight o'clock in the morning, for we were in Surfers Paradise on Queensland's Gold Coast, where we had decided to have a week's holiday. It felt like I was in Guyana because of the climate, vegetation, and some wooden houses on stilts (Queenslanders). As we explored the area later and enjoyed the swimming pool and beach, a question did occur to me: "What were we doing in Port Augusta instead of Queensland?" We did some sightseeing and, of course, visited Dreamworld and Sea World.

Not being accustomed to undercurrents and strong waves, I had an anxious moment when I waded into the ocean with my twenty-month-old daughter. Moira was sitting on the beach as she liked to do while I entertained Nalini. We were standing in the water knee-deep. I was not holding her hand, and I looked away for a couple of seconds. Suddenly, she was not there! A sweeping wave had knocked her over, and she was tumbling in it about three metres from me, wide-eyed and scared. I ran to her and picked her up. Of course, I said nothing to her mother!

South-East Asia

The Irishman, Scotsman, and Indian partners decided they would take a four-week trip to India together and leave the other three of us to run the practice. The senior partner only saw his own patients and had a three-week waiting list, so he was no good to us. They did organise for a locum to help us. He was a retired psychiatrist who was so hopeless at general practice that patients he saw were unhappy and promptly made another appointment to see us. This created extra work for us, so we gave him the sack.

It was a difficult four weeks for Victor and I, as we had to cover the patients of the missing three doctors in and out of hospital as well as our own. The practice had a policy that holidays should be spaced out so that only one doctor was away at any one time, and certainly no more than two. This was ignored. On their return, they were surprised that their next pay cheques were much less than usual and asked, "What have you guys been doing while we were away?" This insinuated that we were having a lazy time, which was not appreciated.

As payback, Victor and I decided to go away together with our wives and my daughter to South-East Asia for seven weeks. The plan was to visit Bali, Singapore, Kuala Lumpur, Penang, Bangkok, Hong Kong, and Manila. The trip was all booked, but unfortunately, Victor became very ill on the day before we were to depart and could not go. Our insurance did not cover us for cancellation, so Moira, Nalini, and I went on the trip.

In Bali, we had a personal tour guide, dressed in a colourful skirt and head gear, showing us the sights in a chauffeur-driven car. We saw the live volcano, a typical family compound with its various huts and temples, plus a wood-carving workshop in addition to various markets and beaches. The tour guide carried Nalini in his arms most of the time.

The next stop was Kuala Lumpur. We had another tour guide who took us to the Batu Caves with its menacing cheeky monkeys, the Selangor Pewter factory, a Batik factory, a rubber plantation, and various other places of interest.

In Penang, the ocean was the warmest I had ever come across. We visited the capital, Georgetown, and the snake temple. That was a freaky and intimidating experience, as one of the snake handlers approached me from behind and quickly wrapped a huge snake around my neck! I froze, and a photo was taken before the snake was removed, much to my relief.

Bangkok was an interesting city. The floating market was an unforgettable experience. The skill of the fast-moving motorboat drivers was impressive, as they weaved their way past the small boats laden with fruits and vegetables for sale. The children climbed from tourist boat to tourist boat looking for money. The people threw coins in the water just to see them dive to retrieve them with great success, despite the murkiness of the water. We saw the Grand Palace and the Temple of the Emerald Buddha, and visited Chang Mai to see elephants at work. Having three tailor-made suits and four trousers in twenty-four hours was impressive.

A cruise on a rice barge travelling through the countryside while sipping a cocktail called Dynamite was relaxing. Dynamite was made with

Thai whiskey and was very strong. I was advised by our guide to have no more than two, but somehow I managed four without falling overboard. The cruise ended with a feast of Thai food and a show with music and dancing.

One night, we arranged for a babysitter and went out to dinner, after which we asked the taxi driver to take us to a nightclub. We went in, ordered a drink, and then, to our surprise, the lights went down and a show started on the stage. It was a live sex performance, during which one of the actresses showed exquisite pelvic muscle control by pouring a bottle of Coke into her vagina and then standing up without spilling a drop! She next decided to shoot a boiled egg out of her vagina into the crowd! They then proceeded to have sex on the stage. It was a shocking but unforgettable experience for us, and certainly far from what we were looking for—a nightclub for some drinks and dancing!

Hong Kong was our next stop, and there, we were shown around by, and wined and dined with, Victor and Anita's relatives. We rode the Peak Train and did some shopping. Staying at the Peninsula Hotel and being picked up at the airport in a Rolls Royce was rather decadent. Having afternoon tea in the hotel lobby rubbing shoulders with VIPs was a snobby affair.

Our last stop was Manila in the Philippines. The streets crowded with Jeepneys that seemed not to follow any road rules was interesting. A trip to some waterfalls where we went under the falls on rafts was a great experience, and so was Pattaya, where I had my first ride on a jet ski—and my first proposition by a prostitute, as I walked along the street with my family! On the beach, the little Thai girls were fascinated by Nalini and wanted to touch her skin all the time.

Trip to Guyana in 1977

It was snowing and cold outside but hot inside the West Indian nightclub in Toronto, with pole dancers, strippers, and lap dancers. We were taken there for shock value by one of my nephews, who obviously underestimated our experience and broad-mindedness. He even cheekily secretly paid for a lap dancer to entertain, and hopefully embarrass, me. He wasted his money.

We were on an around-the-world trip and had a friend, Jenny, travelling with us. She was a nurse who did a locum in our practice and became a friend. She saw this as a golden opportunity to see some of the world. I had left my yellow Jaguar with her parents in Adelaide. Her father took great pride in showing of his new car to his workmates.

Before arriving in Toronto, we had spent a few days in Waikiki enjoying Hawaiian culture, sightseeing, Polynesian shows, and beaches. The weather there was perfect as usual. We even spent time in a disco, taking turns babysitting three-year-old Nalini in the hotel room at the Halekulani Hotel. We had our first experience of beach boys who apparently were making a decent living entertaining rich separated or widowed American ladies. One of them offered Jenny a proposition to accompany her to her hotel room, and for US$30, he would entertain her! She said thanks but no thanks.

Chicago was our next stop. It was freezing, with snow on the ground, a direct contrast to Hawaii. We stayed with one of my medical school classmates (a paediatrician) and her surgeon husband. It was a bit crowded with six of us in a one-bedroom apartment. We managed to do some sightseeing, checking out the city and Lake Michigan.

In Toronto, we were accommodated and shown around by one of my older sisters and her oldest son. Jenny took a fancy to him and said afterward that she would have married him if he had asked her! I suspected they'd had an affair after hearing such an admission.

A phone call came from Guyana while we were pelting snowballs at each other in the backyard of Moira's brother's house in Montreal. It was to tell us that her father had had a stroke in Guyana and was paralysed on one side. He was in his mid-seventies, and so was her mother, who was struggling to look after him. We decided to cut short our stay in Montreal and travel to Guyana.

We stayed with Moira's parents in New Amsterdam and helped look after her father. He was a heavy man, being only five feet two inches tall but about one hundred and thirty kilograms in weight. A neurologist, one of only two in Guyana, travelled from Georgetown to assess him. There was little that could be done apart from rehabilitation. No physiotherapists were available, so we did what we could. Transfers in and out of bed and on and off the toilet were challenging. Jenny's expertise as a nurse was invaluable, and she took to the task with great enthusiasm.

After a few weeks, we wanted to be on our way. Moira's sister and husband came from Barbados to stay with the parents for a few days, and Jenny generously stayed behind while we proceeded to Trinidad. We arranged to catch up with Jenny again in London.

In Trinidad, we stayed with a widowed family friend. We hired a car and drove around the island. Nalini had a wonderful time using a huge cast iron pot filled with rainwater as a swimming pool. These pots were obtained from the sugar estate, where they were used to boil the sugar cane juice to make sugar. At the house, the pot was used to catch rainwater from the roof for domestic consumption.

Our next stop was Barbados. By then, Moira's sister had returned, and we stayed with her. I was impressed that we could drive around the entire island in a few hours. It had wonderful beaches and many luxury hotels to cater to the American tourists. The Americans were choosing Barbados over Jamaica because of the Jamaican government's allegiance with communist Cuba. Many hotels in Jamaica were empty. It was in a nightclub in Bridgetown that I was first exposed to reggae dancing and was shown the dance moves by my sister-in-law. I also tasted Rum Coconut, a cocktail of rum and coconut water served in a green coconut.

During our trip around the island, my sister-in-law took us to a plantation house that was a tourist attraction. Apparently when it was an active plantation during the days of slavery, it was owned by an English lady who was notorious for selecting the best-looking slave to have sex with. Afterwards, she would have him killed! Of course, all the male slaves dreaded this and hoped they would never be selected. I am sure they would have been happy to volunteer if it wasn't for the fact that they would lose their lives afterwards.

The Doctor's Cave Hotel in Montego Bay in Jamaica was our home for the next few days. It was a colonial building with white walls and blue trim and was made of solid concrete. It was across the road from the famous Montego Bay, where we enjoyed sun-baking and swimming. I hired a car, and we visited the famous Dunn's River Falls, with water gently cascading across rocks. We climbed the rocks under the supervision of a guide who carried Nalini in his arms. The water was cold, but it was refreshing and invigorating to stand under the waterfalls.

One night we visited the Pepperpot Club, where one of our favourite bands, the Merrymen, were playing. It was interesting to find that I was the only Indian and Moira was the only light-skinned person there. We were able to practice our reggae dancing to our hearts' content. It was very dark inside, and the only way we knew there were others in the room was when they smiled, revealing their Colgate-white teeth.

Further along the coast was the resort town of Ocho Rios, where we were booked to stay in an apartment. It had a lovely beach. One evening, a cruise ship anchored off the coast, and then there was a hive of activity, as some crew arrived on the beach by tenders and started setting up tables and chairs complete with white tablecloths and flowers. There were torches everywhere, and it created a lovely sight as the sun was going down. The passengers then arrived, dressed in their flowery outfits, and they had a wonderful beach party with great music, food, and dancing. We could observe the proceedings from our balcony. After several hours, they packed up and left. It was a very smooth operation, and they took all the rubbish with them, leaving no trace of their visit.

A day trip to Kingston, the capital, was interesting. We visited the campus of the University of the West Indies and checked out the City Centre. We did not park or walk around, as we were told it was one of the most dangerous and unsafe cities in the world at the time. We were told of incidents where people would have their hand chopped off if they had it hanging out of the car window, to steal their rings and watches!

After a few days, we left for London and reconnected with Jenny. We showed her the sights of London before travelling to Newcastle upon Tyne, taking in the sights on the way. After that, we returned home to Australia.

Medical Conferences in Hawaii

As it was necessary for me to do postgraduate studies, and educational expenses were tax-deductible, I took advantage of combining them with holidays in exotic places overseas and in Australia, including Sydney. Some of these were organised by the University of Southern California and held in Hawaii. In Waikiki, they were always held at the Sheraton on Waikiki Beach. Lectures started at seven thirty in the morning and finished around one in the afternoon. We had the afternoons free to do as we pleased. This was a great arrangement. At dusk, it was time to meet the professors over canapés and drinks on the lawns by the beach. After that, we generally went out to dinner.

Sheraton and Royal Hawaiian Hotels

The first time I went alone, but the second time Moira was with me. The third time I was in between marriages, so I went alone again. The American doctors were busy collecting pieces of paper after each lecture to prove their attendance. This gave them postgraduate points, which they needed to remain board certified. At first, I could not figure out what they were doing. A few years later, that system was introduced in Australia.

The second week of the conferences were on an outer island, once on Kauai and another time on Maui. The lectures there were on two days only, leaving much time for relaxation and sightseeing.

The last time I had a surprise when a friend traced me at the conference to catch up. He and his companion had been at the Cannes Film Festival in France and were travelling back to Australia via Hawaii. We met for a Japanese dinner and had pre-dinner drinks in the courtyard.

A girl sitting alone at a table nearby was observing us for a while. After summoning up enough courage, she approached and asked if she could join us, as she was on her own. My friends dismissed her in a flash, saying they were not interested. I was of course interested, as I was on my own, but I said nothing. I suspected that they were gay, and this was confirmed when I saw that in their room, they only had one queen bed.

Conference in San Diego and the West Coast of America

In 1980, I went to a psychiatric conference in San Diego. It was so boring that after the first day, I did not attend again. Psychiatry was never my field, and I only enrolled in this conference because it was all that was available at the time I wanted to travel and was tax-deductible. Instead, I relaxed by the pool during the day and went dancing in the nightclub in the evening. It was not hard to find dancing partners. I spent one day at the famous San Diego Zoo, and another day, I took a coach trip to Tijuana in Mexico. There I bought a Mexican rug, a poncho, and an owl made of rope, which I still have.

After the conference, I went to Anaheim and stayed at the Disneyland Hotel. I enjoyed the rides at Disneyland. The next stop was Los Angeles, from where I visited Universal Studios and Hollywood. It was rather nostalgic walking along Hollywood Boulevard and seeing the houses of the famous film stars.

I then went to Las Vegas. I had no pre-booked accommodation, so I asked the taxi driver for a recommendation. He took me to a motel beside the MGM Grand Hotel. I checked in, and the guy insisted I had to pay for the first night up front. I did, and when I went to my room, I found it was filthy and poorly equipped. The bed left a lot to be desired. I sat down and thought this was depressing, and I did not come to Las Vegas to slum it. I marched back to reception with my bags to check out. He refused to refund my money, so I lost that. In disgust, I went next door and booked a beautiful room at the MGM Grand.

That evening, I decided to go for a walk along the strip. I had only gone two hundred metres when I was approached by two girls asking if I wanted a party. I was always interested in parties, but I couldn't understand why two complete strangers would invite me to a party. I asked where the party was, and when they said my room, I realised what they were all about. I was so naïve. I declined and walked away.

I saw a couple of wonderful dinner shows at the MGM Grand. One was the Siegfried Follies and the other was the Engelbert Humperdinck Show, preceded by a black American singer who was wonderful. An evening at Caesar's Palace listening to a band and having a meal was also great.

I went on a day trip to the Grand Canyon. It was a combination of a small plane flight and a coach drive. It was something special to see the Colorado River winding its way through the bottom of the canyon.

I then went to San Francisco. There I enjoyed seeing the Golden Gate Bridge and the trams going up and down the hilly streets. Eating along the boardwalk and a cruise on the water were also enjoyable. Everyone, it seemed, was either jogging or roller skating in Central Park. I did go to a nightclub one evening and had a few dances with a young lady who stood out all dressed in white.

After the two weeks on the West Coast of America, I went to see my relatives in Toronto and New York before going to Guyana. My mother accompanied me back to Toronto and then on to Australia.

Early Years in Practice

Konanda Medical Clinic

The team at Konanda Medical Clinic was self-sufficient and gave little cooperation to the other medicos in town. Several new doctors were recruited by another practice in town that wanted to build a clinic to rival Konanda. Many of the recruits were from Malaysia and India, and some were classmates of the doctor there. They created a purpose-built clinic on the west side of Port Augusta, which soon splintered acrimoniously. Consequentially, single-handed practices were set up in various parts of town, and in Quorn some thirty kilometres away. They had a certain amount of cooperation amongst themselves with respect to theatre sessions but did their own after-hours call individually.

Our partnership continued along its merry way until 1982, when two of my partners thought some members were not pulling their weight and suggested turning it into an associateship, where we all contributed equally to the expenses and kept what we earned. The others tried to convince me to this point of view, but I was concerned about their capacity to run a practice. Unable to persuade the partners, the two left and opened their own practice elsewhere in town, taking the practice manager with them.

I stayed with the partnership, but two years later, we realised they were right and decided to change to an associateship. One of the partners was not happy and left for Adelaide. This left the foundation partner, Dr. Yeung, and me in the practice. We reorganised the practice and systematically went about buying out the shares in the building from previous doctors' wives. Once we owned the building, we did some renovations and separated parts of it into two tenancies. One was occupied by an optometrist and another was turned into a dress shop.

We were happy and doing quite well. The bank did a valuation on the building for loan purposes. It cost around $100,000, including renovations. The bank's valuation was $190,000. Not a bad capital gain in such a short time.

Carlton Medical Centre

Another GP in town built a new practice and decided to approach us to join him, as we had the two biggest client bases in town. He could not recruit other doctors, and it did not make sense bringing in more doctors without a patient base. We initially could not see any advantage in joining him, but after numerous approaches over a six-month period, we decided to test him.

We valued our building and put a proposal to him. To do the deal, he would have to buy our building at twice valuation, employ all our staff including the cleaners, and give us a working contract for five years with a right of renewal for another five years. We also had to be paid 70 percent of our billings monthly. He accepted the offer, so we started working with him in 1986.

Without having to worry about practice management, we worked very hard for the next five years and saw a lot of patients every day. We provided a service to Port Augusta Gaol, and Dr. Yeung visited the workers at the Electricity Trust of South Australia on a weekly basis. It was soon evident that the practice lacked proper management, however, and when bills were not being paid and our cheques (wages) started bouncing at the bank, we knew we could not continue there. This gave birth to the idea of Port Augusta Medical Centre, about which I will say more later.

Marriage Problems

Moira and I were busy with our respective practices and probably neglected our relationship a little. People were recognising me and acknowledging me in the street as I went around Port Augusta. We formed many friendships, and many of the patients became friends. We in fact shared some of these patients.

Moira did not like being regarded merely as Dr. Bhola's wife and not Dr. Bhola the dentist. This led to some discontent. It did not help when patients started saying stupid things to her like, "Your husband is gorgeous; he can park his shoes under my bed anytime." One even said to her, "You should take a holiday somewhere by yourself, and I will look after your husband while you are away." This probably made her feel vulnerable and unappreciated.

This led eventually to her having a break by herself in the UK. She took Nalini with her. I was left alone for three months and was convinced she would not be back, so I got involved with a nurse. Eventually, I asked Moira to come back home, as she was very unhappy and depressed. I was not convinced our marriage was over and wanted us to work things out.

She agreed and returned home. Unfortunately, when she found out about my affair, she could not accept it and left again. She set up practice in the neighbouring town of Whyalla, where she lived for several years and eventually married Tony. They seemed happy and are still together.

The In-Between Years

Between 1978 and 1980, I was living alone. I managed to look after myself very well. The need for company and friends to avoid loneliness, however, was very strong. I became what you would call a party boy. I quickly surrounded myself with like friends, and we had many regular gatherings—dancing parties, barbecues, picnics, and dinner parties. I was one of the in-crowd. My house in Stirling North became a party house.

I learnt much later that my partners did not like it. They felt they were missing out, as they were not invited. But then again, they would not have enjoyed my type of parties, where the emphasis was on disco dancing and booze, especially rum.

Once, a few friends were going the Kingoonya races and invited me along. Kingoonya was a railway town but was bypassed by the new railway line. It was dying and only had a pub, a hall, and a few houses. They kept up the tradition of having annual horse races. I travelled up in my Daihatsu F20 wagon with the boot full of Eskys with drinks. After the races, we went to the dance in the hall.

Booze was not allowed in the hall. A band was playing country music. We were going to my car to have our drinks and then returning to the hall but soon got sick of doing that. I poured some Coke out of the bottle and topped it up with rum. As we got louder and merrier, the one local policeman who was on patrol commented with a smile, "I hope it is only Coke in that bottle."

During this time, I had Nalini every second weekend and some school holidays. I tried to give her a good time and would invite some of her friends to play with her and swim in the pool. I spoilt her, in Moira's opinion, as I would buy her many dresses and toys. She was a very easy child to look after.

I recall one night while she was with me, I was summoned to the maternity unit to do a delivery at about two in the morning. I woke her up and took her with me in her dressing gown. She sat in the nurse's station drawing and colouring in her book while I did the delivery.

One of the other doctors arrived and said to her, "Oh Nalini! Your dad must be doing a delivery."

Without taking her eyes off her book, she replied, "Yes, he won't be long now. She has stopped screaming." She was used to this scenario and had experienced it before. She was four at the time.

One evening, I thought I might go to one of the football clubs, as they were the most happening places in Port Augusta on weekends. There was a disco going on at Westies Club. I wanted to dance and asked several girls, but I was turned down by everyone. Apparently, you just don't dance with a well-known local entity like a doctor when you are an ordinary young lady. The girls were happy to dance with anyone else.

After that experience, I decided nightclubbing had to occur in Adelaide, where I was more anonymous. I had a friend called John whom I met when Moira and I went on a cruise of the Pacific Islands on the old ship the *Arcadia*. We were trying to reconcile our marriage, but Moira was not interested at that time. John and I would hit the nightclubs in Adelaide, looking to dance and maybe lucky enough to pick up.

A New Beginning

Our favourite was Regine's in Light Square, which was the in place at the time. It was an old converted church hall that was rather sophisticated and aimed mainly at the thirty- and forty-year-old singles. It was there that I met my future wife and long-term partner, Debbi.

It was late, and John and I had decided to survey the room to see if we could find someone to have one last dance with before calling it a night. I asked Debbi to dance, and she accepted. The song was "September" by Earth, Wind & Fire. We continued to dance, and that song was replayed several times. It became our special song.

While we were dancing, Debbi asked, "What's your name?"

When I said Ram, she said, "Pull the other leg."

I explained rather indignantly that it was short for Ramdyal. Her next question was, "What do you do?"

I said I was a doctor, to which she replied, "Yeah, right, that's what they all say in here to impress."

We decided to leave together to go for coffee at her place, and when I asked the concierge to bring my car, he drove up in my bright yellow Jaguar with its red leather seats. She said, "Well, I now believe you are either a doctor or a pimp."

We got along famously after that, and it was the start of our long and happy relationship.

We saw each other a few weekends in Adelaide and Port Augusta. One day, my receptionist said there was a message from a Debbi who said she would have chicken for dinner. I concluded she was on her way to Port Augusta and got the barbecued chicken. She arrived with her German shepherd in tow and her car packed with all her belongings. She wanted to see me one more time before going back to Tasmania to try to reconcile her marriage. She had been separated after four years.

While she was in Tasmania, we kept in touch. Sometimes her sister Vikki, who sounded just like Debbi on the phone, would have fun with me by ringing me and pretending to be Debbi with lots of lovey-dovey chatter. I could not tell the difference. After leading me on for a while, she would burst out in laughter and pass the phone to Debbi. What rascals they were!

After a year or so, I received a call from Debbi, who said she was faced with a dilemma. She had decided to leave her husband, having convinced herself that the marriage was finished. She wanted to do naturopathy and had gained admission to a course in Sydney, but she thought she might also like to come to Port Augusta. She did not know what to do.

Her friends and Vikki, who was by then in Sydney, wanted her to go there, saying they could not imagine her as a country doctor's wife. I told her to come to Port Augusta, and if it did not work out, she could go to Sydney with peace of mind.

One very hot Friday afternoon, I took time off work and went to pick her up from the Port Augusta airstrip. I waited for hours and wondered whether I had been stood up. I persevered, and in the absence of mobile phones, I had no idea where she was. The office at the airstrip was closed.

After about two hours, a small plane landed, and she disembarked, much to my relief and delight. That night, we had a practice dinner at one of the local hotels, and I invited her along. She was tired from travelling and had only an hour to get ready. She was apprehensive, and quite rightly so, as she faced a barrage of questions from my partners and their wives, who wanted to know everything about her, especially as they had not known she existed.

Debbi, age twenty-four

She conducted herself well and recognised the wife of my Indian partner as her previous English teacher at high school in Launceston in Tasmania. In fact, she also recognised him as the person who threatened to report her to the authorities for being underage in the bar at the racecourse in Launceston unless she told him which horses were hot tips to win the races. Her father was into horse-racing, especially trotting, and would take her to the track to drive him home afterward when he'd had a bellyful of beer. At age sixteen, with P-plates, she was expected to tow the horse float home.

Debbi's Early Days in Port Augusta

Everyone was curious to know who this new gorgeous girl living with Dr. Bhola was—and considering he was such a playboy, would she last? There was no shortage of women warning her about me and my past girlfriends. Two of my so-called friends went out of their way to get rid of her, because I suspect they had their own agendas.

One ex-girlfriend still had keys to my house and would invite herself in to visit us until Debbi demanded the keys from her. My ex-wife even visited with her friend to check whether our relationship was serious. They all underestimated Debbi's strength of character, resilience, and determination.

Some of my women patients were also social friends, and one of them expressed to Debbi how embarrassed she got when she came to me for a pap smear. Debbi reassured her by saying, "Don't worry, unless you have a snapping pussy, he will not remember you from all the others he sees."

Another said to Debbi that she always wore her sexiest nickers when coming for a pap smear, to which Debbi's response was, "He would not even notice them, considering he gets you to undress and dress behind the curtains."

Debbi did not tolerate fools easily, and in time she became known for her curt but honest and appropriate remarks.

There were also a few gentlemen around who thought they might stand a chance of gaining her interest. They took to visiting the house when they knew I was still at work. They were always made welcome, but

Debbi always rang me in front of them to say we had visitors and to come home as soon as I could to join them for a drink. They soon realised she had no interest in them and that we had a sound relationship.

My genuine friends embraced Debbi and made her welcome. She soon developed a circle of friends who became her long-term friends to this day. She was an excellent cook and hostess, having been brought up in the hospitality industry. We threw many wonderful parties which were enjoyed by all. Some went on until the wee hours of the morning.

One memorable occasion was when a certain hospital pharmacist decided to bare all and got into the swimming pool, to be followed by a few others doing the same. The next morning, it was somewhat embarrassing when my housekeeper brought in a pair of ladies nickers, which she found in the hibiscus plant by the pool.

Debbi used to smoke at parties, and I told her I wanted her to stop. She agreed but continued to smoke until one day I'd had enough. In front of our guests, I went up to her and took the cigarette off her, saying, "I do not like to kiss an ashtray, and if you want this relationship to continue, this will be your last cigarette."

She and our friends looked stunned. I was an absolute prick for doing that; I blame it on the rum and Coke. I don't think I could get away with such behaviour these days. But it was, indeed, her last cigarette. If only I could get patients to stop smoking using such bullying tactics!

When Debbi came to live with me, she brought her German shepherd named Ria. I was not a dog lover, but I had to accept her, as it was a case of "I will accept your daughter, but you will accept my dog." It was a fair proposition. Ria was a beautiful dog, and I soon developed a good relationship with her. Unfortunately, she went missing one day and was never seen again. No, I was not guilty! We suspected she was stolen by people who were into dog fights.

My daughter Nalini lived with her mother in Whyalla about eighty kilometres away and came to us every second weekend and some of the school holidays. Debbi was very good to Nalini and accepted my daughter as her own. We always made sure Nalini had a good time and invited friends to play with her.

There were not many jobs available in Port Augusta for Debbi, and when she applied, people's attitudes were, "You don't need to work. You are with a doctor." She did get one job offer working for a training pilot at the airstrip, but she did not enjoy that.

She was very interested in health products and was always visiting the only health food shop in Port Augusta. One day she came home and said, "If that health food shop ever comes up for sale, I want you to buy it for me." A few months later, it came up for sale, and we bought it. She was very happy running it and giving advice to customers. She gained much knowledge from her extensive reading. She even did lectures at ante-natal classes at the local hospital, talking about nutrition for expectant mothers.

She herself became pregnant, and our daughter, Ahsha, was born on January 27, 1983. Ahsha spent many days at the shop. The business was sold a few years later because Debbi became pregnant with our second child, Ramil, and she wanted to concentrate on raising and enjoying her children.

It was time to meet Debbi's parents, who were living in Derby, a small country town in northern Tasmania. They owned a local pub. We arrived by hire car from Launceston to be greeted by her mother, Valerie, who ran the kitchen, dining room, and hotel accommodation. After settling in to one of the hotel rooms upstairs, it was time to face Paddy, the dad. Debbi warned me that he could be gruff and even crude, so I was prepared for him.

I went into the bar where he was serving drinks to his regular local customers. I said hello, introduced myself, and sat on a barstool. The situation was at first tense, with Paddy and I observing each other carefully. They were drinking in rounds, with each one buying a round, including Paddy, who asked if I would like a beer. I said yes, and he poured me a schooner of Boags draught beer.

He went on to explain that Boags was produced in Launceston in Northern Tasmania, whereas Cascade was produced in the south in Hobart. There was some rivalry as to which was the better beer. The Northerners reckon Boags was better and refused to drink Cascade and vice versa. It was a good drop, and I enjoyed it.

There was some polite conversation, and when I bought a round for everyone, I scored so many brownie points that all tension disappeared, and conversation flowed freely. They even told me about the gay people living together in a commune nearby. We got on famously after that.

At about six thirty the next morning, Paddy invited me to go with him to see his horse being trained. It was a cold misty morning, and I looked on as the trainer took the horse through its paces around the track. It was a trotter and not a galloper. We later returned home via the bank in a neighbouring town.

That night, Paddy was going to play competitive snooker in the next town, and he asked me to join him. When we got there, they were one player short, so I was recruited to fill the spot, even though I had not played much before. When asked who I was, he told his mates I was a West Indian cricketer!

I had to think fast when one of them asked my name. I could not claim to be Clive Lloyd or Alvin Kalicharran, who were well known, so I said Faoud Bacchus. He was in the West Indian squad but lesser known, so I was not challenged. We lost the match, had a few beers, and went home.

I must have made the right impression on Debbi's parents, as they seemed to accept me, and we had a pleasant time. Debbi told me that her father had not wanted her to marry her first husband and tried to talk her out of it by saying to her, "Debbi, you can get a bit of stick anywhere, you don't have to marry him for it." He said no such thing about me, so she was pleased about that. They were not at her first wedding.

At the Derby Hotel, there was a wine cellar full of old reds. They were acquired as part of the stock when Paddy and Val bought the hotel. The locals only drank beer, so no one bought red wines except the local priest. The prices on the bottles were the original sale prices and had not changed for years.

Paddy told Debbi to go and get a bottle of wine from the cellar to accompany our Christmas dinner. She was blown out to see all those high-quality wines going so cheap. Apparently, her brother Darrell had been buying them for years and hadn't told her. She was not impressed.

She asked Paddy to sell her some. He told her to take as many as she wanted for the price on the bottles. We selected three dozen, and amongst them were 1973 Hill of Grace and Eileen Hardy's special reserve. Luckily, we had our wagon with us.

Wedding

One day, I came home from work to find half my clothes in a garbage bag, including my work suits that I had brought from the UK. I asked what was going on. Debbi said they were all going to the op shop, as in a climate like Port Augusta, they were inappropriate. She was right. In summer months, with temperatures in the thirties Celsius, I wore long-sleeve shirts, ties, and suits to work. Some were brown. She said a brown man should never wear brown clothes. She set about reorganising my wardrobe very tastefully, and I became a dapper dresser and more casual in my appearance.

After living with me for about two years, Debbi wanted to start a family and came up to me and asked, "Are you going to marry me or what?"

I paused for a moment and then asked, "Why do you want to get married now?"

She said because she wanted kids, and it would be nice if they were not "bastards." I had one child and was not sure I wanted more, but I quickly realised I was being selfish, so I agreed we should get engaged with a view to getting married six months later.

This was on condition that I agree to leave Port Augusta after three years. I agreed, but it was a promise that did not eventuate for another twenty-seven years!

Ram and Debbi's wedding day, June 19, 1982

I did not seek her father's permission. I sent her to the jewellery store with my credit card to pick her own engagement ring, within budgetary constraints. We went out to dinner and became engaged. I did not get on one knee to propose, and I was told I did not have a romantic bone in me. The wedding date was set for six months later, on June 19, 1982.

I told Debbi to come off the pill, as nothing was likely to happen soon. I was wrong. You would be right to assume that a doctor should have known better! She was pregnant within a month, so at the wedding, she was already three months pregnant. The resulting daughter, Ahsha, now takes great pride in boasting that she was at her parents' wedding! She was born on January 27, 1983. Debbi had threatened that if she was born on January 26 (Australia Day), her name would be Matilda.

At the wedding, which took place in our lounge room with a marriage celebrant (the clerk of the local court) and a local photographer, there were about seventy guests. The only relatives were Debbi's sister Vikki and my daughter Nalini, who was the flower girl and ring bearer. Vikki had arrived from Perth by bus the previous night at about midnight and had great difficulty convincing the taxi driver to take her to Dr. Bhola's house, especially as she did not know the address.

The driver knew where I lived and was a patient of mine. He was wondering who the blonde bimbo was who wanted to disturb Dr. Bhola at that hour of the night! He waited until I opened the front door and was relieved when I greeted her with a hug and thanked him for bringing her. We also had a few interstate friends staying at the house.

Debbi washed and groomed her dog for the occasion before she started getting her hair and makeup done—and was furious when the dog came in stinking and covered with filth, having rolled in a dead sheep in the nearby tip! Debbi had to bathe her again.

We decided to serve beer, champagne, and Blue Hawaii cocktails with canapés at home just before the wedding ceremony. We had pre-prepared the mixture for the Blue Hawaii in jugs. It contained vodka, rum, and blue curaçao. This was to be poured in champagne glasses and topped up with champagne before serving.

Vikki was put in charge of the drinks. After about forty-five minutes, she came asking for more of the mixture, as we were running out and it was very popular. We were surprised, as we thought we had prepared enough. There was a buzz all around the lounge. Most of the guests were tipsy, and we then realised that Vikki had forgotten about topping up the mixture with champagne and was serving it neat!

It was then that the phone calls of congratulations starting to arrive from overseas. We weren't even married yet. It was about two hours later when we had the ceremony, by which time the celebrant and photographer were also tipsy. It was a wedding with a difference.

All the guests then got in their cars and drove to the reception at the Standpipe Motel restaurant on the West Side of Port Augusta. Luckily, the cops were not around, as I am sure every driver was over the alcohol limit! The food was prepared by a French chef and was very good. The entrée was a lavish seafood spread, and the main course was various meat dishes.

The music was by the once famous Penny Rockets band, which was reconstituted for the occasion at the request of one of our friends, whose uncle was Brian Penglase, the lead singer in the group. There was much dancing and a few speeches. In the excitement, we forgot to cut the cake, which was done at our home the next day. We spent the night in the honeymoon suite, complete with a bottle of Moët & Chandon, at the Highway One motel, compliments of another friend.

Standpipe Motel

For our honeymoon, we travelled by car to Canberra, and later to our timeshare unit at Vacation Village in Port Macquarie. In Canberra, we ordered a beef Wellington for two, and as Debbi was suffering from pregnancy sickness, I had to eat most of it.

Life in Stirling North

Water started accumulating in the trench beside the road in front of the house, and before long, water was seeping under the side fence into my property. There was no rain in sight, and I could not work out where the water was coming from. It was about two in the afternoon.

The water started flowing faster and soon washed away the dirt driveway into my property and was also flowing across the whole property. The fences were acting as a levy bank, and so the water level in my property was rising. This was causing me great concern, as before long, it was lapping at my back door!

I talked to a neighbour who told me the water was coming from the Saltai Creek up in the Flinders Ranges. He also said that we were living in a flood plain, and it was not unusual to have sudden flash floods when it rained heavily in the hills. *Great*, I thought. No one told me that before I bought the house in Stirling North. I was keen to buy a house, and there were not many for sale in Port Augusta itself. Stirling North was about eight kilometres away at the foothills of the popular Flinders Ranges.

My mother and Nalini in the backyard of the Stirling North house

When I had bought the house, which was built by AV Jennings, it was incompletely landscaped and had fences only on three sides. It was a brick-veneer four-bedroom, one-bathroom house, with no carport or garage. There was also no air-conditioning. It had great potential though.

I summoned assistance from a few friends who helped me remove some of the iron sheets of the fences to allow the free flow of water across the property, and it was a relief to see the water level dropping. The house was spared, but much of the gravel in the driveway was washed away, and the swimming pool—which I had cleaned the day before—was full of muddy water from the flood. After twenty-four hours, the flow of water stopped, and the clean-up started. The pool took a week to bring back to the way it was, using a combination of pumping out mud, super-chlorination, and flocculation.

I had seen many dry creek beds full of rocks of varying sizes and heard about flash floods when it rained heavily in the distant hills of the Flinders Ranges. I was even warned never to camp in creek beds, as your tent could be washed away while you were unsuspectingly asleep in it. I never imagined what it was like until I witnessed these floods.

Once, when I heard that Saltai Creek was running, I drove up to have a look and was amazed that I could hear the roar of the water rushing across the road from a kilometre away. The speed of the flowing water, carrying huge rocks with it, was a sight to behold. I can fully appreciate why people and cars can be washed away by such flowing creeks. Many have even lost their lives in previous floods.

Prior to the flood, I had installed the pool, a four-car carport, a garden shed, a front fence, and gates. I separated the back third of the property into an orchard with thirty-five different fruit trees, complete with an irrigation system. The soil was fertile, as it was made up of silt from years of flooding. I also created a circular drive in the front of the property, with flowering plants bordering it. These put on such a beautiful display that people travelling along the road would slow down to admire it.

In the orchard were nectarines, mandarins, apples, plums, pears, almonds, bananas, apricots, and peaches. At the base of the fruit trees, I planted watermelons, rock melons, and pumpkins, so they were watered at the same time as the fruit trees. I had so much fruit that I gave much of it away to friends and even sold some of the pumpkins to the local grocery store. The largest watermelon weighed forty-four pounds. I was amazed to see warm- and temperate-climate fruits thriving in the same orchard.

When Debbi came along, she thought she would grow a small vegetable garden and had a beautiful crop of about twelve lettuce heads. One day, knife in hand, she proudly went to harvest one for a salad, only to find they were all neatly cropped one inch from the ground, with no leaves in sight. She stooped down to look for footprints, thinking someone had stolen them, when a loud hiss from a wide-open reptilian mouth startled her.

Quick as a flash, she plunged her knife into the head of the creature, pinning it to the ground. She thought it was a snake at first, but it turned out to be a sleepy lizard with a belly full of Debbi's succulent lettuce. That was the end of her attempt at growing a kitchen garden.

A couple of years later, we had another flood. This was handled more efficiently. I had bought a Daihatsu F20 four-wheel drive in case I needed to drive across flooded roads and had large culverts installed in the driveway to allow the free flow of water. I also got a friend to build a dirt levy wall along the fences. We enjoyed living there and had many good parties by the swimming pool. I remember one in particular, a Hawaiian night when friends dressed in flowery clothes with leis around their necks were drinking tropical cocktails and dancing to Beach Boys rhythms. The scene was set by lights shining on the trees and on fountains flowing over the pool.

Another feature of the property was a shade house built one weekend with the help of some friends. Their reward was a barbecue and beers. It was made with pine posts and cladded with pine offcuts with the bark still on. This gave it a rustic appearance. It had shade cloth over the top and inside had a paved central area with a table and two benches made of wood. Railway sleepers formed a border on three sides and housed tropical tree ferns and palms. There were a few citronella bamboo-torches which created a peaceful tropical environment, like some I witnessed in Fiji and Hawaii. The watering system was from above, creating a mist. Debbi and I had many a romantic dinner there, and in fact she was convinced our daughter was conceived there.

The pine offcuts had to be fetched from Wirrabara in the Flinders Ranges. For this, I hooked up my trailer to the Daihatsu. After loading up the trailer, I started on the journey home. I hit a bump on the road, and the front of the Daihatsu became airborne. I had no steering and hence no control. It was an unnerving moment. I slowed the vehicle down, and it came to a stop. The mistake I had made in loading the trailer was that there was too much weight on the tow bar at the back of the Daihatsu.

I had to unload the trailer and repack it, making sure that the load was more evenly distributed.

One night, I was on call for emergencies. At about five in the morning, I was called to the hospital to certify a body in the mortuary. It was that of a man in his forties who had slammed his car at high speed against a coal train travelling from Leigh Creek to the Northern Power Station in Port Augusta. It was at a level crossing between Stirling North and Port Augusta. There were no traffic lights, and no lights along the train on a pitch-black night. The man's face was smashed up, and the top of his skull was missing, exposing the brain. I was so upset I felt sick. When I went home, Debbi thought I had seen a ghost. I couldn't face breakfast.

After that incident, Debbi became worried, as I frequently travelled that road at high speed at night going to an emergency or to deliver a baby. One night about one o'clock, I was summoned to do a delivery and took off down the road in my Mazda RX7 at high speed. I passed a cop car on the way, but even though I was doing 110 in a 60-kilometre zone, I did not slow down. I fully expected the cops to chase me, and I had made up my mind that I would not stop if they asked me to. They did not follow.

After delivering the baby, I said to the patient's husband that if I got a speeding fine, I would pass it on to him. He responded that he was also a cop, and the colleagues who were on the road knew his wife was in labour. They knew my car and that I was her doctor, so they would know why I would be speeding.

After relating this to Debbi the next day, she decided that it was time we moved nearer the hospital. What made her more determined was my boast that I could get to the hospital from home, eight kilometres away, before a lady in labour had another contraction. The result was that she bought a block of land near the hospital and designed and built our family home on Margaret Street in Port Augusta. While the house was being built, we lived in a flat in Port Augusta, as the Stirling North house was sold. Our son, Ramil, was born on August 30, 1984.

Living in Margaret Street

Much time was spent doing research on designs and materials, especially by Debbi. She made most of the decisions and did an excellent job. My only stipulations were that I would like an indoor swimming pool/spa, a bar, a study, and a double garage for my prestige cars. The overriding themes were that the house had to be energy efficient, secure, and practical. The draughtsman had some useful input, and the builder was excited to tackle something out of the ordinary. The kitchen was designed by Debbi and made of solid Tasmanian oak. It was her bit of Tasmania and her pride and joy.

The end result was a very comfortable family home that we enjoyed for many years. Entertaining was easy, and we had many, many gatherings of friends and family. The swimming pool was a big hit with the kids and their friends.

We hosted our medical practice Christmas dinners and some Food and Wine Club dinners at home. It was quite an achievement having an Indian banquet for sixty people and serving international beers to go with the curries, which were all prepared by Debbi. It was one of our contributions to the Port Augusta Food and Wine Club.

This period in Port Augusta was particularly enjoyable for us. We had a comfortable home and a thriving medical practice. We not only went on many overseas trips to exotic destinations but also took full advantage of the very many local attractions. We had many trips into the Flinders Ranges and climbed Wilpena Pound and Devil's Peak. Picnicking at Mambray Creek and Mount Remarkable with friends was a regular weekend pastime. We were members of the Lions Club and the Food and Wine Club.

One day, I decided to buy Debbi some sexy lingerie. I went into the only lingerie shop in town, which was run by a friend. She asked what bra size Debbi was. I said I didn't know. "Well, is she one handful or two?" my friend asked. I said one and a half. She gave me the right size!

Another day, Debbi decided to prune her roses along the drive and cropped them to the ground. The Catholic priest came visiting and said, "They will need divine intervention to survive."

She responded, "Oh! ye of little faith. We'll see." They not only survived but thrived.

We were invited to the wedding of our housekeeper's daughter. It was a typical Italian wedding, and my two children were in the wedding party. My Jaguar was the wedding car, and I was the chauffeur. Later in the evening, during the dancing, Debbi was handed a note by one of the guests. It said, "If you want a gay time, ring this number."

Debbi was furious and showed it to me. I decided to fix the offender and placed an advertisement in the local paper, which said, "For a wonderful time, call me on this number ..." She was kept busy for days answering calls!

CHAPTER 9

SOME FURTHER OVERSEAS TRIPS (1986-1996)

I took regular breaks from my busy work life to spend time travelling with my family to visit relatives and friends abroad

Trip to North America and Guyana in 1986

Our house in Margaret Street was half built when I came home from work one day and told Debbi, "I have this overwhelming feeling that I need to visit my mother in Guyana soon." She was surprised to hear this but was completely supportive and understanding.

A few weeks later, Debbi and I, together with our three children—who were twelve years, three years, and eighteen months—were on our way to Guyana via North America. Our first stop was Anaheim, where we stayed at the Disneyland Hotel in a rather luxurious suite overlooking the dancing waters in the lake, which was set in the beautifully landscaped lush gardens. We enjoyed Disneyland despite the crowds and went on the various rides. Nalini and I returned towards the end of the day, and because the queues were shorter, we went on many rides in rapid succession. We also had a trip to Universal Studios the next day.

New York was our next stop. We stayed with my brother Jack and his family. They were living in a one-bedroom condominium. It had a bedroom large enough to take two double beds, a lounge, a kitchen/dining, and a single bathroom. The building was in a typical high-rise set amongst dozens of similar buildings along the streets. It was difficult to tell one building from another. Being in the middle of winter, the atmosphere was bleak, grey, and cold. There were not many trees or parks, as we were accustomed to see in Australia. The few play courts with basketball rings were made of bitumen.

The first night we stayed in a motel about ten kilometres from this apartment, but we were encouraged to move in with the family, as my brother did not feel right having us stay elsewhere. To accommodate us, we were given the bedroom, and the rest of the family slept in the lounge. Debbi, to my surprise and admiration, accepted this arrangement without any complaints. Many would not have been so accommodating.

Because a hot water pipe ran through the bathrooms of all the condominiums in a vertical fashion, it became so hot that we were perspiring while drying ourselves after a shower. Debbi, being the fixer, rose to the challenge and went to the hardware store, where she found some tape and insulation to wrap around the hot pipe. Problem solved!

One night, we decided to go out for a Chinese meal. I remember that night clearly to this day, not because the food was fantastic, but because it was the coldest I have ever felt anywhere anytime. My nose and ears were burning from the cold. Debbi shared this sentiment.

Equally memorable was the sight of a mountain of black bags filled with garbage in front of each apartment block. Each pile was about eighteen feet tall and occupied the entire footpath. I couldn't believe we humans could generate so much garbage every week!

I felt sorry for my poor brother and his family living in such conditions. He also had an old car that was more trouble than it was worth. We decided to try to help, not that we were in a position to do much, as we were building our house and having this expensive trip. We looked at a few houses for sale and quickly realised this was too ambitious an idea.

My brother offered to repay me the two and a half thousand dollars I had lent him when they emigrated to New York. I could not accept it and said it was a gift. I suggested he use the money to visit Florida and let a friend show him and his wife, Jean, around. I thought being used to the tropical weather in Guyana, they would prefer to live in the warmer climate in Florida instead of New York.

They fell in love with Florida, and to my surprise, signed a contract to purchase a house and land package in Orlando. He needed help with the deposit, so we gave him money we had earmarked for travel expenses and decided to rely on our credit cards instead. The post office transferred his position to Orlando, where he remained until his recent retirement. They have never looked back.

Our next stop was Toronto. There we stayed with my sister Betty. This particular sister had lost her husband at an early age, leaving her to bring up three sons and a daughter. She was always very hard-working and made a success of her life, eventually creating and owning Maple Leaf Wheelchair with her new partner and her sons. This became the biggest wheelchair company in Canada.

I never briefed Debbi on what to expect in Guyana, as I wanted her to experience life in a Third World country for herself. Before we left Toronto for Guyana, Ahsha asked where we were going, and we told her it would be like another Disneyland. As the plane landed at night guided by two rows of rather dim lights outlining the runway at Timehri Airport, she complained indignantly, "Where are all the lights? This is not Disneyland!"

Before we'd left Australia, we had packed several medications in our luggage at the request of my relatives, who could not get them in Guyana. Among them were birth control pills. I had been saving samples of these given to me by drug representatives for some time and had a few dozen packets in Debbi's suitcase. She was also carrying a rather expensive camera. We had been advised to leave all our good jewellery with our relatives in Canada and buy some cheap imitations to wear in Guyana. These had to be declared at the airport on arrival, as visitors were only allowed to take out of the country whatever they had brought in.

The authorities did not check the quality of jewellery, which allowed us to replace the imitations with real jewellery belonging to our relatives. These could be sold abroad to provide funds for those in the United States and Canada. There were restrictions on how much currency could be taken out of the country by visitors or migrants.

Ahsha and Ramil waiting for the ferry in New Amsterdam

It was an unnerving experience for Debbi at the airport, as she was questioned about the purpose of her visit. They were suspicious that she was a foreign reporter because of her camera and would only grant her a one-week visa, while the rest of us could stay for three weeks. This was even though she had already been granted a three-week visa to visit Guyana in Canada. She was expected to apply for an extension from the authorities in Georgetown.

As I was Guyanese by birth, they announced to her that even though the children and I were travelling on Australian passports, we could stay as long as we wished. In fact, they could also detain us in Guyana if they wanted to. This really freaked Debbi out.

We had to delay our trip to my village by twenty-four hours so we could sort out her visa. At the immigration office, we encountered a rather plump African woman of below average intelligence who obviously relished the power she had over people. We tried to explain to her that we all had been granted visitors' visas in Canada to visit Guyana for the three weeks. This seemed just as hard for her to understand as it was for the equally dimwitted officer at the airport. Debbi knew I was getting hot under the collar and frustrated, not to mention embarrassed, by these Guyanese officials. She prevented me from intervening, worried that I might upset them and create more difficulties. At the airport, she was worried about the contraceptive pills in her suitcase, but luckily, that did not seem to concern them.

The officer in Georgetown said to Debbi, "Do you know if I were to burrow a hole in the ground to the other side of the globe, I could be in Australia?" Durr!

Eventually, the visa was granted, especially after Debbi said, "If this is an example of how things are done here, no way will I stay here any longer than I have to, nor will I want to trade Australia for Guyana." She confessed to me later she was already considering making plans for our escape via Surinam if we were detained!

On our way to my village, we spent some time with my sister Seeta and her family in De Kinderen, and with another sister, Gem, and her family at No. 2 village. In my village (No. 47), we stayed at my mother's house. Another sister, Rita, and her family lived in the same village and ran a rum shop. My widowed sister-in-law Baby and family lived across the road from my mother's house.

I was, of course, familiar with the village lifestyle and customs, but it was all very different and fascinating to Debbi, Nalini, Ahsha, and Ramil. I was very appreciative of the way Debbi embraced the Third World experience without so much as a single complaint or criticism. She got used to having roti and dal for breakfast, and curry and rice for the other meals every day. She was still breastfeeding Ramil, as it was a safe and convenient way of giving him milk. We had cloth nappies for him, as disposables were not readily available.

A doctor's wife was not expected to do menial tasks like washing clothes, cleaning, or even cooking. It would have been a disgrace to the family if they permitted her to do these chores. My mother volunteered to help and organised a village girl to do the washing. Debbi refused any help and sat down on a *peerha* (low stool) to beat the clothes on a concrete slab with a wooden beater to get them clean. This was so fascinating to the locals that I think they would have paid a fee to witness this "white gal" washing her clothes Guyanese-style.

One day, news came that petrol had been poured over a three-year-old girl from the village, who was then set alight and burnt to death by some robbers because they did not find what they were after. This freaked us out, especially as we had foreign currency, which was desirable, as the exchange rate was 200 Guyanese dollars to one US dollar. As we were sleeping that night, Debbi passed her hand under my pillow and found a large knife and a machete. She nearly severed her hand in the process and realised that I too must have been worried to arm myself like this.

From then on, she could not sleep at night and lost a lot of weight. The looseness of the bowels from an overload of curries did not help either. In fact, some friends said to her on our return to Port Augusta, "When you left, you looked great and Ram looked washed out, and now he looks great and you look half dead!"

Most people in the village used a long-drop toilet and a shower enclosure in the backyard. Although we had these and Debbi embraced the idea, my mother's house also had a flushable toilet and shower in the house. To use the shower, we had to first pump rainwater up to a tank on the roof, and to flush the toilet, we had to fill the cistern with a bucket. The toilet drained into a septic tank.

The villagers were fascinated by us, especially Debbi and the children. They came around to look at my family at every opportunity. My mother was worried that they would "give them bad eye," so she placed a black dot on the middle of Ramil's forehead. He was a bonny, chubby, healthy-looking baby. One little thirteen-year-old girl took a liking to Ahsha and carried her on her hip everywhere. She took her to her parents' house to see the goats, chooks, and pigs. My mother was concerned that Ahsha would catch lice from her so tried to limit her exposure. This girl brought gifts of fruits, crabs, and coconuts for us.

One day, we had to travel in a hire car from New Amsterdam to No. 47 village. To earn more dollars, these cars would pick up as many passengers on the way as they could possibly fit in, even if smelly, sweaty people had to sit on each other's laps. I negotiated to have exclusive use of the whole of the back seat for my family, all five of us. For this, I was charged the fare for eight people, but it was worth it.

Of course, there were no seat belts or air-conditioning, so the windows were wide open, and the wind played havoc with Debbi's hair. She was fascinated to see the driver sitting on one butt cheek as he drove with one hand on the steering wheel and one outside the window. That was all the room he had. He did a good job avoiding animals, ducks, chooks, and people on the road. Some people were using the road to dry copra (coconut kernels) and paddy! Debbi wrote a letter to some friends in Port Augusta describing her experiences in a very humorous way and apparently had them in hysterics. I never saw the letter.

While in New Amsterdam, we visited the market, where people were selling their produce and handicrafts. We became separated as we inspected the various stalls. Debbi became concerned that she would not be able to find me among all the Indians. Of course, we did not have mobile phones to contact each other.

As she surveyed the scene, she noticed a sea of brown faces all gibbering in Creole, which she could not understand. She was the only white person around. She said it was not hard to spot me at the other side of the market, as I stood tall and was much more smartly dressed and sophisticated than the locals.

Every relative we visited cooked a meal for us, and because we did not want to seem unappreciative, we would eat something. The result was that we were having up to eight meals per day. Not surprisingly, I put on thirteen pounds in thirteen days!

My sister Seeta, her husband, Bhola, and their three sons had decided to emigrate to Australia after we successfully sponsored them. They were to follow us a month after our return to Australia. We attended a religious ceremony at their house. This was a fascinating experience for Debbi and the children. The evening before the service, we helped to prepare food for the many expected guests, and the women were having great fun asking Debbi questions about life in Australia and teaching her Creole words. They were giggling as they compared notes on the names given to women's and men's private parts!

The pundit was put on the spot by Debbi, who asked him why he conducted the service in Hindi, which no one understood. He took the time to explain the service and the significance to her in English, which she found very interesting. She subsequently bought some storybooks to teach the children about Hinduism. I will go so far as to say she knew more about the Hindu religion than I did.

Bhola and Seeta

Ahsha became upset one day when a pet sheep that was tied by a rope in the yard for several days, and to which she had become attached, suddenly disappeared. She found out that it became the curried lamb prepared for lunch. She was not impressed and refused to eat the curry.

We enjoyed our stay and managed to acquire some choice pieces of jewellery before returning to Canada, where we visited Niagara Falls and other tourist attractions before returning home to Australia. My sister and her family followed a month later. Having helped my brother and his family financially, we were not able to give my sister as much help as I had hoped. However, we were able to provide a furnished house for them to live in initially on arriving in Port Augusta.

The important reason for their decision to emigrate to Australia was to keep the family together and to give the three sons every opportunity to get a good education. They took full advantage of this opportunity and ended up with qualifications in electronic engineering, electrical engineering, and computing. The parents made a huge sacrifice for their boys, with

Bhola giving up his job as the headmaster of a primary school in Guyana. He drove taxis at first and later worked as a petrol station attendant, while my sister, who never worked in Guyana, became an expert cook in a roadhouse.

My mother was not happy with my sister and her family moving to Australia, as she remembered how far it was when she visited in 1980. She told my sister she would not see her again. She was right.

In 1987, I was at work one day when I received a phone call from a sister advising me that my mother had passed away from a heart attack in Guyana. I had to visit my sister to tell her the sad news. When I told Debbi the news, she wanted me to stay home, but the only way I could cope was to go back to work and be distracted by my patients' problems. It was a very sad time indeed for us all.

Trip to the UK in 1989

We decided to visit the UK in 1989 for five weeks. Our base was Vikki's place in Surrey, from which we checked out the tourist attractions in and around London. A hop-on hop-off bus gave us a bird's-eye view of central London, but it also made us realise how polluted the air in London was, as we kept getting grit in our eyes sitting on the open top deck. We had dinner in Soho afterwards.

At Hampton Court Palace (home of King Henry VIII), Ramil kept looking behind the old lavish but dusty drapes for ghosts. The tour guide was not impressed with him, as he kept ignoring her and would go behind the chains to get to the drapes. On the grounds of the palace was a medieval fair, with armoured knights on horseback jousting with each other. We had to buy him his own knight's outfit and sword before we could get him to move on.

The London dungeon was so frightening to Ahsha that I had to carry her in my arms, and she kept her eyes closed for the whole tour. Ramil, on the other hand, thought it was great. We visited the Tower of London, Madame Tussaud's, the Planetarium, Buckingham Palace, Westminster Abbey, Big Ben, Trafalgar Square, Whitehall, Hyde Park, and some of the famous bridges on the River Thames.

We hired a car and headed north. Our first stop was Oxford to stay with a niece and her family. We checked out the wonderful architecture of the university buildings, and my niece bought us a souvenir place mat setting featuring some of these buildings, which I still have.

At Stratford-on-Avon, it was interesting to visit Shakespeare's home and Ann Hathaway's cottage. The memory that stayed with me was how low the doorways were. I had to duck as I went through them. People of that era were obviously so much shorter.

In Nottingham, we stayed with my best university friend, Llewelyn, and his family. He was an accident and emergency consultant at Nottingham General Hospital and was the chief medical officer for Donington Formula One Racetrack and for Nottingham Forrest Soccer Club. Before arriving, he had asked me what Debbi liked to drink, and I told him champagne. Debbi was most impressed that he bought her a dozen of the most expensive Moët et Chandon, considering we were only staying two nights.

He asked me to accompany him to Donington Racetrack, and I was impressed with the medical set-up there. Before long, I was in a race car being driven around the track at high speed by a female driver. What an experience! My friend told me he once attended Prince Charles after he came off his horse at polo. He also attended to a spectator having a heart attack.

When we visited an old house full of stuffed animals and antique furniture, Ahsha queried, "Weren't we here yesterday?" We had visited many historic buildings which must have all appeared the same to her. Debbi had a great interest in the architecture of such buildings.

The walled city of York is a must see for visitors. After a day of sightseeing, which included the famous York Minster, we could not find any accommodation, as there was some big tourist event happening. So we set off up the road going north. On the way, we stopped at a motel, and while at the reception area, we noticed all these people going in and out of the motel with their barking/yapping dogs. We had never witnessed anything like that before. It was a motel that allowed dogs to stay with their owners, and they were very busy, as there was a dog show nearby. We made a hasty retreat and set off up the road once again.

Debbi decided we should check out the Durham Cathedral. This we did. By that time, we were hungry and tired. We found a hotel and asked for a family suite. There was none available. We enquired about two adjoining rooms, but the cost was prohibitive. We were just about to leave when the manager, who was observing the proceedings from nearby, approached the receptionist and told her to let us have the two rooms for the price of one. He must have liked the looks of us or took pity on us. We accepted and felt very decadent, as it was a rather upmarket establishment. The beds with their soft cushions and pillows were extremely comfortable.

We took advantage of the indoor heated swimming pool with its Romanesque décor. Ahsha was quite impressed to have a decent shower at last with water pressure that went *psssst* when she turned it on. To add to the decadence, we found a wonderful restaurant and enjoyed a sumptuous meal. By this time, I did not care what it cost.

Newcastle upon Tyne bridge

My friend and former medical school classmate Keith and his family were our hosts for the next few days in Newcastle upon Tyne. Debbi was impressed by the operatic voice of his wife, Marjorie, who sang while waiting for us to front up for breakfast. She was part of the local Gilbert and Sullivan operatic society. Keith was surprised that I told Debbi there was not much to see in Newcastle upon Tyne, as it was an industrial city with lots of abandoned coal mines nearby. I lived there for nine years but did not appreciate the interesting historical sites of the city.

I did, however, go down a coal mine once as part of our industrial medicine studies. That was an unnerving experience as we donned our helmets complete with spotlights and descended in a mine shaft lift to a depth of about half a kilometre in darkness. The coal face was being carved up by machinery, creating a mountain of dust. As I suffer from claustrophobia, I could not get out of there fast enough.

Keith, Marjorie, Debbi, and Ram

Keith decided to prove me wrong to Debbi, so he took us down to the Rocks area of the city to show us the statue of Nelson and the well-preserved part of Hadrian's wall, named after the Roman Emperor Hadrian. There were also the shipyards and the Newcastle Bridge, on which the Sydney Harbour Bridge was designed. Being the docks area, it was complete with brothels, about which many a yarn was spun. The children wanted to see where I studied, so we showed them Newcastle Medical School and the Royal Victoria Infirmary.

We then went cross country via Hexham and Corbridge on our way to the Lakes District. In Hexham, we stopped in a market, and Debbi decided to buy some flowers for a friend in Corbridge. The vendor muttered something to Debbi in broad Geordie, expecting an answer. Debbi did not understand a word and turned to me expectantly. I said, "He wants to know if you would like it wrapped in blue paper or pink paper." Whereupon the guy looked puzzled as he pondered what he just witnessed—a brown Indian interpreting the Geordie dialect to the white English chick!

It was my turn to do some translation for Debbi. I remember her teaching me some Australian slang in her early days in Port Augusta. Patients used words that I had not heard before, like *fanny* meaning the female private part and *nooky* meaning having sex. She even bought me a book of Australian slang words.

In the Lake District, we had pre-booked a bed and breakfast after our experience in York. We eventually found it after going down a few narrow English country roads. Unfortunately, we had to decline the accommodation, as the children were being placed too far from us. After trying a few places, we decided enough was enough and stayed at the upmarket Wild Boar Hotel. We were given two rooms.

We wanted to make a booking for dinner for seven thirty. The receptionist said the children could eat at five thirty, but we insisted that we would all eat together at seven thirty, not appreciating that children are not normally allowed in their exclusive restaurant for fear of disturbing other diners. It explained the horror on the face of the maître d'hôtel when we rocked up saying we had a booking. He cautiously placed us in a far corner of the room just in case.

He then gave menus to Nalini, Debbi, and I, expecting us to order for the two younger children. At this point, Ramil put his hand out for a menu also. He and Ahsha were then given menus. When the maître d' returned to take our orders, he was impressed when Ramil ordered his three-course meal, including the crabmeat soup.

The children behaved immaculately. When I passed my gold American Express credit card to pay the bill, and the maître d' noticed the *Dr.* in front of my name, his whole attitude and demeanour changed instantly, and he invited us to come again. There is really no place for such prejudice and pompousness in modern society.

We went on something that was called a *cruise* on Lake Windermere, but the boat went nowhere, and we were merely served refreshments on board. After that, we visited Beatrix Potter Cottage, where we bought

Ahsha a fluffy rabbit nightdress holder. This she treasured for years. When reading to her at nights at home, I used to lay my head on this rabbit, using it as a pillow, and it would pick up the scent of my aftershave. This gave her a sense of security in bed when I was not around.

Our next stop was Bath, where we had to carry our suitcases up three flights of stairs, as there were no lifts in the multi-storey B & B. The other memorable thing about that B & B was the owner's refusal to refill Ramil's glass of orange juice, even though breakfast was included and all he wanted was orange juice. Nevertheless, Bath was an interesting and delightful city, especially the Roman baths.

Debbi and Nalini decided they had to take the car and find some of Bath's famous fudge. The road near the shop was rather confusing, and with traffic all around, Debbi made a sudden left turn, only to realise she was in a private car park. As she approached the boom gate to the exit, the attendant lifted it to let her out, saying, "Don't worry, madam, it happens all the time."

I am not one to get vibes or feel the supernatural, but the county of Wilshire definitely gave me the creeps. There was an eerie feeling in the entire area, especially when we visited Stonehenge and Longleat Castle. A visit to Longleat Safari Park, with lions climbing on the car roof and peering through the windows, was particularly frightening. I couldn't get out of there fast enough.

We stayed in a hotel in a small town, arriving at dusk. The whole town and the hotel were dimly lit. After checking in, we went to the restaurant for a meal. The man behind the bar was a very glum character, as were the rest of the guests in the restaurant. No one was speaking to each other. The darkness added to the weird vibe.

We quietly had our meal and retreated to our room. Debbi and I then had this brilliant idea (not) to leave the children in the room and go for a stroll along the street. It lasted all of three minutes. We felt so vulnerable in this smoky, dimly lit, and spooky place.

We checked out the sights in Devon before arriving in Cornwall. "I would like a Devonshire tea, please," said Debbi to the man behind the counter in the coffee shop in Cornwall.

He promptly replied, "Madam, it is only Devonshire tea in Devon, and if you are not certain, say English cream tea."

Debbi was amused by this gentle inter-county rivalry.

We had to check out the town of Launceston, as it obviously was the place after which Launceston in Tasmania was named. Here she was corrected again when she announced to the lady in the gift shop that she came from Launceston in Tasmania. "It is pronounced, *Launst*, my dear."

We had to see Land's End having come this far, Penzance because of its history of pirates, and the quaint town of Ool. Our last B & B was interesting in that we spent quite some time trying to find it. We travelled for several kilometres along a narrow windy country road with tall vegetation growing right up to the bitumen. It was only wide enough for one car. I was hoping no vehicle approached from the opposite direction. Fortunately, none did.

The tall white three-storey building was perched on a hill with magnificent views of the ocean, and it had the air of a decadent past. There were only a few guests, even though it had at least fifty rooms. When we enquired about dinner, the look of horror on the manager's face was something to behold. However, he was not fazed by our request and sat us down with a drink as he cooked up a dinner all by himself. It was not a bad effort, either! Debbi took some magnificent shots of the view over the sea from this hotel.

We made our way back to London, and after a few days returned home to Australia. It was a whirlwind trip around England, and I saw more of it than I did during my eleven years' residency there. The main reason was the intensity of the medical course and the lack of finances during my student days.

Trip to Attend My Twenty-Year Medical-School Reunion

Out of the blue, I received an email from a former classmate and his wife (also a classmate) asking if I would be interested in attending a twenty-year medical-school class reunion in Newcastle upon Tyne. This was the first reunion planned since we graduated, and I thought it would be great to catch up with former classmates. This was eventually organised, and in the summer of 1991, Debbi and I went to the UK for a week to attend.

We stayed with my friend and classmate Keith and his wife, Marjorie. Together with my other friend Llewelyn and his wife, Resil, we decided to go for dinner on the Friday night at a nearby town. Resil was apprehensive at first, as she had never met Keith or Marjorie, but we all got on well and had a wonderful time reminiscing about old times and laughing a lot.

The following day, a casual luncheon was organised at the medical school. I went to get a couple glasses of champagne and was waylaid by several friends who all wanted to say hello. After several minutes, I returned to Debbi. Of course, she knew no one, as when I left Newcastle for Australia in 1975 I had a different wife, Moira. In true Debbi style, she was introducing herself to everyone as Ram Bhola's wife and directing them to where they would find a drink.

One gentleman came up to her and said, "You are not the wife he left Newcastle with." He also said to her that he was surprised to find me wearing black leather pants with a stylish white shirt, as I was such a quiet conservative chap at medical school.

Debbi decided to have some fun with him and said, "Well! You should see him in his full black leather outfit on his Harley." He was utterly amazed to hear this, and of course, we never enlightened him as to the truth.

That night, we had the formal ball at a local hotel. We were all dressed in our finery. Debbi wore a dress she'd picked up in Oxford on our way to Newcastle. Llewelyn was in a striking white jacket. The dean of the medical school was present and was the guest speaker. He remarked what a successful year of graduates we were, scattered all over the world, some being professors with outstanding achievements in their fields. We also honoured the few colleagues who had unfortunately passed away.

I was very surprised to find that the classmates who were the academic ones at medical school were the GPs, and the less serious and non-academic ones were the professors of nuclear medicine, etc. I remember after graduation asking one of the eccentric ones what he was planning to do, to which he replied, "I certainly will not be seeing any live patients. Couldn't think of anything worse." He became a professor of biochemistry.

One girl we all regarded as being very boring was a GP in Canada. She kept us amused all evening, and Debbi thought she was far from boring. One of the stories she told was about an advert for condoms. Apparently in Canada, they were called Jiffys, so the TV slogan was, "If you have a stiffy, use a Jiffy."

My classmates were surprised to find me dancing disco-style, as most had never seen me dance. In fact, Llewelyn (who had Mick Jagger-like moves) and I owned the dance floor. One colleague took a fancy to Debbi and asked if she had heard the Billy Joel song "Uptown Girl." He then requested it and wanted to dance with her. Being astute and hurt at the inference that I was a downtown boy, she said, "No thanks, why would I settle for beer when I have champagne?" He was neatly put in his box!

There was a luncheon for all the guests at his house the next day, and again he thought he would try his luck by inviting Debbi to check out his rose garden. She again burst his bubble by saying that it was very nice, but not nearly as good as Ram's back home in Australia.

There have been reunions every five years since, but unfortunately, I have not been able to attend. We were keen to go to the forty-five-year reunion in 2016, but Debbi was too ill to travel and was on chemotherapy. I am hoping to attend the fifty-year reunion in June of 2021.

Family Reunion in Canada in 1996

One evening, I received a call from a nephew in Canada telling me it was ten years since our last visit to Canada and asking when were we planning to go again. I said we had no plans and that there were too many of them scattered across the United States and Canada to visit. I told him if he could get them all together in one place, we would consider it.

He then said it would be his mother's sixtieth birthday in September, and he wanted to give her a special celebration. He asked if he organised a family reunion would we go, to which I replied, "If you do that, we certainly will be there." He did.

Before arriving, we were told there would be about four hundred guests. We assumed some would be relatives and some friends. To our surprise, they all gathered for the party in a large banquet hall, and they were all related. What's more, they were all Indians except for Debbi and a couple who were close friends of my sister.

I was made the MC, which was a pity, as it did not give me much time to spend with the many relatives who had gathered. It was quite a surprise to see that people had travelled not only from all over Canada and America but also from the UK and Guyana. There were people there I hadn't seen for years. In fact, there were some from my village I had not seen since I left Guyana the first time.

Me, Betty, and her son Sookpaul

Debbi did not know many of them and had difficulty understanding their Creole language, so she decided the safest place was behind the bar. She served drinks and enjoyed giving the lads a hard time because they were ordering margaritas, which she told them was a chick's drink, and real men drank rum or Scotch.

There was a lot of food and drink consumed, and all the siblings made speeches. Of course, there was much dancing also. Ramil and two of his second cousins did the Macarena. It was a memorable occasion.

The previous night, we had gathered at a nephew's house for food and drinks. A birthday cake appeared, and we all started singing the happy birthday song. I did not know whose birthday it was until the song ended with, "Happy birthday, dear Uncle Ramdy, happy birthday to you." That was in celebration of my fiftieth birthday, which was back in the April of that year.

It had been a while since I had seen some of my nieces and nephews, so someone had the bright idea of getting me to name them all. I did very well, except there was one young lady I could not place. I thought I knew all of them. It was highly embarrassing for me when I found out she was my eldest sister's daughter. Unfortunately, she was suffering from systemic lupus erythematosus, and this had altered her facial features greatly.

My brother and family from Orlando did not attend the reunion, so I decided to go and visit them before rejoining Debbi and our children, who had travelled to New York by car. We saw some of the tourist attractions while we were there.

One eye-opening moment came when my nephew decided to find a liquor store in the Bronx. He parked the car, and Debbi and I went into the shop. We had to go through a security door, choose our wines, and then hand them over to the cashier through a security hatch. We then went through the security door and paid for our purchase through another hatch before he handed us the bottles.

As we climbed into our car, a large van pulled up and hemmed us in. He was double-parked. My nephew said to the rather large black driver that we were about to leave. He simply showed us two fingers and kept walking. We decided it was better not to argue with him and waited until he returned and drove off before we could leave.

We drove back to Toronto, and I did some of the driving, which was on the wrong side of the road compared to Australia, but with dual carriageways it was not difficult. We stopped to buy duty-free grog in Buffalo on the border between the United States and Canada. I was surprised how cheap spirits were—about US$20 for a four-litre flagon! It was a wonder they were not a nation of alcoholics.

CHAPTER 10

MEDICAL PRACTICE IN PORT AUGUSTA

⊸✺⊶

Practicing medicine in Port Augusta, as in most country towns, was very busy but rewarding. I worked long hours each week. My usual working day started at around seven thirty doing ward rounds at the Port Augusta Hospital. There I might have patients in the various wards—intensive care, surgical, medical, paediatric, maternity, gynaecological, and geriatric. I would review each patient accompanied by the charge nurse and decide what next needed to be done for each one.

Sometimes I had to see a patient in the emergency department or in the renal dialysis unit before commencing consultations at the medical practice, usually around nine o'clock. Patients were booked every ten minutes until one o'clock. I then went home for lunch before returning to the practice to continue consultations until six. Occasionally I had to fit in a house call during the lunch hour or after six o'clock.

Variations to this routine occurred when I was expected to attend an operating session in theatre or do a minor surgery session in the outpatient theatre. Both these activities occurred once each week. One afternoon every month, I visited patients at Ramsay Retirement Village and Nerrilda Nursing Home in addition to seeing a few patients who were housebound. One morning each fortnight, I saw patients at the Port Augusta Gaol. Besides that, emergencies presented anytime, and I would then drop everything and give them priority. Some nights, I continued to work all night in the emergency department at the hospital and still turned out to work as usual in the morning.

It was possible to treat patients effectively every ten minutes at the surgery because the process was highly organised and fine-tuned. The receptionists were very welcoming and efficient at triage. This stemmed from a very capable practice manager who made sure all staff were not only highly trained but also aware of our expectations. They also understood each doctor's idiosyncrasies and needs.

The nursing section was led by a very efficient and experienced registered nurse, which allowed a lot of delegation of tasks to them by the doctors. Being a midwife, she could do much of the antenatal care measurements. Their duties included venesections, wound dressings, immunisations, sterilizations, stock ordering, dealing with pathology results, organising recalls, contacting patients on the doctor's behalf, and helping with medicals and chronic disease management. Patient education was also part of their duties.

Because of the tight schedule at work, I often took work home and would sit at the dining table after dinner with one eye on the television and one doing work or reading medical journals. Sometimes I would have music in the background instead of television. The sort of work I did in the evenings were referral letters for patients to specialists, medical reports for work cover and solicitors, official letters concerning practice management or on behalf of the Flinders and Far North Division of General Practice, of which I was the medical director. By deferring these tasks to the evenings, I could stick to the ten-minute appointment schedule for consultations at the practice. I took great care to run on time and not keep patients waiting.

Because there were no resident doctors at the Port Augusta Hospital, the GPs in town staffed the hospital. They were responsible for admitting, treating, and discharging their patients. They consulted with visiting and resident specialists when needed and assisted in the operating theatres. In addition, they organised themselves on an emergency roster to man the casualty section of the hospital. This meant working all day at the surgery and sometimes all night in the emergency department. They were then expected to work as usual the next day. This meant that at times we had no or very little sleep over a two-day period.

Some of us did obstetrics, and we always delivered our own patients. This meant more sleepless nights, especially for someone like me who delivered an average of ninety babies per year for twenty-five years. That's over two thousand babies in total!

Practice management was my responsibility, whereas my business partner, Victor Yeung, was very good with computers and medical equipment, and he assumed responsibility for these areas. I dealt with staff management, recruitment of doctors, financial management, dealing with the bank and the accountant, and practice promotion. I was interested in local hospital issues and was on the hospital board as the doctors' representative.

I was a member of the three-man advisory group to the medical director of the local hospital. I also wanted to keep abreast of government regulations at the state and federal level. For that reason, I was not only the medical director of the local division of general practice but also a member of the South Australian Divisions Incorporated and the Rural Doctor's Workforce Agency. I wanted to know about any decisions made that would affect my practice.

Much of the day-to-day running of the practice was left to the very capable practice manager, with whom I had frequent short meetings. We also had regular practice meetings involving both doctors and staff. Their input was important to us, and it made them feel part of the team. It was a culture that we promoted and was essential in creating a sense of belonging. This resulted in a happy, motivated, and dedicated team, something treasured by everyone. The staff knew our culture and expectations and did their best to meet them, even down to the cleaners.

To promote this family atmosphere, we had two functions every year, funded by the practice. One was the pre-Xmas dinner and the other was a family day mid-year, when kids were invited. These were special functions enjoyed by all, and they are still talked about to this day. Many old staff and doctors have remained long-term friends, which is a testament to the strong relationships formed during those years.

In the early years of my work in Port Augusta, there was very little cooperation between my early partners and the other doctors in town. Our practice was dominant in Port Augusta and was self-sufficient. We had doctors with varied experience and expertise, so collectively we needed no help from others. We were the United Nations, according to some of the nurses. Some of my partners regarded the others as second-rate doctors.

When Victor and I became owners of the practice after the departure of three of the six partners, we set about creating a more cordial relationship with the other doctors in town. I was keen to get involved in medical politics and to look after the interest of all GPs in Port Augusta and other neighbouring towns. This was achieved, and I gained the trust and respect of all of them. I created a single roster for after-hours emergency attendance at Port Augusta Hospital, enabling doctors to have some time off instead of being on call every night and weekends. I also negotiated a better on-call fee for manning the emergency department.

Ram 1986

Some Memorable Patients (Pseudonyms Used)

Alice

Alice was an indigenous frequent attender of the emergency department, usually in a drunken state anytime day or night. I think she was lonely and used the emergency department as somewhere to get some attention. Her usual complaint was stomach pains and nausea, which we all put down to alcoholic gastritis and gave her the usual treatment with Mylanta tablets. She normally settled with that and would go away happy.

On one occasion, her pain was more persistent and colicky, and she kept complaining after being given Mylanta tablets. My partner, who was on call, told the nurses on the phone to admit her for observation, as it was around two in the morning and he had seen her many times before with the same presentation. He received a call at about six a.m. from a nurse informing him that Alice had had a miscarriage and the foetus was alive! When did she have time to become pregnant, and who was the father?

The doctor attended, and to his surprise, he found a live foetus of about twenty weeks' gestation. After consultation with the retrieval team in Adelaide, the decision was made to do the sensible thing and leave it alone to die in peace, as the chance of a good outcome was extremely low. It took a lot longer than expected, and we suspected it was older than twenty weeks, but malnourished and small for dates. It eventually succumbed. The lesson learnt was to treat each patient's presentation on its merits and don't jump to conclusions without doing a proper assessment.

Mrs. Robertson

Mrs. Robertson was an eighty-four-year-old patient of mine who lived on her own and adopted me as a friend. She always brought a gift for me when she came for an appointment. It could be a piece of cake or some lollies or vegetables from her garden.

When she learnt that I had a small daughter, she started bringing soft toys and books for Nalini also, and always called her Narrele, despite being corrected many times. One day, I decided to do a house call, taking my wife and Nalini to see her. We took her a cake to share over a cup of tea. She promptly put the cake in the freezer and looked for the milk for the tea in the oven. It was obvious to me then how demented she was. She died a year later.

Miss Roberta

Miss Roberta was a girl in her forties and in fact was the granddaughter of Mrs. Robertson above. She was a frequent attender of the various doctors' surgeries in town and the emergency department. She had a drug dependence problem and was constantly looking for codeine-based medications, claiming to have headaches or chest pains or backache. She gradually wore out her welcome with most doctors, mainly because she did not want to follow instructions or take advice. We all tried to help her, but in turn each one of us became so frustrated that we refused to see her.

This became a problem for the hospital staff and administration, as no patient can be refused help in a public hospital. It was frustrating to be woken up at three in the morning to be told Miss Roberta was in casualty with chest pain, knowing it would be fake. It was easy to order two panadeine forte tablets and roll over and go back to sleep. This was okay most of the time, except the one time when she did in fact have a heart attack. The lesson here was to never ignore chest pain but assess each one on its merits.

Miss Gliddon

Miss Gliddon was a problem patient in that she took a fancy to me when I was in between marriages. She would turn up to my house uninvited and always brought gifts for me at the surgery, especially ties and shirts. I tried to stop her by refusing to accept them, but to no avail.

She was not impressed when I started living with Debbi. She kept bringing gifts, and Debbi would dispose of them. She had a minor accident at work and injured her forearm. There were no fractures, but she kept maximising her symptoms, so much so that she had various assessments by specialists and psychologists and maintained that she could not work. She remained on work cover throughout.

She became very depressed and required treatment by a psychiatrist, who put her on antidepressants. These had side effects, and she gained a lot of weight. She became a cat woman and had as many as twenty cats in her mother's house, where she lived. She spent a fortune maintaining them.

I tried to get her to see other doctors, as I felt our doctor-patient relationship was compromised. Her mother pleaded with me to continue seeing her, saying that if I stopped, her mental condition would deteriorate. I placed some conditions—for example, no gifts, no unnecessary attendances, and no contact with my family. The last condition was because she tried to move Debbi on by sending her messages and saying her children were the devil's children.

The scary thing was that one Sunday morning, Debbi received a call from the Catholic priest, who was a friend, telling her not to turn up to church that day, as there was a crazy girl waiting for her and the children at the church. It was Miss Gliddon! I was happy to leave her behind when I left Port Augusta.

Mr. Butler

This patient was housebound with a very bad chest requiring domiciliary oxygen and weakness of the limbs. He had other medical issues and required various medications. To make it easier for him and his wife, I did a house call at six o'clock on a Wednesday evening every month after work on my way home. My car was easily recognised, so the rumour went around town that I was having an affair with Mrs. Butler! I put it down to small-town mentality.

Mr. Thomas

Mr. Thomas was a rather pleasant man in his late seventies with severe chronic bronchitis and emphysema. Whenever he had a viral infection, it went to his chest, and he required admission to hospital for antibiotics plus oxygen. He also had domiciliary oxygen. He was always slow to respond but always recovered enough to go home.

This occurred frequently for years until one day, during my morning ward-round, he asked what I was doing around two in the afternoon that day. I said I was consulting at the surgery. He asked if I could spare him a little time. I agreed, and when I turned up, he had his favourite charge nurse and his daughter there. He got his daughter to bring a few beers and asked us to join him for a drink, as he wanted to thank us for all we had done and to say goodbye.

I asked, "Where are you going?"

He replied, "It's time, Doc, to leave this world. I have had enough."

I said, "But you are getting better, and I was going to send you home tomorrow."

That night, he died. I couldn't believe that someone could will themselves to death like that and had never witnessed anything like it before. Incidentally, there was no reason to suspect suicide.

Mr. Burton

Mr. Burton's wife was in the nursing home, and he visited her every day, spending all day there. He only went home to sleep. His wife eventually passed away. He was so broken-hearted after sixty years of marriage that even though he had no known medical problems, he willed himself to death one week later. Such is the power of the mind. He died at home, and an autopsy found no cause.

The Cooberpedy Patient

A patient presented to me at the surgery saying he had felt unwell for several days and had travelled four hundred kilometres from Cooberpedy to Port Augusta to see a doctor. I assessed him and ran some blood tests. He turned out to be in diabetic ketoacidosis (very high blood sugar). He was not a known diabetic, but if left untreated he would have died in a matter of days.

I treated him as an inpatient at Port Augusta Hospital, and he recovered. He felt so much better that he was ready to go back to opal mining in Cooberpedy. He was so grateful that he handed me a small bag containing some opals. This I gave to Debbi, who had a few set as rings and pendants. We even gave some to a jeweller friend in England.

Miss Maisie

Maisie was an indigenous patient in her late thirties. She presented one evening in casualty very drunk and demanding to see a doctor. When asked if she had a regular doctor, she said no, but she had seen one before. She couldn't remember the name but said, "It's the one who smell like a woman."

The nurses concluded that I drew the short straw, as I liked good aftershave. When I turned up, she said, "That's him, and I want to have his baby!"

Because of the lingering scent of my distinctive aftershaves, nurses would make remarks to their colleagues like, "I gather Dr. Bhola has been to do his ward round."

The Phantom Plumber

HT was an interesting local character. He was your typical Aussie Ocker. I called him the phantom plumber, because when asked to fix a problem in the yard, like changing the filter in the water softener, he would attend and fix it, leaving no trace of his visit. His bill would appear three months later, when his wife had time to attend to it. I would have to ring him up to find out if the job was done, to which his indignant reply would be, "Of course it's fixed. What sort of plumber do you think I am?"

Once Debbi summoned him to check a hot water heater that had suddenly blown up. He came, assessed it, and said, "It's rooted, missis." He disappeared without any further words and returned with a new unit, installed it, hosed down the pavers, and left. The bill came three months later as usual.

One day, he was working on the roof of a building and lacerated his hand on the iron sheets. He came to the surgery and said, "Fix it, Doc. I have to get back to work and finish the job." It was a deep jagged laceration, but lucky for him, the tendons and nerves were spared.

I was drawing up some local anaesthetic when he asked, "What's that for?"

I said, "To numb the area so I can suture the wound."

He said, "Don't worry with that, just get on with it."

I told him the procedure would be painful without it, but he insisted he was not a wuss and to just do it. I decided to test his toughness. He sat there and did not flinch while I inserted eleven stitches. He refused a tetanus booster and a sickness certificate, saying he had to finish the job, as he worked on his own. Most patients would need a week off work. Fortunately, the wound healed well.

The Pethidine Addict

A young indigenous male patient was always presenting to the surgery or the emergency department complaining of a migraine headache and requesting an injection. At that time, pethidine was the drug commonly used. It was highly addictive and gave patients a pleasant euphoric feeling. It is no longer used because of its addictive properties.

This particular patient never seemed distressed with his headache and always reported immediate relief, even though the drug should have taken at least twenty minutes to have an effect. After a few visits, I discussed trying alternative drugs, to which he consented—but he always returned saying they had no effect.

I decided to conduct an experiment with him. I arranged with the practice nurse to give him sterile water injection whenever I said to give him "the usual." It was documented that he received sterile water. This we did several times over a three-month period. He always reported good relief each time. It was obvious he was addicted to having an injection, and it worked if he thought he was getting pethidine.

One day, I decided to level with him and told him what went on, and that the reason for my experiment was to prove to him he did not need the pethidine injections. He was furious and stormed out of the surgery. He returned a week later to thank me for curing his addiction. I am not sure I acted ethically, but it did have the desired result.

The Yugoslav Patient

A middle-aged Yugoslav woman took a fancy to me and started giving me some rather expensive gifts, including paintings. I tried to stop her, but she kept on doing it, saying she could afford it and it gave her pleasure to give me gifts. Debbi was not impressed with this behaviour.

I was relieved when the woman decided to move to live in Melbourne. She invited us to stay with her whenever we visited Melbourne, but we had no intention of taking up that offer. That was the end of that relationship. I guess patients' fixation on their doctors is one of the more annoying, and at times challenging, aspects of the profession.

Mr. Bob Taylor

Bob was a gentleman in his early eighties. His wife had chronic obstructive pulmonary disease and was confined to the house. I did house calls on her when required. Bob was always happy to see me and would proudly give me a tour of his garden, of which he was proud. He would insist I take home some tomatoes, pumpkins, and other potted plants that he had propagated especially for me. He always reserved the best tomatoes for me.

They were married for over sixty years. When she passed away, he was devastated and became very lonely. He left everything in the house undisturbed and would talk to his wife regularly as he went past the chair or the bed that she used.

I decided to continue my regular home visits, and whenever I went, he would insist that I share a beer with him. For this reason, I always visited at the end of the day. He also liked playing his various musical instruments and singing his favourite songs. Sometimes I brought Debbi or my son with me, on his insistence. He also told many jokes.

He was capable of driving and sometimes visited the surgery for blood tests and such. He needed a medical exam for renewal of his driver's licence one day, which he failed. I had to tell him he must stop driving, and I got him some government taxi vouchers. He was not impressed.

One day, he requested a house call. I went there to find him up on his garage roof pruning some trees. I told him it was too risky at his age to climb up a ladder and do what he was doing. He came down. When I asked the reason for his request for a house call, he said he needed to get his prescription filled at the chemist and some "bloody quack of a doctor took my driving licence away so I can't get there." It was payback time. We laughed about it and shared a beer.

One joke of his that I remember was the one about a gentleman who went regularly to the local retirement village to play his ukulele and sing songs to the residents, who looked forward to his visits. One hot summer's day, this gentleman put on his shorts and went to the village. He was sitting on a wicker chair with slats on the seat through which his balls were hanging down.

One old lady was embarrassed for him. When he called for requests for songs, she went up to him and whispered in his ear, "Do you know your balls are hanging down between the slats?"

He said, "No, I don't know that one, but if you can hum it, I will play it."

Mrs. Parkinson

Mrs. Parkinson was a patient and a friend who presented to Casualty bleeding profusely from the vagina. She'd had a hysterectomy by the visiting gynaecologist two weeks earlier. I assessed her and decided she had to be taken to the operating theatre immediately. I summoned one of my partners, who had some surgical experience. There was no time to call the gynaecologist, who was in Adelaide. My partner was to operate and find where the bleeding was coming from, and I was to give the anaesthetic.

I had two drips going and sent a request for four units of blood from the blood bank. She was anaesthetised by me, and my partner set about finding the bleeder, which was somewhere along the suture line at the vaginal vault. There was so much bleeding that he could not see a thing and had to work blindly, trying and hoping that one of the sutures he was applying would tie the bleeder. In the meantime, although I was running fluids into her as fast as I could, her blood pressure was dropping, her pulse was racing, and she was getting very pale. I had visions of my first anaesthetic death.

Everyone in the theatre were horrified. But suddenly, the bleeding eased, and the blood pressure started to climb. She was out of trouble, and we all breathed a sigh of relief. One of the sutures tied the bleeding vessel. That was a close call!

Inmates at Port Augusta Gaol

We provided medical services to the Port Augusta Gaol and conducted clinics there weekly. At first, we were seeing up to forty patients per four-hour session. Many patients faked symptoms to see the doctor to avoid working in the fields. We soon wised up to this and set up a nurse triage system, which reduced the numbers by half.

Many came for sleeping pills and were very persistent to the point of being aggressive. We were reluctant to create addiction problems, so we took a less confronting approach. Rather than refusing medications, we prescribed "yellowdol" tablets. This was the name we gave to yellow vitamin C tablets. The placebo effect worked wonders.

Some inmates wanted tattoos removed. We obliged but had to soon stop when just about every prisoner lined up for the procedure!

There were some high-security prisoners there, like the Snowtown murderers. One indigenous young man was there for stabbing his twin brother to death after his brother had put some sand in his beer while they were drinking in the sand hills. I asked him why he did that. He just smiled at me and shrugged his shoulders.

An amusing situation was when the authorities in Adelaide decided that we were only to see the white prisoners, and the indigenous patients would be seen by the doctors from Pika Wiya Aboriginal Medical Service. They felt these doctors might understand the needs and culture of those patients better than us, even though we had been treating indigenous patients for years before that. The irony was that we were the coloured doctors, and the Pika Wiya doctors were white and had no previous exposure to indigenous patients.

Baxter Detention Centre

I had negotiated a contract to provide medical services to Baxter Detention Centre, and we took turns visiting twice each week. The patients were from all over the Middle East, and some required interpreters. I found them to be very demanding. They wanted all their problems fixed while they were in detention, free of charge. They did not understand the concept of a waiting list for non-urgent problems and would attend every few days to ask when they would be treated, even though they were already on the surgical and dental waiting lists. Interestingly, some of their problems were longstanding and were present for years before they left their country.

One of our doctors was Muslim, and they expected him to help them get out of detention and acquire resident visas. He was so stressed by their demands that he refused to visit them anymore.

Management decided we could perhaps do some consulting in each security wing instead of bringing every patient to the clinic. During one such visit a tall, strapping, fearsome, bearded Arab decided he must see the doctor at once, even though he did not put his name down on the list before that day, as he was meant to do. The nurse told him he had to follow procedures and would not be seen. He did not accept this and was about to make a scene. I think he was bored and wanted to buck the system and throw his weight around just for the fun of it.

He became very aggressive and threatening and would not accept that he couldn't see me when I was just there. To defuse the situation, I intervened and saw him straight away. He received two Panadol for his imaginary backache and went away happily.

My Indigenous Experience

Before the establishment of the Pika Wiya Aboriginal Medical Service, the indigenous patients attended our surgery and the other surgeries in town. They formed about 7 percent of the population, although this varied from time to time, as they were an itinerant population and sometimes went walkabout to remote towns to visit relatives. Sometimes those from the outback came into Port Augusta for shopping, visiting relatives, seeking medical attention, or attending special events like NAIDOC (National Aborigines and Islanders Day Observance Committee) week.

I had some families that travelled from outback towns like Maree, Leigh Creek, Andamooka and Cooberpedy, often by bus overnight, to see me for medical treatment. It was interesting that many of them never attended the Pika Wiya Health Service but stayed with me. Others went there for free medications but came to me for assessment and prescriptions. Some attended there mostly, but when they felt very sick, they wanted to see a "real doctor," meaning one of us. Somehow, they had less respect for the Pika Wiya doctors, partly because those doctors changed often.

I wondered if some of them identified with me because of the colour of my skin. On a few occasions, I had to nip in the bud any romantic ideas towards me. They certainly supported the West Indian cricket team against the Australian cricket team, which I believe was on racial grounds. A few of the girls would hang around the hotel lobby where the West Indian players stayed to try to contact them.

I found them to be very appreciative and respectful. Unfortunately, many were addicted to alcohol, which led to problems such as fights, serious injuries, and other health issues. The incidence of diabetes, hypertension, infections, and kidney problems was higher amongst them than the non-indigenous population.

I particularly enjoyed delivering their babies. Deliveries were generally quick. Their tissues were so much more elastic compared to the white patients. I often stated that they had not lost the ability to breed. They were a shy race and, as a mark of respect, never looked me in the eye.

Culturally, some of them had the attitude that what's yours is mine. This was evident when a few teenagers decided to help themselves to music books from my wife's music store, and when confronted, said, "What you gonna do about it?" They generally received only a warning from the police. Many were involved in petty crimes like breaking and entering. As a result, many ended up spending time in the Port Augusta Gaol. In fact, about 70 percent of the inmates were of aboriginal descent and were there for petty crimes.

When I played cricket, our team sometimes played against the indigenous team. It was amusing that when we had a drinks-break, they had a cigarette break instead. They were gifted athletes and were well represented in many football teams across the country. Debbi loved to have them on her netball team.

Some Memorable Medical Encounters

The First Death

I was a first-year medical student working in a nursing home in Northumberland when I witnessed my first dying patient. The elderly gentleman was in end-stage heart failure and was unconscious. His breathing was rapid and rattly, and he was blue.

I was worried and decided to call the doctor, expecting him to do something. He attended, took one look, and did nothing except say, as he walked away, that the patient should be gone within two hours. He was right.

It was upsetting for me, and that image stayed with me for some time. It was not until I became a more senior student that I learnt to deal with the dying patient.

Twin Presentation

One day I was on call and was summoned to the emergency department to find a female patient in advanced labour. She was from Port Lincoln and had been admitted for rest at the Women's and Children's Hospital in Adelaide at thirty-four weeks' gestation, as she had a twin pregnancy and mild hypertension.

She decided she wanted to go home, took her own discharge against medical advice, and boarded the train to Port Lincoln. She went into labour, and the train guard decided she had to be dropped off at Port Augusta and be assessed at Port Augusta Hospital. She was too far advanced in labour to send her anywhere or to have her retrieved. I had no choice but to deliver her twins, a task normally reserved for specialist obstetricians.

I summoned a team of four doctors and decided she had to be delivered in the operation theatre instead of the labour ward. We were four GPs acting as anaesthetist, obstetrician, paediatrician, and surgical assistant. One of my colleagues delivered the first twin, which presented head first, but the second baby was lying transversely and could not be turned around to be deliver head first or breech, so it had to be by caesarean section.

Fortunately, all turned out well, but the outcome could have been very different. Some patients just do not appreciate that their irrational decisions can place GPs in difficult situations, and themselves at risk.

Breech Delivery

The phone rang, and when I answered it, the midwife said, "Dr. Bhola, your patient is ready for delivery." I enquired who was the patient, as I was not aware that I had a patient in labour. I was informed that she had just arrived and was fully dilated, meaning she was ready to deliver the baby. When told her name, I said I did not even know she was pregnant, even though she and the whole family were my patients.

She was a sixteen-year-old rather quiet, shy girl from a very pleasant family. She was so frightened that she had told no one about the pregnancy and had not sought any medical help. Her parents had no idea she was pregnant. She'd started to wear loose clothing that hid her enlarging tummy.

The baby had a foot protruding from the vagina, so it was a footling breech presentation, and time was of the essence. Again, this is a problem for a specialist obstetrician and not a GP. Fortunately, I had done a breech delivery before and witnessed others, so I knew what to do. I got the midwife to summon another colleague in case I needed help with resuscitating the baby. The delivery went according to plan, and my colleague congratulated me on a job well done.

The baby came out screaming, which was a welcome sound. It was only 2.5 kg. The delivery might have had a different outcome if it was a bigger than 3.5 kg. Interestingly, all breech deliveries in first-time pregnant mums are now done by elective caesarean sections.

Shoulder Dystocia

The third obstetric case that caused me some angst was a delivery that was going very well with the head delivered easily, but the shoulders got stuck. The umbilical cord was tight around the neck and had to be cut. This meant the rest of the baby had to be delivered as soon as possible. But no amount of tugging at the head would allow the shoulder to come past the pubic bone, despite a large episiotomy. The baby was blue, and the midwife looked horrified.

I was sweating, with thoughts of my first neonatal death and a coronial enquiry going through my head. I managed to get my index finger in the axilla of the baby, and as I pulled hard, there was a crack. I knew that I had fractured something. After that, the shoulder collapsed enough to allow the baby to be delivered. It required some resuscitation but was okay. The right humerus had an undisplaced fracture, but fortunately no nerve damage. I explained to the parents that the fracture was a blessing and prevented a dead baby. I reassured them that it would heal without any adverse outcome. They understood and were extremely grateful.

My son, who had a similar birth, ended up with a weak left arm due to nerve damage. My colleagues expected me to sue the obstetrician involved and were surprised when I did not. I understood how easily one can find oneself in this situation, having had the above experience.

Incinerated Patient

As I arrived in casualty there was an awful smell of burnt flesh throughout the area. I found an indigenous patient groaning in pain from burns to virtually 100 percent of his body. He had been brought in by ambulance, having been found near a campfire in the sand hills near the Aboriginal Reserve, just out of Port Augusta. He was extremely drunk and had rolled into the campfire.

I contacted the burns unit in Adelaide, who advised me they had nothing to offer him and to let him die in peace. This occurred about an hour later. This presentation remained imprinted in my mind forever. The smell lingered for hours.

Gunshot Suicide

I was called one night to pronounce a patient dead in her own home. It was a sixteen-year-old who was lying at forty-five degrees in her bed, with her head on the pillow. Beside her was a shotgun. Her open mouth revealed a large hole on her hard palate, where she had aimed the gun as she pulled the trigger. It was a very upsetting scene for me, the ambulance, and police officers.

Good Samaritan Act on an Air Canada Flight

"Is there a doctor on board? If so, please see the air hostess."

This was the announcement over the intercom on an Air Canada flight I was on, travelling from New York to Toronto. I waited to see if an American or Canadian doctor would answer, as I was not registered to practice over there. The call was repeated a second time. I waited. When it was made for the third time, my wife, Debbi, said I had no choice but to answer.

I went and found that a patient on board was having difficulty breathing. She had an oxygen mask on. She was in heart failure and was going to see her son in Toronto. Her GP had given her some morphine syrup and other medications.

I checked her and found that she was hyperventilating from anxiety. She only required reassurance and a little more morphine, after which she settled and completed the journey without further problems. On disembarking, I was given a bottle of champagne by the air hostess.

A month later, a letter from the CEO of Air Canada arrived at my home in Australia, thanking me and saying it was reassuring to know that there were still some doctors around who would answer a Good Samaritan call.

Scalped

I was called to attend a patient one evening in the emergency department. There I found an obese, drunk, middle-aged indigenous lady swearing at the nurses and accusing them of talking about her. "You are no better than me just because you are white. Stop talking about me. I may be black, but my cunt is as pink as yours" she was saying.

I told her to stop being rude if she wanted me to treat her. She obeyed and started singing. She had been hit by someone with a piece of wood, perfectly descalping her. The scalp flap could be lifted off the skull bone from the forehead to the back of the head. There was a lot of dried and clotted blood on her hair, clothes, and the barouche.

I did not use any local anaesthetic and stitched her up in layers. I placed sixty-five sutures in her scalp, and she did not flinch once. She had enough self-administered general anaesthetic on board and sang throughout the whole episode.

Road Accident

My children were watching the local news on television while Debbi was preparing dinner. They were shocked to see me on television and told her that Dad would be late for dinner. I attended a road accident site ten kilometres out of Port Augusta. The ambulance officers wanted a doctor on site, so I went with them in the ambulance. We had to extract the driver from his car. Fortunately, all went well, and the patient survived.

Coal Train Incident

It was around five in the morning when I was called to the morgue at Port Augusta Hospital to pronounce a patient dead. He was driving on Highway One towards Port Augusta at 110 km/hr and had slammed his car against an unlit coal train carriage travelling from Leigh Creek to the Northern Power Station. There were no warning lights or barriers. It was a dangerous crossing.

Strychnine Poisoning

A lady was brought into casualty one afternoon when I was the doctor on call. She was on a barouche and was very agitated. She said, "Do something, save me, I do not want to die. It was a mistake." On questioning her further, I found out she had taken strychnine to poison herself but had a change of mind immediately. There was no antidote to strychnine, so there was nothing I could do but watch her die. This only took about four minutes.

The Jordie Patient

A patient started consulting me because he heard I had graduated from Newcastle Upon Tyne and he was from that area. He was on worker's compensation for a long time with a bad back supposedly from a work incident. There was very little to find on examining him. I was not convinced by his story but had no option but to issue further work-cover certificates for the moment.

One evening, I attended a local pub where a band was playing, and there he was strutting his stuff on the dance floor with no apparent discomfort. As soon as he saw me, he limped off the dance floor. He never came to me as a patient again.

Filleted Patient

A young man stooped to climb over the lower rung of a fence made from railway sleepers when the one on the upper rung fell and filleted his back. The bony spine was exposed under the large flap of skin and muscles. We administered painkillers and had him retrieved to Adelaide.

Road Accident near Tenterfield

We were on our way to the Gold Coast by car, travelling in convoy with another family, when we came across a motor vehicle accident. There were two injured people in a two-car collision. One ambulance was on site, with two ambulance officers. It was on an isolated stretch of road. The nearest town was Tenterfield in New South Wales. No police were in attendance.

One person had a back injury with a suspected vertebral fracture. Any movement caused him pain. The other was very irritable, restless, and agitated. He had some bleeding from one ear, which suggested a significant head injury. He needed urgent transport to the local hospital and retrieval to a major hospital as soon as possible. He kept saying, "Please help me."

There was only one available ambulance, so both patients had to be transported together. I accompanied them in the ambulance and arranged to meet my party in Tenterfield, where we had booked a motel to spend the night. The nearest hospital was located there.

The patient with the spinal injury was feeling every bump on the road. The ambulance officers decided to travel slowly because of him, even though I tried to impress on them the urgency of the other case. The head injury patient was getting more restless and agitated, pleading for help. He appeared very frightened and knew he was in serious trouble.

When we eventually arrived at the hospital, the town's only doctor, an elderly man who had been warned of our situation, was there dressed in his suit and had made no effort to prepare for our arrival. The head injury patient was unconscious by this time and needed intubation. The doctor made no attempt to help and took some time to find an endotracheal tube and laryngoscope to intubate the patient. This was left to me.

I asked him to contact Sydney and get a retrieval team there. The patient arrested, and we could not resuscitate him. The spinal injury patient was retrieved instead. I was disappointed with the outcome and the handling of the whole situation. I needed a stiff drink, which Debbi kindly provided.

Recognition for Long Service

After more than thirty years of working in Port Augusta, the Rural Doctors Workforce Agency decided to present me with a thirty-year service award. This was done at the Hyatt Hotel in Adelaide.

Ram Bhola, Bob Cooter, and Devinder Grewal received Service Awards

My immediate family; my partner, Victor, and his wife, Anita; the practice manager; and a few close friends were allowed to accompany me. Some other doctors also received awards that night. The awards were presented by the South Australian Minister of Health, and the master of ceremonies was a local TV news presenter.

I was asked how I came to be in Port Augusta and what had kept me there so long. I told the story of how I thought I was going to somewhere like Coolangatta, which everyone thought was hilarious. I mentioned the satisfying type of work in rural and regional areas.

CHAPTER 11

LIFE IN PORT AUGUSTA

Life in a small country town can be enjoyable and interesting.

Climate

Being on the edge of the desert, there was wide variation in the temperature from day to night, by as much as 25 to 30 degrees at times. The summers were very hot and dry. Temperatures could get up to high forty degrees Celsius. The winters were cold at night but sunny and pleasant during the day. Spring and autumn were perhaps the best seasons. Rainfall was low. The plants that survived best were natives, such as eucalyptus trees, that required little water.

When I first arrived, there were not many trees, but the local council set about greening Port Augusta and planted many trees. There was an enthusiastic parks and gardens officer who made it his personal goal. By the time I left, the results of his efforts were obvious. The climate lent itself to outdoor life and activities.

Friends and Family

The people of Port Augusta were very friendly and accepted us readily. Never have we experienced any racial discrimination. We made many friends from all walks of life—from Catholic priests (even though I was a Hindu) to train drivers, fitter and turners, teachers, bank managers, businesspeople, nurses, pharmacists, optometrists, doctors, laboratory technicians, store attendants, housewives, and pastoralists. We were happy to make Port Augusta our home and took a long-term view.

With this outlook, we became involved in the local community. I played cricket with a local team and joined the Lions Club. Many of my patients were Italians, who often invited us to Italian Club functions and to play bocce. Debbi became involved with the Red Cross, the Caritas Caterers, the Quilting Club, the Swimming Club, and the Netball Association. She played netball and badminton at a very high level and later was a netball coach for a local club and an Adelaide club. She was a state level-two coach.

We were friendly with couples of similar ages and family situations, and many had young families with children in the same classes as ours at school. Our children spent time at each other's houses and had sleepovers regularly. We had an indoor swimming pool that was a great attraction to the kids. Debbi kept spare bathers and towels to cater to the influx at times. My children loved to have swimming races with me and play Marco Polo. They also liked me to swim with them on my back. There were many barbecues and family picnics in various locations in the nearby national parks and creek beds, where the children looked for tadpoles as the parents sampled a wine or two.

The swimming pool/spa was a place for adult entertainment also. I remember two Irishmen swimming in it in the heart of winter, saying how refreshing it was and seeming immune to the cold—or too drunk to notice. This only confirmed the statement "as mad as an Irishman."

One Indian friend would sit in the spa drinking champagne and shouting to Debbi in the kitchen for a refill, much to her amusement. She would reply, "Yes, my lord." On another occasion, a friend dressed in her Sunday best dared me to throw her in the pool. A great mistake! I grabbed her from the back, lifted her, and lowered her into the pool, much to the surprise of everyone. How mean of me!

Another night, we all went out for dinner and came back to our house. It was not long before, fuelled by alcohol, someone had the bright idea of going skinny-dipping and was quickly followed by the rest. One female guest spent most of the time under water, checking and comparing the crown jewels of the male guests!

We had some great parties at our houses. The emphasis was on dancing to Motown, reggae, and English pop music. Alcohol and food were always in abundance. Sometimes we had a theme to our parties, and we always seemed to have more fun when we assumed another identity. I had several identities over the years; a baby in nappy, complete with a bonnet and dummy; a voodoo high priest from Haiti, complete with dreadlocks and beads, looking for a virgin to sacrifice; and one of the Three Wise Men from the East carrying condoms for distribution to prevent any more "virgin births." This last time we marched through a teacher's convention singing "We Wish You a Merry Christmas," and the principal later told Debbi that I made a great wise man and that our entrance was very timely, as the presenter was rather boring.

As country doctors, we were often invited to Adelaide for a weekend of postgraduate lectures by one particular drug firm. They put us up at the Grand Hotel in Glenelg and provided us with accommodation and meals at no cost to us. On the Saturday nights, there was a themed dinner meeting. One time in the middle of winter, we were asked to dress in beach gear for a beach party. We had no idea where we were going and were taken by coach to the Hilton Hotel in the middle of the city. The nightclub was set up as a beach scene, with sand and palm trees.

I was drinking rum and Coke. After a while, I went to the bathroom, slipped into my flowery pants, and put on my dreadlocks and sunnies (Bob Marley, eat your heart out). When I returned to the dance floor, no one knew who I was!

On another such occasion, we were asked to do karaoke, and I can't believe I had the courage to get up and sing "The Banana Boat Song" by Harry Belafonte, considering I can't sing and am tone deaf! I even dressed like Harry Belafonte. I did have Debbi by my side for moral support and a heap of alcohol on board for Dutch courage.

Debbi as Cher, Ram as a Rastafarian

Ram as one of the Three Wise Men

Progressive dinners were also great fun, and for these we often hired a bus to go from house to house. It was a great way of distributing the workload, so everyone had fun. Interestingly, one such dinner ended up in the local cemetery, where the headstones glowed in the moonlight while we consumed liqueurs and chocolates.

Debbi and I were members of the local Food and Wine Club. This only happened in the later years, as our previous medical partners did not want us to be members so we could be on call while they enjoyed the dinners. Another friend later sponsored us, and we were accepted. Debbi became secretary of the club and a valued member because of her organisational skills. We organised some great functions.

One time, Debbi felt enthusiastic and cooked curries for about fifty people. Dinner was in our family room, with furniture borrowed from the local primary school. Three of us were waiters. We served imported beers from all over the world. Everyone thought the food was great. It was a testament to Debbi's capabilities, which I will talk about later in this book.

On another occasion, we served a potent rum cocktail called Bhola Bomber which we perfected ourselves as a pre-dinner drink. This occurred in our backyard, with a musician providing background music, before we boarded a coach and went to the Willows Restaurant in the Flinders Ranges near Quorn. The food and atmosphere were great.

The third function that stands out was when we decided to have a Thanksgiving dinner in a local grand home, which was vacant at the time. It had been the home of the head of the Commonwealth Railways and was called Eleura Lodge. It once had the best gardens in Port Augusta, and many wedding photos were taken there. The retired gardener from there became my gardener in my first house in Stirling North near Port Augusta.

For this party, a few of us dressed up in stars-and-stripes aprons to serve as waiters. We served pumpkin soup with cornbread, followed by pork spareribs from the Pink Pig Restaurant in Adelaide and vegetables including corn on the cob. Our daughter collected the spareribs packed in eskies with ice and brought them up in her Volkswagen beetle. She confessed later that the smell of the food was too much for her, as she was hungry, and she had to stop en route to sample a few spareribs. The evening ended with someone playing the piano and all of us singing.

At the end of some days, the doctors would go and have a few beers at a local pub. I usually got my secretary to ring Debbi and tell her I had to go to choir practice so would be late for dinner. Debbi knew what that meant, but my secretary thought for years that I was in a real choir. We bought a round of drinks each and drank them rather quickly so we don't keep the wives waiting too long. The drinks would hit us on our way home.

One afternoon, the temperature was forty-six degrees Celsius, and even though we were all fully booked, no patients turned up. We decided to go home via the pub for some cold beers. As we walked on the road, we could feel that the bitumen was soft under our shoes.

Sometimes our friends arranged for several families to spend a weekend at homesteads in and around the Flinders Ranges. Everyone took food, including meats for the barbecue. Everything was pooled, and we prepared and ate meals together. The kids ran around and had a great time. We went for long walks and in the evenings sat around the campfire, enjoying a few drinks and telling stories or jokes after a hearty barbecue meal. The homesteads were so large that each couple had a bedroom, and the kids shared the lounge. Sometimes we used shearer's quarters. Having outdoor showers with rainwater added to the charm.

A couple of times, we went to Falls Creek, which was organised by two of our ex-teacher friends who used to be involved with outdoor education. We drove in convoy, stopping at Shepparton overnight and at Brown Brothers winery to get some supplies. At the tasting counter, an elderly gentleman was so impressed by my daughter Nalini that he gave her a special bottle of orange muscat and Flora dessert wine. When we asked another attendant how could he do that, he replied, "He can, because he owns the winery." It was Mr. Brown himself!

We stayed in a virtual hostel and did much of the catering ourselves. The building was cold, and the kids spent much time in the drying room in the evenings to keep warm. We had several layers of clothing in bed. Skiing was fun, and the kids benefitted from attending ski school.

I generally stuck to the green runs but was encouraged once to try a blue run. Momentary lack of concentration saw my skis pointing down the slope, and I took off at great speed, out of control and gaining momentum. I knew this would not end well. All I could do was head for a large mound of soft powder snow and crash into it. Luckily nothing was broken. All my friends could do was laugh at me.

On another occasion, I fell, twisting my right knee and tearing the medial meniscus. Debbi had a worse accident when she slipped on ice and landed on her back, as she was carrying several skis for the kids. She suffered a whiplash injury and had to wear a neck brace all the way home. Our skiing days were now over, as we couldn't take the chance of further injuries.

Regular Breaks from Port Augusta

Our life in Port Augusta was busy. I worked long hours, and we socialised a lot. We felt the need to escape at every opportunity and made regular trips to Adelaide on weekends. This occurred at least once per month. We went to good restaurants, movies, shows, museums, the zoo, sports, sightseeing, beaches, and friends' homes. Our friends used to say we saw and enjoyed more of the city than they did, even though they lived there.

Sometimes we went interstate to Melbourne or Sydney. We also made trips to the Gold Coast, Sunshine Coast, Cairns, the Barrier Reef, and Perth. We owned timeshare weeks in Port Macquarie and Coolangatta and spent much time there. This allowed trips to theme parks. Sometimes we took friends and relatives with us. We all loved bodyboarding and did a lot of this, even in Hawaii, fetching our own bodyboards.

There were a few interesting moments on the road from Port Augusta to Adelaide. One night, we were on our way and came across a mice plague. There were millions of white mice lit up by car lights as they ran across the road, and we could not avoid running over them. They were eating the wheat in the nearby farms. Another day, there was a plague of locusts, which made such a mess on the front of our car that we had to stop every few kilometres to clean the windscreen.

Once I hit a galah at high speed, and it became embedded in the grill of my Jaguar car. Blood was spattered all over the bonnet. I was on my way to pick up Debbi in Adelaide. She had left home early and travelled by bus to do some business. I decided that I would surprise her by booking into the Hyatt for the night. I checked in and left some clothes in the room before going to pick her up in Currie Street. I turned right into Currie Street from King Willian Street, ignoring the flashing "no right turn" sign. A policeman followed me, and when I stopped, he decided to lecture me. He did not see the blood all over the bonnet!

I got annoyed and said, "Just fine me and let me go on my way!" I was furious.

I picked Debbi up and told her the story. She thought I had the ticket in my shirt pocket and tried to grab it, but it was the booking slip from the Hyatt, which I did not want her to see. I grabbed her hand and lost concentration momentarily. I ran into the car in front of me at low speed and broke his rear light cover. He noticed the blood and gave me some weird looks.

Not wanting to engage that policeman again, I paid the driver fifty dollar to get his light fixed, and he accepted. I said to Debbi that I was stressed and needed a drink before driving home. We went to the bar at the Hyatt and had strawberry daiquiris. After the second one, she said no more, as I had to drive home. I ignored her and had a third, and then went up the lift to the first floor, where we had a wonderful meal in the Shiki Japanese Restaurant. She then realised we weren't driving home that night. She was relieved and relaxed to enjoy the night.

Once, we had an amusing moment at Adelaide Airport. I can still picture the face of the girl at the business class check-in counter when Debbi and I rocked up to check in our clothes, which were in large striped plastic bags. It was the best way of fetching bulky winter gear for the snow.

Gypsy Wagon

One weekend, Debbi organised for us to explore part of the York Peninsula near Minlaton by Gypsy Wagon, which were available for hire at the time. Debbi, Ahsha, Ramil, and I arrived at the farm and received instructions on how to handle the horse and harness it to the wagon. We went along a set route, spending the first night in a cabin.

We had to feed and water the horse after unhooking the wagon. I had no idea how to handle the animal. Luckily, Debbi was used to handling horses, as her parents owned racehorses, and she could even ride them. It was a large draft horse who knew the route and did not need much guidance where to go. She had only one speed—slow and steady. She kept farting at regular intervals, which smelt terrible.

The wagon was comfortable, and we enjoyed the experience. The second night was near Cockle Beach. We cooked our meals on an old plough dish on an open fire. It was rather pleasant sipping our wine around the fire before retiring to bed in the wagon. We walked on the beach the next day, and the children collected seashells.

The third night was in a house, and our hosts brought us a home-made cake. We played cricket in the yard before returning to the farm.

Debbi on the Gypsy Wagon

Sports

As mentioned before, I played cricket with a local club. One day, Debbi came to see me play and was impressed with my batting. I had scored fifty-four runs when a blowfly went up my nostril, and I accidentally swallowed it. This was so off-putting that I got out the next ball. Debbi took great delight in telling our friends about this incident. Playing cricket allowed me to associate with a great bunch of local people who invited me to barbecues at their homes.

Apart from recreational swimming and bodyboarding, I also played squash socially. I had a natural aptitude for the game. Although I did not practice much, I could give A-grade players a run for their money. Debbi thought I had the ability to be a world-class player.

I played with a female theatre nurse who was an A-grade player. Sometimes she would beat me, and at other times, I would beat her. In theatre, we would give each other a good ribbing. One day she challenged me to a match, which was to take place the next day. That evening, we were at a party together, and she decided to make me drinks of rum and Coke. She was deliberately spiking my drinks, and I had too many. This was her tactic to make sure she had the upper hand.

The next morning, I felt awful, with a severe hangover, and thought of cancelling the match. Then I decided I should teach her a lesson for doing that to me. I psyched myself up and was determined to prevail. That I did. She could not believe it when I gave her the worst thrashing that she had ever had. Such is the power of the mind!

Debbi played netball and badminton with local clubs and was good at both. She made many good friends, and this helped her to integrate with the local community and to have some outside healthy interests. Many local people loved her and thought she was not aloof like some of the other doctors' wives.

Water Activities

Fishing

Port Augusta being at the top of Spencer's Gulf, it offered a variety of water activities. I was not into fishing but went a few times with friends in their boats. I was too impatient to be a fisherman, in that I got bored and ready to quit if I didn't get a bite within a few minutes. I was happy with the company and always willing to man the bar (esky with beers).

Once Debbi and I went out with the Catholic priest in his old boat and spent much time bailing water out of the leaky boat to stay afloat. As if the threat of drowning was not enough, we were nearly asphyxiated by the diesel fumes from the outboard motor. It was rather embarrassing after a few beers to go to the toilet, which involved hanging your butt over the side of the boat while everyone looked the other way!

Waterskiing

A couple of friends had boats and were willing to teach us to waterski. This was a challenge, and it was often difficult to get our heavy bodies out of the water, but it was great when it happened. We enjoyed it, despite Debbi straining her forearm muscles and me twisting my knee, aggravating a previous cartilage injury. It was safer to ride in the sea biscuit behind the boat and just as much fun. Considering my fear of sharks, it was surprising I did not do a JC (Jesus Christ) and walk on water when I fell off. I also had a go on a jet ski a few times and thoroughly enjoyed that. I should have invested in one of those when I was younger.

Beach Activities

After waterskiing, we often had a sausage sizzle on the beach and a dip in the sea as the sun went down. The kids loved jumping off the jetties.

Horseback Riding

Once we were holidaying in Queensland and decided to go horseback riding. I had never been on a horse before and saw this as a new experience. Debbi, on the other hand, could ride horses, having done so many times in her childhood.

The guide chose our horses in keeping with our previous experience. I was given a large sluggish horse, which I was told was unlikely to throw me off. I was happy about that. I mounted the horse, and we set off on our tour along a dirt path.

My horse being slow was last of the pack. She insisted on doing her own thing and did not respond to me pulling on the reins to go right or left. She had a mind of her own. Nor could I get her to speed up to catch the rest of my party. She must have had a Taurus star sign, as she was both stubborn and controlling! She insisted on taking me into the bushes, where I had to wave my hands to avoid being hit in the face by the low-lying tree branches.

I still ended up with scratches all over my arms and face. Everyone thought that was hilarious. That was my first and last horse ride.

Visiting Students, Doctors, and Relatives

Our practice was a teaching practice, and we often had students from Adelaide and Flinders Universities, in addition to countries like the UK,

Germany, France, and Sweden. Doctors in training for general practice were also regularly posted to the practice. Sometimes we shared students attached to the hospital and the Royal Flying Doctor Service to give them a more varied experience. They were all treated very well by our doctors, nurses, and staff.

I often took students home to share an evening meal with the family, and at Christmastime, those stranded in Port Augusta were invited to share Christmas dinner with us. We also made sure they saw some of the local sites of interest. A few of the students invited us to their parents' homes in Adelaide for dinner to show their appreciation. Some of these relationships lasted well after these attachments. I am often approached at medical gatherings by these former students.

One female student stands out in my memory. She was extremely good-looking and was my shadow for a couple weeks, which meant she went home with me for lunches and dinner. Debbi was recovering from giving birth to our son and was not feeling very sexy by comparison. She was jealous, and I did not appreciate this until later, when she mentioned it to friends,

CHAPTER 12

INVESTMENTS AND ENTREPRENEURSHIP

Before arriving in Port Augusta, I was an employee in the UK. Taxes and other contributions were taken out of my salary. At Konanda Medical Clinic, I was initially salaried during the probation period of four months, and after that I could buy into the practice for $2,500. This changed my status to self-employed, and from then on I was responsible for my own taxes and was not entitled to paid holidays or sick leave.

No one explained the taxation system to me. I knew nothing about provisional tax. I was receiving a monthly income that was far greater than what I had in the UK. I thought, *How wonderful!* We started going on holidays and bought a house and a Jaguar car, thus fulfilling a long-held ambition. I spent everything I earned.

At the end of the year, I got a shock. I had earned $48,000 for the financial year, and the tax was $46,000, comprising of $23,000 income tax and $23,000 provisional tax for the following year. I had to get a bank loan to pay the tax. I was not happy.

Negative Gearing

I thought there must be some way I could reduce my tax bill, so I had a discussion with my accountant. He said as a doctor, apart from claiming a deduction for professional fees and related expenses, there was little I could do. He followed that with an explanation of negative gearing. This interested me, and I wanted to explore this option.

He referred me to a real estate agent client of his, a very personable Greek gentleman, who found me my first residential investment. I subsequently bought several more through him. They were negatively geared, and he managed them for me. I saved some tax and was benefitting from capital gains.

I thought this was great and did some more buying and selling. At one time, we had eleven properties. Then we started to sell the cheaper units and bought more expensive ones—not necessarily a smart move, as the cheaper units gave a better return and were easier to rent. Most were good-quality properties in good locations.

Hallett Cove Shopping Centre

My real estate friend encouraged me to move into commercial property investments, explaining that the returns are generally better and they can be less of a hassle. I followed this advice and bought a shopping centre he found for me in Hallett Cove. I had to sell my residential holdings and borrow a large sum of money to do so.

This proved my undoing. I did not know enough about the finer points of commercial investments, such as the strength of the tenancies and their ability to pay the rents and afford increases as per the leases. The result was a lot of unpaid rents, vacancies, and no increases in rent. On the contrary, we had to reduce rents. Some tenants were fighting with each other over what they could sell and expected us to fix the problem, but we had no cooperation from them. A few tenants just vacated the premises overnight and disappeared owing rent.

This investment was a disaster for us, as we had to subsidise the property heavily, especially in a very high-interest-rate environment. In the end, I had to do some negotiations with the mortgagee to avoid bankruptcy. Debbi had not been in favour of this deal in the first place, and the agent said to her, "Get out of the kitchen if you can't handle the heat." I should have listened to her. This venture set us back ten years in our investment portfolio.

Debbi took on management of the shops, as the agents were not doing a good job and to save costs. This was very stressful for her and resulted in many day trips to Adelaide to sort out problems. I regretted putting her in that position. This centre nearly bankrupted us. It was on Ramrod Avenue, and Debbi said she hoped it was not the "rod that broke Ram's back."

The initial idea was to leave Port Augusta and open a surgery in our shopping centre. We even bought a house in the area but then had a change of heart. We paid too much for the house and had to sell it at a loss. In the end, we accepted a lower price and acquired another shopping centre in Prospect in the deal.

Prospect Shopping Centre

This building housed the original RM Williams store. It had several tenancies and was not a bad investment. We lost a few tenants and gained others. One shop could not be rented for some time, so we had the not-so-brilliant idea of establishing a laundromat there. It meant we had to look after it. Poor Debbi had to go and clean it at five in the morning before getting the kids off to school—an imposition she did not need. We eventually sold off the equipment and closed it.

One tenant, who occupied the upstairs, had a room that he refused to let us inspect, and for good reason—it was a drug lab. One tenant downstairs was up late in her dog parlour when she heard a few Harleys in the car park and footsteps on the roof. They had climbed up the fire escape around the back. A few minutes later they were gone, no doubt with their supplies.

One day, Debbi was cooking in our house in Port Augusta, and on the television screen was a photograph of our shops on the national news. There was a drug bust by the police. When that tenant left, there was a white powder all over the air-conditioner and ducts in the roof space. It was an interesting experience. We eventually sold the shops and just broke even. It was a pointless venture.

Land at Pennington

After much effort, we eventually sold the Hallett Cove shops in exchange for some money and six blocks of land in a housing estate in Pennington. We should have built houses on those blocks and sold them, but we were so eager to rid ourselves of the whole affair that we sold them to consolidate our position. We managed to get rid of some debts, which allowed us to start moving forward again with our investments.

Timeshare Units

In 1982, I saw an advertisement in the paper for timeshare units at Vacation Village in Port Macquarie. This was one of the first timeshare developments in Australia. The concept of pegging holiday costs appealed to me, and I bought two units sight unseen. Debbi thought I had flipped my lid, but when we went and stayed there, she was sold on the idea. We eventually bought two more weeks there and two others in Broadbeach. Later, we bought another, and two in Beach House in Coolangatta. We made full use of all these units and exchanged them overseas in Hawaii, Spain, and Mexico, as well as within Australia. We particularly liked staying at Beach House and have gone there every year since 1987, sometimes twice each year.

The timeshares never gained value and could not be sold easily, because many more had been built all over Australia. The annual maintenance costs kept going up. We eventually swapped them for a point system, which allowed more flexibility.

Gold Coast Property

We got carried away one day and bought an old house on a large piece of land along Kennedy Drive on the Gold Coast. Unfortunately, the council changed the zoning, and we could not build units on it as we had planned. Besides, the house was eaten by white ants and had to be demolished. The land was sold at a loss—another dud investment. You win some and lose some.

A Music Store, Curry House, and Chinese Takeaway

My sister and her family were sponsored by us and came to Port Augusta in 1986. Because of their ages, it was hard for them to find suitable employment at first. He drove taxis and did some relief teaching, but he did not like teaching because of unruly kids. They needed to earn enough to support their three boys. My sister could not find work.

We were stuck with the lease on a shop where we ran a music store. We had been encouraged to open this store by a friend who was managing a music store that was closing down. We bought the stock off the vendor. I think our friend wanted continued employment and so told us it was a good business, but that was not the case. Just imagine me delivering pianos to people in my trailer in my spare time! I even started to learn to play the organ, but the teacher decided to encourage me to stop wasting my time and his, as I had no time to practice and was making no progress. We eventually sold off the stock, as it was running at a loss.

We then had the brilliant idea of opening a curry house for my sister and her husband to run. It was called Seeta's Curry House. They tried their best, but my sister was lacking in energy, and Debbi had to help in the shop, something she was not expecting. It turned out that my sister was severely hypothyroid. She improved with treatment, but not before we closed the shop and rented it as a Chinese takeaway. The landlord would not let us assign the lease, so we had to see it to the end.

The operators of the Chinese takeaway could not pay the rent, and in the end, closed the business. They paid the back rent with their car and some cash. I gave the car to my sister and her family.

Shell Roadhouses

A friend of ours who lost his job as a motel operator for a syndicate of which he was a part was interested in buying Shell Port Augusta West Roadhouse, which was on the market. He did not have enough money, so he encouraged me to come in as a silent partner. He and his wife took a salary and managed the business. I agreed to join them on the proviso that they employ my sister in the restaurant and my brother-in-law in the shell shop. Debbi helped in the office.

This arrangement worked well at first, and we got enough return to pay a loan that was secured by my Hallett Cove house. The dividends started to dry up, however, after Debbi stopped working there on my encouragement, as she and our partners did not see eye to eye. Debbi wanted to put the stock on the computer for stock control, but the partners objected.

Later, there were some blatant irregularities going on, which were obvious to my relatives. Expenses were put through the business that were their personal expenses; friends were sold stock, and payments in cash were retained by them. They even tried to dismiss my relatives because they were reporting to me, and I would ask questions. My response was, "They stay, or else I will sell our half of the business to them for one dollar, and they will be your partners."

They were, in fact, very good workers. My sister was not used to handling beef or pork and had never cooked the fast foods sold in roadhouses. Being a Hindu, she did not eat beef or pork. Yet she embraced the requirements of the job so well that she could multitask and was reputed to make the best steak, egg, and bacon sandwiches in the place. The threats stopped, but they did not stop giving my relatives a hard time. Eventually I got a couple, another set of friends, to buy them out.

Shell Meteor came up for sale, and we were encouraged to buy that as well. We had to mortgage my sister's house to fund it. The deal was they would live in the house on site and work there. This worked well for a while, but again, the returns were not great, and we eventually sold out. Again, there were some partnership issues. Fortunately, my sister and brother-in-law continued to be employed until their retirement and relocation to Adelaide. There is much truth in the saying that one should never mix business and friendship.

Medical Centres

Konanda Clinic

As doctors left the original practice, Victor Yeung and I bought them out one by one. We eventually owned the practice and the building and proceeded to renovate it and create some tenancies. This doubled the value overnight without much cost.

We ran this practice until 1986 when we joined Carlton Medical Centre in another part of the town. We worked there until 1991.

Port Augusta Medical Centre

While we were working at Carlton Medical Centre, two blocks of land came up for sale on Gibson Street in Port Augusta, and Debbi decided we should buy them. They were well priced at $23,000 and $14,000, the latter having a condemned house on it, which we demolished. We renovated the other house and rented it.

Debbi's idea was to buy them just in case we needed to create another surgery. It was brilliant foresight on her part. When it became apparent that we were not happy in the other surgery, we had plans drawn up for a purpose-built surgery. Debbi had a lot of input in the design, materials, and finishes, and did a brilliant job. I designed the consulting and treatment rooms.

After seeing the plans, Dr. Yeung agreed to join us. Together, we created a state-of-the-art surgery, which was used to help set the standards for accreditation of general practices by the Royal College of General Practitioners. Together with our doctors and staff, we ran a very happy and efficient surgery from 1991 to 2007.

Port Augusta Medical Centre

Ram and Victor with Dr. John Thompson (centre) at the opening of the Port Augusta Medical Centre

We later acquired a cottage on either side of our property and two blocks of land across the road. This enabled us to create more car parks and to extend our building twice to house a growing practice. One cottage created a doctor's residence and a laboratory tenancy. We eventually had fourteen doctors in the practice.

We sold the practice in 2007 and the building in 2012. The land across the road was sold separately, and the cottage was sold and turned into a dental practice. We made good profit from the whole Port Augusta Medical Centre venture thanks to Debbi's foresight.

CHAPTER 13

FAMILY SEPARATION 1996

Debbi and I had decided we would like to send our children to a private school in Adelaide for secondary education. We had placed their names on the waiting lists of several schools. Debbi went to an all-girls school in Tasmania and did not enjoy the experience, so we wanted co-ed schools. Pembroke and Westminster were the standout choices for us.

We thought we would send Ahsha and Ramil boarding but had not decided initially at what stage. In 1995, Debbi decided Ahsha should go at the beginning of year seven as a boarder. We then thought it would be a shame to separate them, as they were very close and would miss each other. Westminster school was willing to have them as boarders, but Ahsha was not happy with the boarding facility. She preferred the boarding house at Pembroke. Westminster would take them both, but Pembroke had no space for Ramil.

It was decided that Ramil would go to Rose Park primary school in the meantime and Ahsha would go to Pembroke. But then we had the problem of where Ramil would live. Debbi decided she would move to Adelaide to look after them and started to look for a house in the area. She found one in Dulwich that she liked but thought we could not afford it.

I came down to Adelaide for a medical conference, and unbeknown to Debbi, attended the auction. The auctioneer had reached the point of accepting a bid but went inside to talk to the vendors, as they do. On his return, he asked for any further bids, and having worked out that it was a good price, I stuck my hand up offering a further $1,000. No one else bid.

I then realised I had just bought a house. I had not made any arrangements with my bank and had no money for the deposit. I negotiated a three-month settlement and asked that my deposit cheque not be presented for four days, as I had a term deposit maturing then. I did not!

They accepted, and I then started to panic. It was a Saturday. I rang Debbi and said, "You will never guess what I have done."

She, being so astute, said, "How much did you pay for it?" She knew exactly what had transpired.

We put our heads together and, between borrowing money from her parents and raiding the credit cards, we covered the deposit. I then arranged a mortgage with my bank to settle three months later.

Debbi moved down to Adelaide in January 1996 with the children, who both started at Pembroke. Ramil managed to get a space in year five at Pembroke, as another boy was leaving with his parents to go to Fiji for a year. This was the beginning of our separated life, which proved to be a difficult time. I was working during the week in Port Augusta and coming home on weekends. Debbi and the children went up to Port Augusta on weekends when I was on call. It meant a lot of travelling for both of us.

I was looking after the gardens and pool in Port Augusta and had a housekeeper. In Adelaide, I spent hours in the gardens to establish and maintain them. We did a lot of renovations and improvements to that house. Debbi worked hard in the gardens to improve the soil and inside the house. In fact, one neighbour said she worked like a man when he noticed her moving mounds of mulch from the driveway to the garden beds. He wished he had such a worker on his property in the country.

9 Dulcie Street, Dulwich

This arrangement did not allow me to be involved much with the children during the week, so I tried to make up for it in the weekends by attending their sports.

After nearly twelve years of commuting twice a week between Adelaide and Port Augusta, we were starting to ask ourselves how much longer we were prepared to do this. I calculated that I must have made the trip about fifteen hundred times. I would get up at four thirty in the morning and, after a shower, set off for Port Augusta, arriving at the hospital around seven thirty, before any of the other doctors, to do my ward rounds. After that, I would start consulting at the surgery at nine.

It was very difficult to leave home at that hour. Debbi would wave goodbye to me, and I would be in tears as I left. She would ring me after a couple of hours to find out if I was okay and how far up the road I had travelled. Sometimes I could not speak to her, as I was so choked up. It must have been equally difficult for her. I gather she also shed many a tear and became depressed.

On arrival in Port Augusta, the family home, which we still had, seemed sad and lonely. Once again, it was emotional as I rang her to say I had arrived. Once I started work, I would settle down and start to count the days before I returned to Adelaide on Fridays. I would have the car packed in the morning with whatever I had to take back to Adelaide, including my washing. I would work through the lunch hour so I could make a hasty getaway at three thirty. Snacks, lollies, drinks, and loud music kept me awake during the drive.

I was so tired that I once fell asleep at the traffic lights at Gepps Cross. It was only for a short while, and I woke up to the green light without the car behind beeping me. When I mentioned this to my chest physician, he ordered sleep studies, which were done at Burnside Hospital. They were normal. I was just exhausted.

Debbi and I talked on the phone for hours every night after dinner discussing the day's events. Neither of us wanted to hang up. I learnt later from our children that she was lonely and depressed much of the time and resorted to a glass or two of wine in the evenings to help.

I had so little to do with the children's school (Pembroke) that Debbi was attending parent/teacher and other social gatherings by herself. Many thought she was a single parent. In fact, there was a group of Pembroke parents who were single and had social meetups to which she kept being invited. She had to tell them that she was, in fact, married.

Temptations were ever present for both of us, and I was glad that we survived unscathed. My children told me that there were many students at school who came from broken homes. Some of those parents got together, resulting in large families with children from previous marriages, somewhat like the Brady Bunch.

CHAPTER 14

MELROSE PARK AND PARADE MEDICAL CENTRES

———◦◆◦———

Dr. Yeung was in a similar situation. He and his wife had done the same as us, but starting much earlier, as they sent their children to Adelaide from primary school. We both wanted to spend more time with our families in Adelaide.

Melrose Park Medical Centre

Dr. Yeung found an advertisement for the sale of a house in Melrose Park in Adelaide that had been a doctor's surgery. One day, the doctor had had enough and simply walked out, telling the staff he wouldn't be back. After three months, he decided to sell the building. He did not ask for any goodwill. He had physiotherapists and a massage therapist working there on a casual arrangement.

We bought the building and tried to resurrect and promote the practice. The patients had scattered, so it was going to take some time and effort. We did some renovations, with Debbi's assistance, and started to take turns working there, making sure one of us was in each practice at any one time. We changed the name to Melrose Park Medical Centre from Winston Avenue Medical Clinic. We had one of our ex–Port Augusta doctors who had relocated to Adelaide working there and later recruited two more GPs. It was not busy enough, and I was not prepared to waste my time there when I had so many patients waiting to see me in Port Augusta. Besides, it required subsidising by the Port Augusta Medical Centre.

I lost interest, and it became obvious that it was not going to do well. We ended up selling the practice and the building to the two new recruits at cost. It was a fruitless exercise for us, and we were back to square one.

We were still trying to find a way to spend more time in Adelaide and negotiated to do sessions at Morphettville Medical Centre for Foundation Health Care. The other doctors were not happy with us being there, as they were not busy enough, so I moved to Prospect Medical Centre and Dr. Yeung stayed there.

This was a poorly run practice. I knew I would not last. I think we were too spoilt having been used to being our own bosses and running a state-of-the-art practice of our own. We soon left and bought the Parade Medical Centre.

Parade Medical Centre

The Parade Medical Centre in Beulah Park had been on sale for a while. The GP owner was feeling burnt out. He had started the practice in 1988 and ran it with his wife as practice manager. It was in an excellent position, and he had a few part-time GPs working with him. There were also rooms leased to a dentist. A podiatrist and a massage therapist were on periodic tenancies. We saw this as a more promising practice than Melrose Park.

We negotiated to buy the business in 2004. He was reluctant to sell the building at first, but on Debbi's insistence, he agreed to sell it at valuation. We were not keen on the deal without the building, as we could see potential that required us to own the building. We wanted to do some alterations, and having the constraints of a landlord would have made it difficult.

We proceeded to move walls and got rid of the podiatrist and massage therapist immediately. The dentist had to be coerced, and eventually her lease was bought out. We created an extra three consulting rooms and an extra treatment room. All the doctors and reception staff stayed with us. We appointed a new practice manager. We changed the billing policy to bulk billing all pensioners, health-care-card carriers, Commonwealth seniors, and children under sixteen. This was a master stroke. As news got around, we began to attract a lot more patients.

Dr. Yeung and I started to work alternate weeks in Port Augusta and Adelaide, thus enabling us to spend more time with our families. We alternated so one of us was in each practice at any one time. This arrangement worked well for a while. We often passed each other on the road between Adelaide and Port Augusta and had our practice meetings by the roadside around Snowtown.

Another GP on Norwood Parade was looking for a change in her situation. She ran a practice for years employing a few part-time doctors. She did all the management herself and was burnt out. The landlord kept increasing her rent, and the lease was due to be renewed.

I proposed to her that we amalgamate the two practices. She agreed, and we took on two of her part-time GPs and a senior receptionist who eventually became our practice manager. Because of the alterations we did to the building, we could accommodate them.

Dr. Yeung and I found some outside work at Workcare SA. Another popular GP from our Port Augusta practice was relocating to Adelaide for her son's education and started to work with us at the Parade Medical Centre. All the above changes and the creation of more car parks outside enabled us to run a very successful practice. The turnover trebled within a year.

The doctors were making more money and were happy. Some decided to stop working elsewhere and started working full-time with us. Drawing from the lessons learnt from the Port Augusta practice, we created a happy working environment. The Port Augusta manager and a senior receptionist spent time in our Adelaide practice and helped to introduce some of the systems we had perfected.

Around 2006, Dr. Yeung was keen to relocate to Melbourne, where his daughters had settled. As per our unwritten agreement to sell together when one of us was ready to move on, we started trying to find a buyer for the Port Augusta practice. We approached Primary Health Care and set up a telephone link with Ed Bateman, the big boss, who was a difficult, arrogant person to deal with. He only wanted to buy Victor and me, not the practice. He would then locate us in one of his Adelaide practices. He placed no value on our business and had no interest in our buildings. The meeting ended abruptly after just two minutes.

After approaching several other local prospective buyers, we eventually negotiated a deal with IPN (Independent Practitioner Network). After doing their due diligence, they agreed to buy both practices or neither. This was unexpected, as we wanted to retain the Adelaide practice. We were offered a better price if we sold both and agreed to work part-time in both practices for six months and another four-and-a-half years in the Adelaide practice. We agreed and in fact visited the Port Augusta practice for about eighteen months.

After five years, Dr. Yeung left and I continued to work, reducing hours progressively until in the end, I was only doing twelve hours a week. Dr Yeung sold his half of the Parade building to us. We had already sold the Port Augusta real estate to an investor at a reasonable price. In the preceding years, we had also sold our Port Augusta family home and lived in the cottage beside the surgery, which was divided into two residences. We occupied one, and Dr. Yeung lived in the other.

After a while, Gribbles Laboratory offered a good rent for my half, which Debbi had set up very well. We accepted the offer and lived for a while in the Flinders Hotel in the main street. This was unsatisfactory, so we rented another unit until a townhouse, which we bought off the plan, was completed on the West Side foreshore. It was a beautiful townhouse with good views of the Spencer Gulf and Flinders Ranges. Debbi set it up beautifully and was tickled pink that she had a loo with a view! It was very comfortable.

From there, I often walked to work going over the old bridge. We spent a few days there every fortnight. While I worked, Debbi did her studies. She was doing an external course at the University of South Australia in tourism and event management, which she eventually completed. This townhouse was later sold when I stopped visiting Port Augusta.

In 2016, IPN did not renew their lease on the Parade Medical Centre and relocated the practice to a purpose-built building on Portrush Road in Trinity Gardens. The name was changed to Trinity Gardens Medical Centre. It was their biggest mistake, as many of the doctors, staff, and patients did not follow. That practice has not picked up in nearly four years. The location was not as good as the Parade site. The culture of the practice is all wrong, and it was not a very happy place to work. There was frequent staff turnover, including managers. I worked there for nine months and went back to help on two occasions for short spells.

I eventually stopped working and retired to look after Debbi, who became unwell, as I will describe later in this book. We eventually sold the Parade Medical Centre building, which was demolished and a new building erected in its place to house the Dulwich Bakery. Some of the floorboards were used in the new building to make tables and chairs and shelves attached to the walls. It is interesting that our previous staff and doctors from both our practices have remained friends and socialise regularly.

CHAPTER 15

THE GREAT SHOCK (SARCOIDOSIS)

At around age fifty years, I developed a mild chronic cough. It was more like a need to clear the throat now and again. It became part of my existence, and I did not notice it on a day-to-day basis. My father-in-law commented that I still had that cough whenever he visited. I did not place any significance to it, as it did not affect my performance in any way.

As the years went by, I started feeling very tired and put it down to working long hours for many years. I regarded myself as a country doctor burnt out from burning the candle at both ends for years. I then developed an unusual symptom in that every time I drank rum, my voice went hoarse! It became a source of amusement and conjecture as to the cause.

Debbi decided to organise a holiday so I could rest. Her parents came over to look after the children, and we went to Guam for two weeks. En route, I organised an ear, nose, and throat consultation in Adelaide. The specialist found a nodule on one of my vocal cords but thought it was insignificant, and as we were going on holiday, he did not take a biopsy. This symptom did settle eventually.

In Guam, we stayed at a very nice hotel. They were doing some renovations, and we received a warning and an apology for any inconvenience. We were not impressed with the room, which stank of cigarette smoke even though we were supposed to have a non-smoking room. We requested another, but the staff were not cooperative. We were tired so, we decided to rest and sort it out in the morning. Debbi said, "Don't unpack the suitcases."

At about five the following morning, we were awakened by the sound of drills and a jackhammer. This was the last straw. With a determined look, Debbi marched down to the reception desk and demanded to see the manager. I was worried about this confrontation and conveniently stayed several paces behind. She made her feelings known firmly and succinctly. The result was that we were given a large suite with ocean frontage and received a large bowl of fresh fruits and an invitation to a cocktail party that evening.

The hotel lounge and casual dining area on the ground floor was being renovated and had to be ready for the grand opening in two days. We doubted that it would be ready. It was impressive to see tradies working day and night, some tiling while others painted. It was indeed ready on time for the grand opening; I lost my bet. It would never have happened that quickly in Australia.

I was so tired that I was sleeping fourteen hours a day. Debbi was left to amuse herself and went shopping and checking out the local area. We ate Japanese every night, as there was an abundance of good Japanese restaurants.

There was a hurricane heading towards Guam, and people were keen to get off the island. We were due to leave the next day and waited anxiously. We had visited a rather quaint place called Setti Bay a few days before, and I'd bought a souvenir T-shirt depicting the bay. We managed to leave Guam on time but heard on the news that the hurricane struck the island and a huge tsunami wiped out Setti Bay. I treasured that T-shirt for years.

I still thought I was just burnt out until one day, when I was travelling by a small plane from Adelaide to Port Augusta, I felt I could not get enough air. I thought something was not right. Around that time, a blood test showed current glandular fever infection. Debbi reported that I had the "death rattles" at night. My cough was more constant and productive. I was having night sweats, and the bed sheets were stained brown. Debbi joked that I was losing my brown colour.

I decided to order a chest X-ray on myself, and this showed a widened mediastinum (centre of the chest). The radiologist suggested a CT scan, for which I went to Adelaide. There, the radiologist put up all the films on the viewing boxes and called me in. I could see many enlarged lymph nodes in the centre of the chest. He did not know how to convey the bad news to me, so I helped him out by saying, "You're thinking lymphoma, aren't you?" He confirmed this, but when I told him about the glandular fever, he said that might explain it. We decided to repeat the CT scan in three months.

The repeat scan was unchanged. It was being read by a different radiologist who concluded that we were looking at a picture of sarcoidosis. When I asked why, he said because his chest CT looked just like mine, and that was his diagnosis. He advised me to see a chest physician, Dr. Peter Robinson, who agreed that this was the most likely diagnosis.

I had lung function studies that confirmed some restrictive airway disease. There was fibrosis, and I was functioning at 70 percent lung capacity. He wanted histological confirmation before deciding on a treatment plan.

I was referred to a thoracic surgeon for a mediastinal lymph node biopsy. I was freaking out about this procedure, as it was in an area we referred to as tiger country, with major blood vessels and nerves in the vicinity. I must have looked petrified, so he asked me if I had any concerns. I asked about the risks, and he merely said, "Well, I haven't lost a patient yet." That was meant to be reassuring, but all I could think about was *there is always a first time.* Moreover, we all knew that if anything was to go wrong, it would be with doctors or nurses as patients.

The procedure went well and confirmed the diagnosis. Dr. Robinson started me on a course of steroids for six months. I felt better within twenty-four hours and had lots of energy. My appetite increased, and I started gaining weight, as patients do on long-term steroids.

I continued carrying a heavy workload. Regular follow-ups with lung-function studies, chest CTs, and blood tests were done every three months.

I looked like someone dying of cancer. I lost a lot of weight after stopping the steroids and was grey in the face. I was breathless on exertion. Many patients noticed this but did not know what to say. A few long-term ones were brave enough to ask if I was okay. Many thought I had cancer. I was on holiday once, and the rumour around the town was that I had died from cancer!

Debbi was very worried about me but did not show it. She too thought I was dying and shed many a tear in private. I now learnt that she was counselled and supported by our daughter, Ahsha.

After six months, Dr. Robinson ceased the steroids because of the risk of long-term complications and commenced methotrexate in reducing doses over a twelve-month period. This seemed to halt progression, and I stabilised. I have been stable since but still functioning with 70 percent lung capacity. Follow-ups are now less frequent.

This whole affair was a massive wake-up call for me. It suddenly occurred to me that if I were to die, Debbi could not meet the financial commitments we had. I was carrying massive loans for our investment property portfolio. I had the cash flow to meet these commitments, but Debbi would not.

I had given up our life insurance policies just before that, because I felt we had enough assets and the premiums were stepped premiums that were increasing every five years. They had reaches $40,000 per annum. I felt Debbi had longevity on her side, as her mother, auntie, and maternal grandmother lived into their nineties. On the other hand, she had those on her paternal side who were less lucky, and many died of various cancers.

I had fortunately kept my income-protection insurance going. I decided to change our circumstances so that, should I be unable to work, this insurance would meet our living expenses. It was generous and worth $13,000 per month. To achieve this, I sold everything and paid off many loans. I only retained the surgery investments, our homes, and our cars.

The other major change was to reduce my workload. I progressively dropped activities such as anaesthetics, obstetrics, emergency medicine, and medical politics. My colleagues, especially those from overseas, were eager to pick up extra work and gladly filled any vacancies created by me cutting my workload.

Debbi and I saw the movie *The Bucket List* with Morgan Freeman and Jack Nicholson. We thought we should have a bucket list of our own. I asked Debbi to do one, and I did one too. It was amazing that we had about 80 percent correlation between the two lists.

We created a master list incorporating all that we both wanted to do. It involved travelling far and wide, both overseas and within Australia. Some of these adventures are mentioned in the following chapter. We decided we should give this some priority instead of delaying it and then having regrets if we never got around to it. I had seen too many patients who were putting off travel until retirement and never managed to realise their dreams because of changed circumstances. Our children were getting independent by then, so it was easier for us to take off whenever we felt like it. In retrospect, this was one of the best decisions we made and was timely, as you will realise as you read on.

As I was spending up to three hours per week on maintaining our two houses, we decided first to sell the Port Augusta house and later the Adelaide house. I wanted a lock-up-and-go lifestyle so that we could be free to travel without being a burden to our children by asking them to look after properties. Debbi was less inclined to sell her Dulwich home, into which she had put so much effort, but she went along with my wishes.

We bought a large apartment in the brewery complex at Kent Town. It was a lovely apartment on the fourth floor with three bedrooms, two bathrooms, a large lounge, a family room, and four balconies. There were two car parks. All the rooms had wonderful views of the parklands and the Adelaide hills. The garden setting was beautiful, and the entertainment complex had a swimming pool, a sauna, a spa, and a gym. I made full use of the facilities and felt that regular swimming, a more relaxed lifestyle, and more rest were instrumental in helping me to stabilise my sarcoidosis.

We travelled extensively and were having three holidays every year, many of our trips being overseas. After six years in the apartment, where we made many friends and attended many social gatherings, I found Debbi looking in the real estate section of the Saturday paper and dragging me to open inspections. When I asked why, she admitted that she would prefer to live in a house again. We eventually found a suitable one in Kensington Park and put it on contract with a two-month settlement. We then engaged an agent to sell the apartment while we went away on holiday to North America to visit my relatives.

Our friends in the Brewery complex were not happy to see us leave, as we were part of the social group and took an interest in the running of the complex by being on the board of management. We owned a second unit in the complex, where our son lived.

The house at 2A Alpha Street, Kensington Park, was a beautiful, large, two-storey townhouse. It was very comfortable, and we set it up beautifully with our furniture and artwork. We enjoyed the home and had many family gatherings there. It was easy to maintain, which left us plenty of time to enjoy it and to continue our bucket list.

After Debbi passed away, I sold the house and lived temporarily in an apartment in East Park on Dequetteville Terrace. This was a convenient location within walking distance of the city, botanical gardens, and the east Parklands. Attending the Fringe Festival and Womadelaide was easy from there.

Alpha Street House

Debbi had helped me to find the East Park apartment, as she thought I should sell the house when she was gone. It looked too small when completed, so we signed a contract for a larger one off the plan in Norwood. That has now been built, and it is very lovely and comfortable. I am living there at present and find it a very convenient location.

CHAPTER 16

THE BUCKET LIST (1996 TO 2018)

Trips on our bucket list started while we were still living in the house at Dulwich and continued while we lived in the Brewery apartment and the house in Kensington Park. It was particularly easy when we had the lock-up-and-go lifestyle in the apartment. We visited many interesting places and did many interesting things.

I do not want to appear boastful or bore you with too many details, so I will only mention some of the highlights of our trips. We were grateful that we did so much travelling and felt we had not missed out. It was a great decision to embark on such a bucket list while we could. We have probably covered about 80 percent of what was on our list. The places we visited many times because we liked them or had relatives to see were Tasmania, Singapore, Hawaii, the United States, Canada, the United Kingdom, Coolangatta, and other timeshare resorts in Australia and overseas.

Trips that I would like to mention in more detail, I have separated as land trips and as cruises. I have not gone into too much detail about each place, as this was not meant to be a travel guide, but I merely wanted to mention the places we visited and some funny moments we enjoyed.

Land Trips

Uluru

Though I'd lived in Port Augusta for many years, I had never gone to Uluru. Debbi and I flew to Alice Springs, where we stayed for a few days and checked out the sights before flying out to Uluru. We were there for a few days and visited Uluru at sunrise to appreciate the changing colours. Afterwards, we went on a conducted tour around the base of the rock. It was very interesting and informative.

I was surprised by the number of overseas tourists there and had a conversation with some folks from Trinidad. They were intrigued by the fly mesh we had over our faces and thought *What a good idea!* as the pesky sticky flies were bothersome and attacked our eyes and nostrils. We explained to them the Australian salute to keep flies from getting into their eyes, ears, and nose. They bought some mesh for themselves.

We had a champagne dinner under the stars with white tablecloths and waiter service—very decadent. A trip to the Olgas and Palm Valley were equally interesting.

One evening, we went to a restaurant where we had to barbecue our own steaks, but salads were provided. An English couple did not know what to do, so I volunteered to cook their steaks, and we sat with them for dinner. He said he would tell his friends in the UK that he had his barbecue cooked to perfection by an Indian doctor in the Australian outback. To him, this was incredible.

Lord Howe Island

Debbi was always interested in seeing Lord Howe Island, because the whole island is an eco-friendly national park. I was attending a weekend medical conference in Sydney, and we extended our trip to go to Lord Howe Island for a week.

We were met at the airport by our hostess in her four-wheel drive, and she took us via the grocery store so we could get some supplies before it was closed. Our accommodation was a self-catering house, which was quite comfortable. The whole place was hilly, and we could walk or use the complimentary push bikes to get around.

We were impressed by the abundance of kentia palms and the absence of flies, snakes, and stinging insects. There were a few restaurants, which took turns opening on different nights and provided complimentary transport back to our accommodation. There were not many tourists, as the infrastructure could only support about four hundred people, including the locals.

There were two high peaks on the island, and we decided to attempt to climb the less hazardous one. Much to our surprise, we made it to the top and appreciated some wonderful views from there.

The beaches were good, especially Ned's Beach, where fish and small sharks swim around your legs in the shallow water. It was still freaky as they brushed past our legs looking for feed. I felt uncomfortable with the little sharks!

The honesty system in place for renting wetsuits and snorkels was great. We could use them and leave the money in a tin. People pulled up their canoes and left them on the beach overnight. It took me back to my childhood days in Guyana, when you could leave your house wide open and go away for extended periods, and no one stole or interfered with your stuff.

New Zealand—North Island

I was told New Zealand was a beautiful country and that they were geared up for tourists. I thought the experience of a camper van holiday would be unique. A camper van appealed to me more than a caravan or tents. Some years before in Port Augusta, we had bought a camper trailer and taken it to a West Beach caravan park in Adelaide for the weekend. It was so cold and windy that the canvas walls and roof flapped about in the breeze, keeping us awake all night. It was not my kind of holiday, so the camper trailer was promptly sold.

We organised for our friends Peter and Mary to accompany us to New Zealand and decided that we would spend two weeks just exploring the North Island and leave the South Island for another time. We booked two four-berth vans and flew to Auckland, where we spent the first night in a hotel. We walked around the waterfront in the evening and had a great meal in an Argentinian-style restaurant with a wonderful array of barbecued meats.

The next morning, we were picked up and taken to the camper van hire place and found out that they did not have any four-berth vans and had upgraded us to bigger vans for the same cost. We did not mind, as these had a shower and toilet and, of course, more room. It was a shock that we had to give a deposit of $3,000 each on our credit cards as security, however. This put a dent in our credit card balances before we even started the holiday.

Peter decided it would be safer if we booked to stay in caravan parks overnight as we went around. This arrangement worked well, as we used their bathroom facilities and kitchens and could empty our septic tanks on site. This was a task we did not relish.

We headed north in convoy, spending the first night near Whangarei before travelling to Paihia. What a delightful place Paihia was! There we travelled by ferry across to Russel, and after inspecting the old buildings in this rather quaint little town, we settled down to a rather lengthy lunch in the al fresco area of the local hotel. It was so relaxing (or was it the three bottles of wine?) that we were in no hurry to leave.

We went on a jetboat ride dressed in our raincoats and life jackets. Peter, Debbi, and I went, that is—Mary was too chicken to go. She missed out. It was an exhilarating ride with a very skilful pilot. The bay of islands was beautiful to see. There was a market with some interesting local products and arts and crafts. Debbi bought some pieces to make a quilt.

One day, we went to see the re-enactment of the signing of the Treaty of Waitangi. This treaty was signed on February 6, 1840, between the British Crown and the Maori chiefs, and it is regarded as the founding document for the establishment of New Zealand. That day is celebrated every year by New Zealanders and is a public holiday.

The re-enactment was done for tourists and took place on the original site in Waitangi. It was great to see the fearsome Maori warriors in traditional dress and painted bodies. They were suspicious of the British. We volunteered Peter to be the white person representing the British Crown. He later admitted that he nearly shat himself when he came face to face with a Maori warrior, with his wide-open eyes and protruding tongue, doing a war dance and shouting a war cry.

We were told we must see the ninety-mile beach. This is best done in a specially modified coach that can travel on the water's edge. We booked and went. On our way, we came across some huge sand hills, and people were riding toboggans down the slopes, which seemed like a lot of fun. Along the beach we stopped to collect Pipis or small clams (*Vongole* in Italian) for our tour guide. They were plentiful and found just under the sand.

We travelled back towards Auckland along the western coast, not wanting to retrace our steps. The landscape was drier and less interesting, but we did come across a caravan park that had a swimming pool that was fed by a natural spring. The water was almost too hot to tolerate.

We then proceeded to the Bay of Plenty, bypassing Coromandel Peninsula, as the weather was too wet and the roads were only accessible with four-wheel vehicles. We stayed in a caravan park on the hilltop overlooking the beach at Whakatane. It was a lovely spot, and we went for walks on the beach. The highlight of this stop was the four German ladies in the camper van next door, who were uninhibited and walked around their van hanging out their washing etc with either only knickers or sometimes nothing on!

Our next stop was Rotorua, after we had travelled through some beautiful countryside with waterfalls and natural springs. After checking in to our caravan park, we went to the reception to enquire where the interesting sites were. The charming receptionist, in her broad Kiwi accent, said, "Some mud ponds are just around the corner, and there is a peeble beach nearby." It sounded like a *people* beach, and we wondered *What's a people beach?* as most beaches are for people. We soon realised she meant a *pebble* or rock beach and joked that we might be able to have some "fesh and chups" (fish and chips) there. I actually love the Kiwi accent.

The whole place smelt of rotten eggs caused by the release of hydrogen sulphide (not sulphur, as most people think) due to geothermal activity in the area, as evidenced by the smoky bubbling mud pools everywhere. I wondered what the long-term health implications from this exposure to hydrogen sulphide would be. It did take me back to those chemistry experiments at high school and the fun we had releasing hydrogen sulphide gas on our unsuspecting classmates.

Ignoring the smell, Rotorua is a must-see for tourists visiting the North Island. It was very interesting visiting the Thermal Valley and witnessing the way of life of local Maoris in their natural environment. Seeing them using hot springs for cooking and bathing was very interesting, as was the live theatre performance by the natives.

The health benefits of bathing in the natural springs have been known for centuries. The hot natural springs shooting up towards the sky and the technicolour mud ponds were awesome sights. I will not go into more details of the region, as these are available on the web. We had some of the best restaurant meals in the main street of Rotorua.

Lake Taupo came next. We were told while cruising on the lake that it was created by a volcanic eruption that was so huge it was seen as far away as Italy. The depth is unknown, and it is a freshwater lake. Trout were introduced into it, and now trout fishing is enjoyed by many. We stayed in such a nice caravan park that we extended our stay by another night.

Mary had a school friend in Hastings she wanted to visit. After passing through Napier, we arrived at Hastings and had lunch in his restaurant in the main street. That area was not as picturesque as other parts of the North Island.

The windy city of Wellington was next. It is a very interesting and lovely city. The waterfront offered a wide variety of eating places. The Mount Victoria lookout offered picnic areas and panoramic views of the city. It was accessible by cable car.

We then embarked on the long drive back to Auckland via Palmerston North, Wanganui, New Plymouth, and the industrial city of Hamilton. The drive was rather long and tedious, so it was punctuated with regular stops for coffee, lunch, bathrooms, or just to stretch the legs. Peter had a low back problem, and I was pushing him all the way. He tried to keep up but suffered with backache after some of the long driving spells. We returned the vans in Auckland and flew home having had a wonderful experience.

New Zealand—South Island

My daughter Nalini had her graduation ceremony and became a fellow of the Australian and New Zealand College of Radiologists in Christchurch, New Zealand. Debbi and I saw that as an opportunity to visit the South Island. We flew to Christchurch a week early, hired a car to drive around, and stayed in motels on the way.

We first went to Mount Cook, where we booked a helicopter flight to see Mount Cook up close and personal. It was our first helicopter experience, and I was rather nervous at first. We landed on Mount Cook and walked on the snow. We imagined Gandalf of *Lord of the Rings* on the top of the mountain, the movie having been filmed in the area. It was simply stunning. We also landed on the Franz Josef glacier.

That night, we had very little sleep, as the young Chinese couple in the room next door was on their honeymoon and displayed great stamina all night. The walls were paper-thin.

We drove through some wonderful picturesque countryside, stopping for meals in cute cafés in quaint country towns. We visited the site where some Hobbit scenes were shot and eventually arrived in Queenstown. We enjoyed a drink and lunch by the lake, and as we were walking along the street, Debbi suddenly said, "Wait a minute." She disappeared into a shop.

I followed a few minutes later and found her paying for a stuffed toy called "Big Ears." She was buying it for her sister Vikki in London, who'd had one she was attached to as a child. It had fallen apart, which made Vikki very upset. Debbi posted it to Vikki, who was over the moon when she received it.

With Queenstown as our base, we drove to Milford Sound. We boarded a small boat and travelled amongst the huge peaks, observing some beautiful waterfalls that covered us with a fine mist. It was a cloudy day, and it felt surreal.

In Christchurch, we were impressed by the beauty of the city centre. This was before some of it was destroyed by earthquakes. We bought some quality clothing—raincoats, gloves, shorts, and merino wool jumpers.

The graduation ceremony went well, and I felt very proud of Nalini's achievement. The after-dinner speaker was a highly motivated New Zealand mountaineer. The impressive thing was that he was a bilateral amputee who had climbed to the top of Mount Everest and other mountains. He described the trials and tribulations of the Everest climb. It was mind-boggling.

We were joined for dinner by a medical-school classmate of mine who lived in Perth, Western Australia. He was a radiologist and a member of the college board. He in fact became the president a few years later.

We returned to Adelaide but have since returned to New Zealand, circumnavigating the islands on a cruise ship. We revisited many of the cities we had seen before and some we hadn't seen previously. We particularly enjoyed visiting some of the wonderful boutique wineries, kiwi plantations, and historic buildings. Until then, I had not realised kiwi fruits grew on vines.

Darwin

I always thought that I would enjoy Darwin, being that it was tropical like Guyana. We had friends who moved to Darwin and kept inviting us to visit them, but we always seemed too busy. In semi-retirement, it was time to tick this off the bucket list. In fact, we visited Darwin twice: the first time to check out the city and the second time to join a cruise to some of the Aboriginal communities in Arnhem land. The cruise will be described later.

Our first trip was an eye-opener. I quickly realised that Darwinians were a breed of their own—a young population sporting gorgeous tans and with wardrobes filled with shorts and T-shirts, not forgetting the ubiquitous wife beaters. The weather encouraged outdoor living.

We visited some great restaurants and had a crème Catalan that scored a nine out of ten in a Spanish restaurant. The Aboriginal art galleries had some fantastic artworks, but they were on the expensive side. Mindil Beach sunset markets were worth visiting. I was disappointed that we just missed a concert by Jessica Mauboy, a fantastic singer. Our friends' families had fallen apart, so we saw a few of them separately for lunch and sightseeing.

Cooberpedy

Even though I had lived in Port Augusta for many years, I had not visited Cooberpedy. I had patients who travelled regularly from there to see me in Port Augusta. Debbi and I decided to visit, and I wanted to experience sleeping in a dugout.

We booked a room at the Desert Cave Hotel. After a wonderful meal in Umberto's Restaurant, we retired to our room. It was rather unnerving to be in a room with no natural light. When I turned all the lights off, it was so dark that I could not see my hand held in front of me. I could not sleep there unless I left the bathroom light on with the door ajar.

We booked some tours and found it a unique and interesting place. Some of the things we did were going down a working opal mine, visiting an underground home, and visiting the Serbian Orthodox Church. We also looked at opal shops and the underground art gallery at the Desert Cave Hotel.

The trips to the Breakaways at dawn and dusk were something special. This was part of the dried-up inland sea. The colours of the rock formations were stunning, and it was unreal to think that we were driving on what was once an ocean bed. I did not realise that the inland sea connected to the Gulf of Carpentaria, and this explained why we had so many salt lakes in the middle of Australia. The dog fence, I am told, is the longest wooden fence in the world. It was erected to keep the dingoes north, thus preventing them from attacking the sheep further south.

I have visited Cooberpedy several times since and have taken visitors, including overseas relatives, who all found it very fascinating.

Arkaroola

I had heard what an interesting place Arkaroola was, and after having had a few trips to peaks in the Flinders Ranges in our Land Rover and observed the magnificent views, we thought a trip to Arkaroola was beckoning. We took my parents-in-law with us in our Holden Avalanche and went via Wilpena Pound.

We had an overnight stay at the Blinman Hotel. There, Debbi visited the graveyard. She always had a fascination for graveyards and loved reading the inscriptions, especially on very old graves, as she tried to link people in small-town cemeteries.

The bitumen suddenly stopped, and we had to travel on unsealed roads for some distance. We eventually arrived and checked into the motel. After dinner, we visited the observatory and had a fascinating view of the stars on the Hubble telescope.

The next day, we went on a trip to one of the highest peaks on a specially modified four-wheel-drive vehicle. It was a hair-raising ride as we travelled over large rocks on a winding track along the mountainside.

We were swaying from side to side on the hard bench seats, bumping each other every few seconds, and laughing all the way. We had to hold on tightly. The vehicle seemed to be on a forty-five-degree incline at times, and all we could see ahead was the sky. The expansive view of the surrounding hilltops covered with colourful blossoms was simply stunning and worth the trip.

We walked along creek beds while on a tour of the surrounding area and even went on a scenic flight over Lake Frome. The pilot was the owner of the Arkaroola Wilderness Sanctuary.

On our way home, we had a puncture and could not find a tyre to replace the spare, because they were special nineteen-inch low-profile tyres. We had to drive to Adelaide without a spare but luckily made it without further incident. The lesson here is, "Do not go to the outback with fancy cars or fancy tyres."

The Great Ocean Road

A drive along the Great Ocean Road on Australia's southern coast was as enjoyable as it was beautiful. I have travelled along it on a few occasions, the last time being a few years ago when a few of my relatives from New York were visiting. We took them to Melbourne, and after seeing the sights there, including a cruise on the Yarra River, we went on a bus tour around the city and then onto the Great Ocean Road.

Mid-morning, my niece offered me a French pastry. When I asked where she got if from, she revealed a bag full of goodies she had pinched from the buffet breakfast counter. I knew she was careful with money and was worth several millions. That spoke volumes about her character.

We passed through several interesting townships like Torquay, Bells Beach, Lorne, and Warrnambool. We saw the Twelve Apostles and walked in the Great Otway National Park. The beaches on the way were spectacular. We stopped for coffee and cakes compliments of our witty and knowledgeable driver/tour guide. My nephew was not well, so he rested and did not do some of the walks. This was in direct contrast to his sister, who was manic and had to see everything. They both, however, thoroughly enjoyed the experience and were grateful to Debbi for organising it all.

The Sydney Olympics

In 2000, the Olympics were held in Sydney. My son Ramil was very interested in seeing the American Dream Team play basketball. We were lucky to get tickets, considering we applied late. We had tickets for the quarter-finals of basketball, athletics, and indoor volleyball. It was a real privilege to see Kathy Freeman win the 400-metre race in her spacesuit. We also saw all the top basketball teams in the world play, especially the American Dream Team.

The organisation of the Olympics was very impressive. The way the large crowds were handled, including train transport between the city and Olympic Park, was something to behold. We were lucky to have had the use of a friend's apartment in the Haymarket area, as accommodation was hard to find.

The Australian Open Tennis Grand Slam

I have always been a tennis fan and rarely missed big matches on TV between the world's top players, especially the Grand Slams. We decided to go to Melbourne for the Australian Open and bought tickets for the quarter-finals. Our hotel was within walking distance of the Australian Open tennis courts. We had a wonderful two days seeing players like Andy Murray, Stan Wawrinka, Li Na, Ashleigh Barty, Roger Federer, Rafael Nadal, and Novak Djokovic.

Melbourne Cup Day

Melbourne Cup Day is such an iconic event in Australia, and the nation stands still during the Melbourne Cup race, the longest horse race in the world. Just about everyone has a flutter on this race, even non-gamblers like me.

We decided this was an event we must attend at least once, so we organised a trip with our friends Sandra and Stuart. We stayed centrally in a hotel and trained it to Flemington racecourse. It was a glorious sunny day. We were dressed up for the occasion and enjoyed several champagnes on the grass in front of the stadium. The atmosphere was electric, and we had a great time. It would have been better if we'd won some money, but sadly, we did not.

That evening, we had a nice Chinese meal before going to the theatre to see the wonderful *Jersey Boys* live. It was a great way to finish the day.

Melbourne Cup Day—Debbi and Ram

Tahiti

Ever since childhood, after reading such books as *Mutiny on the Bounty* and *Coral Island*, I have had a romantic fascination with tropical islands, especially Fiji and Tahiti. I have visited Fiji several times and was never disappointed. The opportunity came to visit Tahiti when we decided to visit my relatives in North America, travelling with Air Tahiti Nui, which offered very attractive business class fares to New York via Papeete. We decided to have a stopover for a week and arranged a swap at a timeshare resort on the island of Moorea.

We arrived at around ten at night in Papeete and had great difficulty locating our connection to Moorea. One airport employee sent us to one end of the terminal, then another one directed us back to where we had come from. Eventually, we had to walk through a garden path to find a young lady waiting for us. She hurried us onto a plane, saying we were half an hour late.

There was only one other passenger on the flight. The pilot was a man in his late thirties wearing shorts, a flowery shirt, and a scruffy beard. I am sure he was a surfer by day!

The plane was more like a crate with wings. The sides were open— thank God for seatbelts! It flew no more than a couple of hundred feet above the sea and was very noisy. At least it had two engines. I was expecting that we would dive into the water at any minute, especially if the pilot forgot he was not on a surfboard.

The twenty-minute flight felt more like twenty hours. You can imagine the relief when we landed on a dimly lit airstrip with a great thud and a continuous clanging of metal as we taxied towards the terminal, or more correctly a tin shed. That was not the end of the drama.

It was dark, and there was hardly anyone else in sight. The other passenger was being met by his partner and child. The plane was returning to Papeete. There were no taxis in sight. We asked if the other passenger was going anyway near our resort and could give us a lift for a fee. Fortunately, it was on our fellow passenger's way, there being only one road circling the island.

We arrived at the resort, and the driver would not accept American or Australian dollars, so we had to go to reception and exchange our US dollars for Pacific Francs. We checked in and were directed to our room, which was basic but comfortable. It was after midnight, and we were hungry, but the restaurant was closed and packing up. There were two guests gaffing, having finished their meals.

We approached the staff and asked if we could have a meal. Fortunately, they offered burger and chips, which we accepted gratefully and enjoyed. We were tired and went to bed as we reflected on the day's events, realising how vulnerable we were and what chances we had taken. We could have ended up as reluctant kidney donors!

The drama hadn't quite finished. We were awakened at about four in the morning by two roosters having a competition as to who could crow the loudest. All we needed was a braying donkey and some Indian music, and we would have thought we were back in Guyana. In fact, I felt we were in Guyana when we got up in the morning, looked out at the vegetation, and felt the warm climate.

There was only one shop nearby, which opened at seven thirty in the morning and closed at ten. It then reopened at four in the afternoon until six thirty. We had to get some supplies in. The Chinese owners sold everything, including grog. They lived upstairs. The highlight of the day was their French pastry: vanilla or chocolate, freshly baked. These were so good that if you did not get there by eight a.m., they were sold out. They were the best pastries I have ever had. I was there at seven thirty every morning!

We had a wonderful quiet time relaxing and cooking our meals. One evening, we felt like going out and asked the receptionist for a recommendation. She said everyone went to the flash restaurant up the hill, which was owned by the same man who owned the timeshare resort. She recommended that we try a little restaurant a bit farther up the road, but we had to swear to secrecy, because she would lose her job if the owner found out.

The owner was one of the two men sitting in the resort's restaurant the night we arrived. This gentleman came to the island and established a vanilla plantation, which he still owned. I gather Tahiti produced a large proportion of the world's vanilla.

On arrival at the restaurant, guess who was there eating—yes, the owner and his friend. We ignored them. There were no other diners. We were recommended the seafood paella and crème brûlée for dessert by the waitress, who was also the owner and chef. We waited a long time for the food, but it was worth it. It was simply exquisite, and I had to give it 10/10. I have since measured every paella and crème brûlée against this standard.

As we waited for the food, we sipped an exquisite French wine, which we finished before the food arrived and had to order another round. We noticed some chickens and sheep in pens adjacent to the restaurant's dining room, which was an open-air affair.

Another day, we went for a long walk, ending up at a wharf where fishermen were unloading their catch. We asked in English if we could buy some fish. Fortunately, the French-speaking monsieur understood. He not only filleted the fish but packed it in a plastic bag full of ice. On our way home, I saw some pineapples for sale. They were small but had a strong aroma, indicating that they were sweet. I wanted one, as we were leaving the next day, but the vendor had them in bundles of four and would not separate them. He would have charged me for four even if I only took one! I took all four, and just as well. They were so sweet that we ate them all in one sitting.

We left to spend a couple of days in Papeete before proceeding to New York. There, we visited an open-air market and realised the likeness of Papeete to Georgetown in Guyana. We had lunch in an upmarket hotel, then swam in their pool and used their pool towels. That was rather nice and refreshing, as it was a warm and humid day.

Paris

I have been to Paris several times and have always enjoyed my visits. In fact, it was Debbi's most favourite city. Several times, we visited the usual tourist sights, such as the Eiffel Tower, the Arc de Triomphe, the Louvre, the Champs-Élysées, Notre Dame, the Palace of Versailles, Montmartre, Moulin Rouge, and Place de la Concorde (previously Place de la Revolution, where Louis XVI and Marie Antoinette were executed).

One time we stayed in an upmarket, rather sophisticated, and of course expensive hotel in the Opera area. Another time, we stayed in a cute and interesting boutique hotel in Montmartre. I will not describe the virtues of each place we visited but will relate some interesting or hilarious experiences we had.

One day, we decided to have lunch in a restaurant that looked interesting. We looked at the menu, and not thinking clearly and feeling like a steak, were influenced by the photograph of a dish that took our fancy. It was *cheveaux*, and it was still bleeding when it arrived! I noticed how lean it was. We called the waitress and said we liked our steak medium to well done. She corrected us by saying it was *cheveaux* and took our plates away. When she returned, they were no different. It suddenly occurred to us that we had ordered horse instead of steak. We quietly paid the bill and left, much to the waitress's surprise.

We ordered morning tea in a café. There was a plateful of French pastry on the table. We thought it was complimentary and proceeded to eat several—and were surprised when we were charged for them.

I got a severe telling-off by Debbi for leaving her as I wandered around the viewing platform of the Eiffel Tower, taking in and photographing the views in every direction. An older Indian tourist must have taken a fancy to her and was following her around, standing so close to her that it made her uneasy. He may have thought she was on her own. Of course, she handled him with her usual firmness by saying, "If you treasure your private parts, keep your f— distance from me." He did, as he was shocked that a lady could speak to him like that.

For years, Debbi had said that when she got to Paris, she would buy a handbag from the Louis Vuitton store on the Champs-Élysées. That day had arrived. We were surprised to find a long line of shoppers trying to get into the store. They only allowed six people at a time, after six people exited the store.

After what seemed like a lifetime, and me complaining that this was ridiculous, as we were doing them a favour and not the other way around, we entered the store. All the way around, we were accompanied by this pest of a salesman who kept asking if he could be of help. I think he did not trust us and thought we might steal one of their precious bags.

Debbi was interested in a particular design, as she had bought one before in Singapore and loved it so much that it was worn out. Our local shoe repair person refused to patch it up anymore. They had changed up the design and she was disgusted, so we left, much to her disappointment. Nothing else was acceptable.

To appease her, I took her to a lovely restaurant near our hotel. The head waiter did not seem to like us—maybe because I was coloured or we spoke English. After the entrée, he asked us how it was, and I replied, "Trés bien, monsieur, merci!"

He gave us a big smile, and from then on, he was more friendly. He was even more gushy after I gave the pianist a few euros and waved my American Express gold card at him, having added a tip to the bill. He even opened the door for us and said, "Please come again." What a prick!

We went on an adventure taking the train and getting off at Bastille, where we had a rather nice lunch, before we found a shop that was selling some rather nice French design clothing at reasonable prices. There I bought a jacket and some shirts, which I still love wearing to this day. After leaving the shop, I could hear Bob Marley's reggae music, so we followed the sound and came across a one-man band. He was dressed like Bob Marley, complete with dreadlocks and colourful clothing. I stood by him and danced to the music. I chatted with him afterwards and found out that he was from Senegal. I gave him a tip, for which he thanked me.

My brother, who lived in Orlando, Florida, never liked long flights, so I had not been able to get him to visit Australia or even to meet us in Hawaii. My sister-in-law was always keen. During one of our visits to Orlando, we asked him if he could go anywhere in the world, where would he go. He said to the mother country. I thought he meant India, but he meant England. We put him on the mat, saying, "If we organise it, would you all meet us in London?" To this he agreed. We organised it and met them in London the following year. I have described this trip to the UK elsewhere, so I will only describe our experiences in Paris.

He wanted to see Paris and Amsterdam, but we only had enough time for Paris. He had studied English history and wanted to see some of the places he read about. We took the Euro Rail from St. Pancras in London to Gare du Nord in Paris. It was an interesting trip, and mind-boggling to think we were travelling under the English Channel. It was certainly more efficient than flying, as it went from city centre to city centre. In Paris, the airport is a long way from the city, as we had found out on a previous trip.

Debbi had done her research and got us Metro cards to use on the Metro de Paris, so we took the train from Gare du Nord to Montmartre, where our hotel was. It was exciting making the right connections to get there. Our stop was within walking distance of our hotel, which was fantastic. Le Chat Noir was a cute boutique hotel that was once a brothel servicing the Moulin Rouge area. We checked in and then went for a walk.

We had booked a city tour for two in the afternoon and were to be picked up from our hotel. We waited and waited, and eventually our tour van arrived. The tour guide was not impressed with us, as he had come for us before and could not find us. Of course, we had forgotten to adjust our watches to Paris time, which was later than London. The other tourists in our party were not amused.

We did the tour, which included a cruise on the Seine and a tour of the Eiffel Tower. We were to meet our bus at the end at a certain spot. We arrived there and, again, waited and waited. In the end, we got fed up and took a taxi back to the hotel. We had still not adjusted our watches to

Paris time. You would not believe we were intelligent university graduates. What a joke!

The taxi trip was interesting in that we had to go around the Arc de Triomphe, where no less than twelve avenues converge. No one gave way, and it was chaotic. Everyone seized an opportunity as they weaved a path around this roundabout. We felt our fate was entirely in the hands of the taxi driver. No wonder no insurance company provided cover for driving in this area.

That evening, we had tickets for a dinner show at the Moulin Rouge. We had dinner, and then the scantily clad dancing girls appeared. They were topless. This was too much for Jean, my sister-in-law, who kept her eyes fixed on the floor and missed the entire show. She was embarrassed. By contrast, my brother kept his eyes fixed on the stage and enjoyed the entire performance.

We went on a walking tour the next day around Montmartre and rode the funicular. The walk then took us up a hill, and Jean and I were struggling. So when we came across a cute little hotel on the way, we decided to stop and have a drink. We waited for the party to return. That was a more civilized way to go. Jean later managed to buy some souvenirs for her family back home.

Barcelona

Barcelona is a very impressive and interesting city with a rich history. It is one of our favourite cities in the world, and we were fortunate to have visited it four times, the last time being with our friends Peter and Mary. The first time was on our way to Amsterdam to join a scenic river cruise from Amsterdam to Budapest. We arrived at the airport from London and boarded a taxi to take us to our hotel, which was on the famous La Rambla strip. The taxi driver spoke no English, so we had to point to the address of the hotel on our booking sheet.

En route along a busy road, we could see another taxi cutting in front of our taxi, which took no evasive action and collided with it. The two drivers got out and started shouting at each other in a heated fashion in Spanish. Neither was impressed and blamed each other. This went on for about fifteen minutes before we could proceed.

There was a music festival around our hotel, so we could not be dropped off at the door but had to get off two streets away and walk the rest of the way, laden with our luggage. The hotel was a boutique hotel. Our room was small but comfortable and had a tiny en suite. The lift was so small that we had to go up one at a time with our luggage.

After getting settled in our room, we went to check out the surrounding area and found Placa Catalunya, where we listened to some wonderful music by one of Spain's famous and well-known singers. We then walked along the famous La Rambla, enjoying seeing the street performers and human statues. The human statues were so good that I was staring at one trying to decide whether he was alive when he winked at me.

I was engrossed looking at a street performer and nearly jumped out of my skin at the sound of a loud whistle just behind me. Unknown to me, another performer had crept up behind me to scare me. He then said, "Be careful. I could have robbed you." I quickly checked my pockets, as pickpockets were active in the area and generally worked in groups.

It was then time for some tapas and sangria. We found a restaurant along La Rambla and soaked up the view and the atmosphere.

After a sumptuous cooked breakfast in the hotel the next morning, we went to meet our tour guide in one of the many plazas. After a while, this rather good-looking young lady arrived by bicycle and introduced herself as our guide. She had no other clients, so we had personalised service as we wandered the streets around the Bario Gottico, the ancient Roman quarter. We tasted tapas, virgin olive oil, cheeses, and freshly roasted nuts, and checked out various buildings, including her school. She pointed out the famous plazas, and at Plaça Reial, we watched some dancers.

The next day, it was time to check out the rest of the city, and for this we got some hop-on-hop-off bus tickets, as this was the best way to get around. We were fascinated by the various buildings demonstrating the famous Gaudi architecture, including the Sagrada Familia, which was still under construction. We visited Parc Gruel, the home of Gaudi, with its extensive landscaped gardens.

One day, we took a bus tour to Montserrat, home of the Black Madonna or Virgin Mary. It was a very impressive place. The Black Madonna was disappointingly smaller than I expected—a bit like the *Mona Lisa* in the Louvre in Paris.

We tried black paella made with squid ink but were not impressed with it. We enjoyed the variety of tapas, especially one mid-morning when we sat in one of the famous squares and decided to have sangria and tapas while we watched a free performance by some singers and dancers. Debbi found the famous Desigual brand of clothes and bought a few pieces, some as gifts for the family.

Once, Debbi booked us into a hotel called El Castel, which was away from the city centre. It was once a castle and had beautiful outdoor areas where we sat sipping wine and soaking up the atmosphere. It had an underground nightclub. We found jacaranda trees with their purple flowers and were surprised to learn that they were in fact not native to Australia or Spain, but to South America. The buffet breakfast at this hotel was fantastic and offered the best ham I have ever tasted.

The last time we visited Barcelona was with Peter and Mary at the end of a Mediterranean cruise. We acted as tour guides and had a wonderful time. Mary still recalls being served sangria in what looked like a fishbowl. It contained one litre of sangria, and we had to help her finish it.

The Rockies in Canada

Peter, Mary, Debbi, and I decided to do an Alaskan cruise and combine it with a visit to the Rockies. Debbi, my son Ramil, and I first visited the relatives in America and Canada via Hawaii, and after seeing Ramil off in San Francisco on his way back to Australia, we flew via Seattle to Victoria. There, Peter and Mary were waiting for us to arrive at the hotel.

Our tour guide, Max, who was gay, met us and explained the tour through the Rockies. We visited Butchart Gardens and did a tour of Victoria Island in a horse-drawn carriage, while Mary and Peter did a scenic seaplane flight. We boarded the coach and went by ferry to Vancouver on the mainland.

We then commenced our two-week tour of the Rockies, visiting Whistler, Lake Louise, Columbia Icefield, Banff, Jasper, and Kamloops. The highlights were the blue Lake Louise, the Icefields Parkway (where we walked on the Athabasca glaciers after being transported there by specially modified four-wheel-drive vehicles), black and brown bears along the roadside, the quaint town of Jasper, and of course, the train ride through the mountains from Jasper to Vancouver.

In Jasper, we found a pub where a band was playing. We had some drinks and then left, leaving Debbi's handbag on the seat. We were lucky to find it still there and intact ten minutes later.

In one town, we visited a laundromat where "Mrs. Fluff and Fold," as she was called, did a bag wash for a few dollars. All the hotels we stayed at were top class, and the meals were wonderful. The coach driver handled all our luggage from the coach to our hotel rooms and back.

The Rocky Mountaineer trip was iconic and one of those must-do life experiences. Gold-leaf tickets were a must, as you could see the tops of snow-clad mountains through the glass roof, unlike the red-leaf seats. It was rather decadent to have champagne and hors d'oeuvres before dinner. The wines with the sumptuous meals were of good quality. We were even treated to afternoon tea with scones, jam, and cream.

In Vancouver, we saw the city highlights, including the site chosen for the forthcoming Winter Olympics. We were, however, horrified by the number of drug addicts begging in the streets.

The UK and Ireland

We were happy when my brother and sister-in-law agreed to join us for an Insight coach tour around the UK and Ireland. We met them at Heathrow and took the underground to Kensington, where we had booked hotel accommodation at the Holiday Inn. The only difficulty was managing the huge suitcases they brought, as we had to go up and down some stairs at the tube stations.

Debbi's sister Vikki and her husband, Bob, booked into the same hotel for a few nights so they could spend some time with us. My niece Devika and her husband, Raj, travelled into London to join us for dinner. The next day, we went on the hop-on-hop-off bus in the pouring rain to see the sights of London—Big Ben (Houses of Parliament), Buckingham Palace, Trafalgar Square, 10 Downing Street, St. James's Park, Pall Mall, Westminster Bridge, Tower Bridge, Tower of London, Southbank, Oxford Circus, Piccadilly Circus, Westminster Abbey, St. Paul's Cathedral, Harrods, and the Bank of England. We also went on a cruise along the Thames River and did a tour of Buckingham Palace. My brother loved it all, as it was his wish to visit those places.

We boarded our coach and set off north, visiting Stratford-upon-Avon to see Shakespeare's residence and Ann Hathaway's cottage. We then proceeded to the walled city of York and visited York Minster before travelling to Durham and Newcastle upon Tyne, where I had attended university many years prior. Our journey took us via Ashington to Edinburgh in Scotland.

We had tickets to attend the military tattoo in Edinburgh Castle. It poured with rain, and we were given plastic ponchos to wear. The rain did not spoil the enjoyment of this iconic show. However, we were late in returning to our coach, which left without us. We were lucky to catch up with it along the road, as the traffic was at a standstill.

We proceeded to St. Andrew's and saw the famous golf course. St. Andrew's is regarded as the birthplace of golf. We then made our way through the Scottish countryside, staying at some interesting country hotels. Our tour guide was a very funny lady who kept us laughing most of the way, making the long days on the coach tolerable. We travelled through to Carlisle in the picturesque Lake District before heading south to Liverpool.

In Liverpool, we visited Abbey Road and the studio where the Beatles started their career, plus other interesting sights. After that, we proceeded to Blackpool, visiting the famous pier before crossing the Mersey and going to northern Wales to board the ship across to Ireland. It was a rough crossing, but we survived.

Life in Ireland seemed a lot slower than England, and I was surprised to find a certain sadness in the vibe of the whole place. We enjoyed the visit and saw places like Dublin, Limerick, Tipperary, Killarney, and Waterford, famous for its Waterford crystal. We tasted Guinness and visited a whiskey distillery, a horse stud, and Blarney Castle, but we did not manage to kiss the Blarney Stone. In Dublin, Debbi visited the National Archives, where a very helpful lady guided her to find a lot of information about her ancestry, her father being from Killarney.

We returned by ferry and felt very seasick on the way. Our next stop was in Cardiff in Wales. The huge colliery spoil tips were impressive. It made me remember the disaster in 1966, when the village of Aberfan near Merthyr Tydfil was buried by ash. The city had several interesting sights. I was interested to see Cardiff University, as I had applied to go there to do medicine. Eerie Stonehenge was our next stop, followed by Winchester and its famous cathedral.

The tour ended in London. We visited a cousin who had been particularly close to Jack back in Guyana. We stayed overnight with them and enjoyed their hospitality before Jack and Jean returned home to Orlando. We spent a few days with Vikki and Bob before leaving for Adelaide.

Cruises

South Pacific Cruise on the Pacific Princess—The Love Boat

This was our first-ever cruise, and we were with Mary and Peter. We were very excited to be going on a cruise. The ship was the lovely *Pacific Princess*, which was used to film the television series *The Love Boat*. We were expecting to see Captain Stubing around the ship. The décor resembled a French château.

After boarding, we thought it would be nice to watch the boat leave the dock in the beautiful Sydney Harbour. Champagne in hand, we went to the top deck and danced to the sail-away music in one of the lounges at the front of the ship. It was fabulous to see the Sydney Harbour Bridge and the Opera House disappear in the distance.

As we went through the Sydney Heads, we became quieter and quieter, as we all started to feel sick and did not want to own up to it. Peter was the only one who was okay. Mary, Debbi, and I returned to our cabins to lie down.

I felt bad about Peter dining by himself, so I decided to join him. I only ordered some soup and, according to Peter, looked greener by the minute. I had to make a hasty retreat to my cabin. We dosed ourselves with anti-sickness medications and felt good after that.

We visited Poum and Noumea before setting sail for the Isle of Pines. In Poum, we were welcomed by local musicians. I started to dance to the music, and Peter joined me. The natives thought that was fabulous and taught us some of their moves. Noumea was our next stop, and there we did some sightseeing.

The ship travelled overnight and docked the next morning. I looked out of the window and thought this was familiar. Hadn't we been here yesterday? Yes, we were back in Noumea, because wild weather prevented us from going to the Isle of Pines. We were not told this until the morning so as not to disturb us. We went ashore again and this time did some shopping, as we had seen the sights the day before.

We thoroughly enjoyed the cruise, appreciating good food and wines and seeing some wonderful shows. We also did a lot of dancing every night. I brought back six souvenir cocktail glasses, which I still have.

On our journey back, we passed Lord Howe Island. Debbi said that she would like to visit there one day, and later, we did.

Mediterranean Cruise on Royal Caribbean's Mariner of the Seas

Through our timeshare membership and with Vikki's help, we managed to get a very good deal on a fourteen-day cruise of the Mediterranean, starting and finishing in Barcelona. Our first stop was Nice. I was not impressed by the pebble beach with only one small area of sand that seemed like it was transported there from elsewhere. I guess I was spoilt, being accustomed to beaches in Australia, which are sandy and quite expansive.

Paying to have a pee was the pits, especially when you didn't have small change and the lady attendant would not let you in unless you paid beforehand. You had to declare whether you needed a number one or number two. Of course, you only got given toilet paper for an additional fee if it was number two! The local market, however, was good.

From there, we went by coach to Monaco. I was impressed by the cleanliness of the city state. It was good to see the Monte Carlo Formula One street circuit and the Grand Casino. Everything was rather expensive. It was there that I first saw an Audi Q7 and thought what a beast of a car it was. I just had to take a photo of it.

We then proceeded to the Port of Livorno, from which we did a tour to Florence. There we saw some impressive buildings and churches. The leather goods were exquisite. We saw the Leaning Tower of Pisa and thought it was smaller than we expected.

After that, we went to the port of Civitavecchia and had a full day touring the city of Rome. What an impressive city that is. The highlights were the Trevi Fountain, the Forum, the Amphitheatre, the Vatican, and the Sistine Chapel. Walking all day on cobblestones was not good for the feet. Finding toilets was a challenge, and we had to visit gelaterias so we could use their toilets. We did not mind, as we found the best gelato, called dolce de leche.

Napoli was next. It was an interesting city, and as we went around, we thought of it being Mafia territory and felt a bit uneasy, for no reason at all. We knew Italians were good builders but were mortified at the bare electrical wires tied in huge bundles hanging from one building to the next.

The visit to Pompeii was an eye-opener. To see the level of sophistication that city had reached two centuries ago was truly mind-boggling. The drainage and sewerage systems, the steam baths, the amphitheatre, and the stores were well developed. The building that surprised me was the brothel, which had several rooms. Above each doorway was a picture illustrating the specialty of the girl who offered her services there!

Next, we were in Palermo in Sicily, another Mafia stronghold. It was interesting to see Mount Pellegrino, where the famous sparkling bottled water originated. We had a lovely lunch in a classy hotel by the sea. We then sailed back to Barcelona, enjoying all that the ship had to offer, before flying to Paris and then returning home from London.

Alaskan Cruise on the Carnival Spirit

We followed up our Rockies trip with a fire-and-ice cruise on the Carnival *Spirit*, taking us from Vancouver to the inside passage of Alaska and then returning to Vancouver. It then continued to the Hawaiian Islands. We were travelling with Peter and Mary.

When we boarded the ship, Mary had a meltdown and couldn't cope with the décor. It looked like an Egyptian palace, with a lot of bling and gold statues of pharaohs. She was nearly in tears. To add insult, we all noticed that the bedside lampstands in the rooms seemed like phallic symbols. I think she was about to refuse to go on the cruise; she only settled down when Debbi took her down to the ship's atrium bar and gave her a glass of champagne. After that, she settled, and we had a wonderful cruise.

The cruise went to Ketchikan, Juneau, and Skagway before entering Glacier Bay National Park. We found the local Alaskans to be a breed of their own, or as Debbi described them, "hicks from the sticks." Their accents were a drawn-out drawl. They stared at us as if we were from another planet. The towns were truly outposts from a bygone era. One even had an old-fashioned brothel.

I was suffering badly from my first attack of gout in one of my big toes and walked slowly with a limp. Every step was painful. This was very amusing to the rest of my party. They decided that I needed a wheelchair and procured one from the ship to take me ashore. I would not let Peter push me, as he was too eager and heaven knows where I would end up. Debbi did the honours.

I bought a walking stick in a local store. It was made of beautifully carved wood and had an eagle's head to hold on to. Unfortunately, I gave it away to the cabin steward at the end of our cruise, as it was too difficult to bring home.

We went up further north by small float plane. The land was covered in snow and was very desolate. It was like nowhere else on earth we had visited. There was an oil rig and the odd truck in an otherwise barren landscape. Unfortunately, Mary did not enjoy this flight, as she had travel sickness due to the bouncy ride.

Another tour took us on a huskies' ride, and we learnt a lot about these amazing animals. Disappointingly, it was not on a sledge but on a cart on wheels.

On the ship, Peter and I were in the spa one day when we were joined by this rather large overpowering American lady. She was one of a group of Bible bashers (or as Debbi named them, "the hallelujah sisters") who were on the cruise and went to great lengths every night to dress up for cocktails and dinner and hundreds of photographs.

That day in the spa, the lady asked Peter, "Have you found God yet?" with a serious face.

Peter, beaming from ear to ear, replied, "No, I didn't realise he was missing, but I promise to look for him. He may be in the cabin next door to mine."

She gave him such a piercing look that Peter appeared positively frightened. That was worth seeing, as there were not too many people who could do that to him. He was so uncomfortable that we had to make a hasty retreat to the change room.

Another interesting group on board was some folks from Calgary. They drank a lot of beers and danced the night away. We were very confused, as they seemed to partner with a different person each night. *Swingers!* we thought.

All these groups left the ship in Vancouver, but we continued via Seattle to the Hawaiian Islands.

Hawaiian Cruise on Carnival Spirit

Having completed the ice part of the cruise, we were on our way to the fire part. We had five days at sea before arriving in Hawaii. We were drinking Nobilo Sauvignon Blanc from New Zealand every night with our meals. Our drinks waiter told us that they only had six more bottles on board, as they did not get their delivery in Seattle, and there were others on board drinking it. We bought all six, much to the disgust of the others.

In Hawaii, we cruised around the islands of Maui, Kauai, and the big island of Hawaii before finishing up in Oahu. In Maui, we spent time at my favourite beach, Kaanapali, to which we travelled by local bus. In Kauai, a taxi took us to a lovely beach and returned for us later. Peter and I enjoyed the waves while Debbi and Mary sat under the palm trees on the beach. The waves were throwing us around. We were having a wonderful time. The hems of our bathers filled with sand, and we could not understand how this was possible. We were exhausted and could hardly walk after such frolicking in the waves, much to Mary's amusement.

We were in a shop later, and I was enjoying the music so much that I asked the shop attendant who was singing. She said it was a group called Ekolou, a popular Hawaiian band. I asked where I could buy their CD and was directed to a music store. The taxi driver took me there on the way back to port. It was my hobby to collect music from different places I visited.

The next stop was the Big Island, which was like a moonscape. I knew a beach where, on a previous visit, we did some bodyboarding and Ramil and Ahsha had their first surfing lessons. We took a taxi and found the beach. The waves were powerful, and again, Peter and I were in it having a whale of a time.

Suddenly, Peter was quiet. He lifted his hand up to show me his little finger, which was crocked. He had a dislocation. Quick as a flash, I told him to take a big breath, and I reduced it, much to his surprise and relief.

We called it a day and walked up to a hotel on top of the hill. We ordered a mai tai cocktail each, and they were so good that we ended up having four each. Peter did not feel any pain after that.

The cruise ended in Oahu, and Peter and Mary booked into the upmarket Halekulani Hotel while we stayed at a timeshare resort nearby. We had a whole two-bedroom apartment. We visited the international market, eating and drinking more mai tais and buying souvenirs.

One evening, we decided to try some authentic Hawaiian cuisine and asked the taxi driver to take us to a local restaurant. It was a very popular place in one of the local suburbs. The food was interesting. Mary was not impressed and refused to taste anything. She sat with a face like thunder throughout the meal, which I must admit we did not enjoy.

Another evening, we went to the Hawaiian Cultural Centre and enjoyed the fantastic evening performance. It was a celebration of Hawaiian culture. We flew home after that.

European River Cruise—Amsterdam to Budapest on a Scenic ship

I would rate the river cruise from Amsterdam to Budapest as the best cruise we have ever done. We did it with Mary and Peter. Debbi and I flew to London and then on to Barcelona before flying to Amsterdam via Madrid.

In Amsterdam, we were unexpectedly met by a chauffeur in a luxury limousine who took us to our ship. Peter and Mary arrived a few hours later. The price was all inclusive and covered our accommodation, wines with meals, all meals, and all tours. The staff were mainly Bulgarians, including the captain. They were very friendly, welcoming, and efficient.

Our cabin was well-appointed and comfortable. The shower was a bit small, in one corner of the bathroom, and had a curved door. One had to reverse out of it. I couldn't help wondering how a big person managed. The toiletries, however, were of high quality.

The first night, we remained docked, giving us the opportunity to explore Amsterdam after dark. The four of us set out to find the red-light district, which was only a short walk away. On our way, we came across a huge multistorey bicycle park the likes of which we had never seen before. I wondered how one found one's bike amongst the thousands parked there.

The red-light district was an eye opener. It was interesting to see beautiful girls on display in the windows. But don't be fooled, as the ones displayed were not the ones available to clients. This was the experience of my godson during his trip. He was not impressed when presented with a fat ugly chick instead of the gorgeous one on display in the window. That's advertising for you!

The coffee shops were interesting places, as you could buy pot there with no questions asked, and that was their main trade. We were not made to feel welcome looking just for coffee. The following day, we had a tour visiting a cheese factory, a clogs factory, and a village with windmills.

Our tour took us to various interesting cities along the Rhine, Main, and Danube Rivers. We travelled mainly at night, toured during the day, and went through several locks on the way. Our entertaining tour guide was a Dutch lady. She was very knowledgeable and multitalented. She told jokes, gave us a history lesson on the various castles we saw, and sang to us at night. Every evening after dinner, we had outside entertainers—local Bavarian bands, comedians, glass blowers, etc. We also had the opportunity to dance once we had enough alcohol on board.

One evening, the captain addressed the group. His English was limited and delivered with a broad Bulgarian accent. Mary and I had great difficulty restraining ourselves when he kept saying, "If you need anything at all, just ask my screw." He meant *crew*. Everyone else was silent and listening intently as he gave the safety instructions. I had to avoid eye contact with Mary, or else we would have embarrassed ourselves by bursting out in laughter.

Another evening, we dobbed Debbi into singing "Waltzing Matilda" with the band. She did a wonderful job but was not impressed the next day when an American couple, who drank several bottles of whiskey in their suite every night, said to us that it would have been good if the girl who sang "Waltzing Matilda" the night before knew the words! They did not realise it was Debbi. She was ropeable!

We visited Cologne, Rudesheim, Wurzburg, Bamberg, Nuremberg, Regensberg, Passau, Melk, and Vienna before arriving in Budapest. The scenery along the rivers was just stunning. The rivers were the main route for moving cargo and were very busy. I was impressed by the dexterity of the captains manoeuvring their various crafts on the waterways.

For the tours we had coaches going to various places, and we had to choose our preferred tour the evening before. We were provided with headsets so we could hear the commentary by the tour guides, many of whom were locals. Some tours included lunch.

We visited a brewery and were each given a glass of the local brew. Debbi and Mary were not keen on drinking beers, so Peter and I had to reluctantly help them. One evening, we attended an opera, which was a lovely experience.

Nuremberg, the site of Hitler's military parades, was a place with a rather depressing vibe. The buildings where the various trials for war crimes were conducted were pointed out to us. They'd just had a music concert on the parade grounds, and the whole place was covered with rubbish. It was in direct contrast to what we were used to in Adelaide during the Fringe and Womadelaide festivals.

In Melk Abbey, one of our group fell and hurt her back. She was distressed and could not walk. I thought she might have slipped a disc. The two heroes sprung into action. Peter got a wheelchair from the coach, and we put her in it. She was a big girl, and Peter had to push her up a steep hill to get her back on the coach. I was worried he would slip backwards and lose control, so I was pushing Peter from the back, much to Mary's amusement.

On board, we assisted the woman to bed, having given her two Panadeine Forte from my first-aid bag. We felt conned when three hours later, she was strutting her stuff on the dance floor with no apparent discomfort.

Vienna is a beautiful city. The central square where there was a statue of Mozart was inspiring. It had a beautiful vibe. The World Cup was on and being televised on a big screen in the square. There were food booths, and in one there was a mouth-watering pig spit roast. Peter and I just had to try some with sauerkraut on bread. The vegetarian Mary was disgusted. To add to her amusement Peter then ordered not one but two disgustingly rich creamy desserts for himself in a nearby coffee shop.

The Bratwurst Boys—Ram and Peter (left to right)

A visit to Schonbrunn Palace, home of the famous Habsburg family, showed the opulence and decadence of the royal existence at the time. It was interesting to learn that Queen Margaret of Austria had ten children and tried to dominate and control other European countries, especially France and Spain, through their marriages and her own marriage. Marie Antoinette was one of her daughters.

It was unreal to find ourselves in Salzburg city and to walk around the gardens where *The Sound of Music* was filmed. We even sang "I Am Sixteen Going on Seventeen" in the famous gazebo used in the film.

It was spring, and Debbi was suffering severely from hayfever caused by the white blossoms on the river. She had to take antihistamines.

Budapest, the capital of Hungary, is made up of two districts connected by the nineteenth-century Chain Bridge. Buda is the poorer hilly area, and Pest is the flat richer area. Buda's old town going back to Roman times was interesting. The prominent parliament building on the riverside is featured on many travel brochures.

After leaving the ship, we went by coach to Prague as an extension of our holiday. What an interesting city that is. On our way, we stopped at a roadhouse and were shocked to find a turnstile at the entrance to the toilets. You had to pay using tokens or local coins. This was the same roadhouse where my friend Janet tried to go through the turnstile with another person, as she did not have a coin. To her shock, she was immediately grabbed by a large scary woman pointing a finger at her saying, "You pay!"

In Prague, we walked over the Charles Bridge, visited St. Vitus Cathedral and Prague castle, and checked out some markets. In the cathedral grounds, Peter spotted a pickpocket and made him so uncomfortable by keeping a close eye on him that he left the area. King Wenceslas Square in the centre of town leading up to the parliament house was a lovely area, but we were surprised by the presence of many African gangs at street corners. Debbi bought a few paintings and colourful candleholders. In one building, it gave us a laugh to see a huge horse mounted upside down and a man riding on its tummy.

After Prague, Debbi and I went to Paris, and Peter and Mary went to Rome before returning home to Adelaide.

New Zealand Cruise on Royal Caribbean's Voyager of the Seas

We had already been on holidays around New Zealand but agreed to go on a cruise with my sisters Betty and Seeta and their families. Debbi and I met Betty and Singh in Sydney and showed them the sights for two days before the cruise. It was nice to spend time with them on board and to see some sights that we may not have seen before.

Seeta was not into gambling and frowned upon anyone who was. Consequently, Betty and Singh would sneak out to the casino after she went to bed. Betty and Seeta did not care for formal dinners and preferred the variety in the "gobble and go" smorgasbord, so we often ate without them, as we quite liked the waiter service. The cruise went around the South and North islands before returning to Sydney.

Caribbean Cruise with Carnival

In 2013, we went to visit my relatives in North America, and my brother and sister-in-law decided to join us on a cruise of the Caribbean. We flew to San Juan in Puerto Rico to board the ship. The itinerary took us to St. Thomas, St. Marten, St. Lucia, Barbados, and St. Kitts.

I was surprised to find that many of the traders in the ports were Indians from India, and they all seemed to sell the same things. It was disappointing, as the souvenirs were not locally made but imported from overseas. In a square in St. Maarten, a reggae band dressed in brightly coloured clothing and sporting dreadlocks was playing in the street. Jack and I started to dance and amused the crowd. In St. Lucia, we hired a taxi to go to the top of an extinct volcano, but the road was so windy that Jean felt sick. We decided to turn back.

Jack and Ram dancing in the street

In Barbados, we were met by Mary Rose, Moira's sister, who drove us around in her little car. We visited some caves and a pottery shop before having lunch at her house. It was a West Indian dish. Her partner was rather shy and said very few words until he found out that we liked rum. He became much more sociable after we had a few shots. Debbi got him to show her his vegetable garden and instructed him on the use of sheep dip to get rid of lice from his fowls.

The weather was perfect, and the beaches were great. The people were friendly, wearing huge smiles. We enjoyed the facilities on board the ship. After returning to San Juan, we flew to New York, and Jack and Jean returned to Orlando.

Art of Arnhem Land Cruise on the Orion

Cruises on the Orion in Northern Australia were always very expensive, normally about six thousand dollars each for fourteen days. An opportunity came for us to attend a medical conference on board on the *Orion*, and the fare was only half the above. We booked and flew to Darwin. We had dinner with some friends who lived between Adelaide and Darwin and joined the cruise the next morning. Our medical group was only six plus our partners. We only had to spend three hours per day for four days doing case presentations followed by discussions.

Our cabin was fantastic and easily the best cabin I have had of any of the cruises we have done. The ship was a great little ship and carried about one hundred passengers. I was worried that it might bounce around on the high seas, but it did not, as it had fantastic stabilizers. We had guest lecturers on board who were well versed in the Aboriginal culture and local flora and fauna. They conducted free lectures on board for those who were interested.

We also had Terry, an Aboriginal elder, on board with his Italian wife, Clely, who was initially a tourist and fell in love with the place. They gave us an insight into life in those communities. They even taught us a few words in their language and to dance Aboriginal style. We were even shown how to play the didgeridoo. They also took us to visit their family home, which was a cave, and gave us a blessing. I got on well with Terry, who tried to encourage me to work in the community as a doctor.

The cruise first went to the Tiwi Islands (Bathurst and Melville), and we checked out the local communities. The other places we visited were Maningrida, Yirrkala, Nhulunbuy, and Thursday Island. We saw the locals doing their paintings, making didgeridoos, and dying and putting patterns on materials. We even saw schoolkids making paintings using rocks. The ship had to travel into international waters due to some regulations, so we went towards Borneo but never docked anywhere.

We had to use Zodiacs to get ashore, which was exciting, as we felt we were in a James Bond movie. We knew there were crocodiles around but did not see any. However, there were a few "logodiles" (logs of wood in the water that resembled crocodiles).

Debbi wished she could join in the activities with the locals. We bought a painting from a local painter who was so pleased that he danced around showing off his money to his friends. In one gallery, Debbi spotted an exquisite painting with a price tag of two thousand dollars. It was very intricate, and she remarked it was the best painting in the gallery. We thought of buying it but decided to look around first. Some Americans heard Debbi's remarks, and by the time we came back to the painting, they had bought it!

After Thursday Island, we travelled by boat to Horne Island to catch a flight to Cairns, from which we flew home.

Singapore–Vietnam–Hong Kong on Holland America's Volendam

We had been interested in going to Vietnam for some time. The opportunity came in February 2014 when we found a cruise going from Singapore to Hong Kong via Malaysia, Thailand, Cambodia, and Vietnam. We flew to Singapore, where we spent a couple of days at the Furama Waterfront Hotel. From there, we enjoyed Clarke Quay at night and cruised along the Singapore River on a Bumboat. The views of the Marina Sands Hotel from the water was fantastic, as was the Merlion Fountain and the restaurants along the riverbanks. After a hearty breakfast the next day, we boarded our ship.

In Penang, we visited the markets and some historic colonial buildings. In Ko Samui, we travelled on a rice barge to a market and were bothered by some rather large mosquitoes. A coach tour took us to a place where we saw the locals working with coconuts and were treated to trained monkeys climbing the trees and picking coconuts. We did not do the tour to Bangkok, as it would have been too tiring for Debbi. Instead we explored the port area.

Similarly, we only saw the local market in Sihanoukville in Cambodia and did not do any of the tours on offer. We were struck by the poverty of the place. The marketplace was very crowded, and we had to be careful of pickpockets. There were some small monkey bananas that took our fancy. We bought a hand of some thirty bananas and wondered what we were going to do with them, as we could not take them on board. As it turned out, we had no trouble eating the lot.

We had several stops around Vietnam at Phu My, Nha Trang, Hoi An, Danang, and Halong Bay. We did not do the tours to Ho Chi Minh City or Hanoi, as they would have been too tiring for Debbi, who was having a break from chemotherapy. We were surprised by the progressive vibe of the country and the many mopeds on the streets. People did not wear helmets and were fetching furniture, large baskets, and boxes full of provisions, and sometimes had a whole family on one little moped. The skilful manoeuvring of the mopeds and the respect shown to other road users allowed for the orderly flow of traffic. We learnt that when crossing the street, just keep walking and do not turn back, as the riders would drive around and avoid you.

There were some beautiful sandy beaches in places like Nha Trang and Hoi An. Many good-quality hotels lined the streets. The buildings were evidence of a colonial past. We did not tackle the tunnels, such as the Cu Chi tunnels, as it would have been too strenuous. Shopping for clothes and silk and embroidered products was good, and we bought several pieces. At the embroidery factory, it was particularly impressive to see girls doing such intricate and delicate work with a great deal of skill and patience.

At Halong Bay, we boarded a small vessel and travelled amongst the large rocky outcrops. It was a very peaceful experience. We were approached by people in boats selling fruits and vegetables—a sort of floating market. There were many larger vessels doing overnight and three-day cruises on the bay.

Throughout the cruise, we enjoyed the facilities on board and of course ate a lot. They had my favourite bread pudding served with vanilla sauce. I think I could have easily been persuaded to have it for breakfast, lunch, and dinner. We swam and enjoyed the spas and sauna. The night shows were of a high standard, as was the music on board, allowing us to do some dancing.

We then docked in Hong Kong. This was the end of a wonderful, enjoyable, and interesting cruise. We had arranged to stay in a hotel and explore Hong Kong for a few days. The harbour with the light shows on the high-rise buildings were impressive. After a ferry ride across from Kowloon to Hong Kong Island, we went on a bus tour around the island. At a market, Debbi saw some leather handbags with brand names going cheaply, so she bought several. Of course, they were fakes and fell apart when she tried to use them, much to her disgust.

A ferry ride took us to Macau. There we toured the island and some of their famous casinos, before seeing the famous show entitled "The House of Dancing Water" in the City of Dreams. It was very impressive and featured, divers, acrobats, dancers, circus performers, actors, motorcyclists, and over eighty gymnasts on a stage that transformed into different sets. It was a pool that changed to a stage in seconds. We had to use the blankets supplied so we did not get soaked, as we were near the stage.

The ferry was crowded with Chinese from mainland China who went there to gamble. It was also Chinese New Year, so there were many street performances and decorations everywhere. After a wonderful few days in Hong Kong, we flew back home to Adelaide.

Venice, Rome, and Greece, Then On to Barcelona on Holland America's Noordam

Having completed the cruise from Singapore to Hong Kong in early 2014, and having booked a trip to India later that year, we at first refused an invitation to go with Peter and Mary on a cruise of the Mediterranean Sea in June of 2014. They were so disappointed that I felt bad and soon decided to join them, thinking that Debbi was sick and we should do as much as we could and not worry about the future. We flew to Venice after going to London to see Vikki, and Peter and Mary flew to Milan and trained it to Venice.

We arrived first and checked into a hotel called Ca Doge, which was selected by Peter for its central position on Piazzale Roma, not far from the cruise terminal. We did not realise it had only two stars until we arrived. The reception was a poky little room, and our room was in a building across a car park. There was no concierge service, and we had to fetch our cases above our heads, as the cars were so poorly parked with only inches between them. On the steps of the building was a drunk finishing off the remains in his wine bottle as he stared at us. There were no lifts of course, so we carried our cases up the stairs. The room itself was comfortable and clean.

After getting settled, we checked with reception to see whether Peter and Mary had arrived. They had, so we went to surprise them. Mary opened the door with a dazed look on her face, and Peter was in the shower shouting, "Mary, there is no hot water. Can you tell reception?" The room was small and dark. We decided it was not a good time to visit so left them to it.

We thought that the hotel was one star if that! We renamed it "Ca Dodge." We felt better about it after a few drinks in our room—thank heavens for a stocked bar fridge. After a leisurely stroll, we found a rather beautiful restaurant with an open-air dining area, where we enjoyed a sumptuous meal accompanied by a bottle of Chianti. The owner was particularly friendly and allowed us to choose some dessert compliments of the house.

The next morning, we took a water taxi from across the road to St. Mark's Square. The trip was beautiful, and it was a pleasant sight to see Mary and Debbi semi-reclining at the back of the boat with hats, bright shirts, and dark glasses on. They looked like the ultimate tourists.

There were lots of pigeons on the square, and we loved the fantastic old buildings. An orchestra was playing classical music in an upmarket alfresco-style coffee shop. We decided we just could not miss the experience, as there was no charge. Well, so we thought—until we received the bill for our coffee and cakes!

We then walked along the narrow streets checking out the shops. One was selling caps, and we could get names embroidered on them if needed. We found a yellow one and had Max's (our grandson) name embroidered on it. Lunch was at a cute little restaurant, after which we walked back to our hotel and checked out the stalls on the square. There was a political demonstration going on at the time.

The next morning, we made our way to the dock via monorail and boarded the ship. The cruise was two separate cruises back to back. It first went from Venice to Livorno and then on to Civitavecchia before going to Naples and Palermo. We then returned to Rome. The second cruise went to Greece, Turkey, Tunisia, France, and Monaco before ending in Barcelona.

In Turkey: Debbi, Peter, Ram, and Mary

Having been in the area before, Debbi and I did not go back to Florence, the Leaning Tower of Pisa, Rome, or Pompeii but checked out the areas near the ports. However, we did go on a local tour bus through the streets of Naples. Walking along one of those streets, we came across a coffee shop advertising Leghorn Punch, an espresso coffee liqueur drink. We decided to try it and ordered four, which we enjoyed sitting on chairs and tables on the pavement in front of the shop. They were so good that we had another three each, much to the surprise of the bartender, who had told us they were very strong.

Visiting Olympia in Greece where the Olympic games started was interesting. The running track was just dirt, and the spectators sat on raised mounds along the track. It was mainly athletics, and the runners ran naked. Maybe they felt they could run faster naked without wind resistance against their clothes. I hear bike riders now shave their bodies so they can go faster. I don't quite get the logic, as they are not naked.

The modern Olympic stadium in Greece is now in Athens and is an impressive set-up. The changing of the guard at Parliament House in

Athens was interesting to watch, with their funny stepping. The Acropolis was certainly worth a visit.

We visited Rhodes, Mykonos, and Santorini. We were there in the day, but I think we needed to be there in the evening to appreciate the Greek food in the tavernas on the beaches at sunset, with Greek music in the background. We nevertheless enjoyed a seafood lunch at one of the restaurants on the seafront in Mykonos. The skill of the waiter who shelled our crayfish was impressive.

Santorini, with its white and blue theme, was pretty. We did not do the donkey ride up the hill but walked up instead. We walked around the winding streets checking out the shops, and I persuaded Debbi to buy an outfit she absolutely loved and has worn on many occasions afterwards. We had lunch in a beautiful restaurant overlooking the sea.

Tunis in Tunisia was the next stop. We were impressed by the evidence of Roman presence in Carthage. The drainage and irrigation as well as the water supply systems were very interesting. It was a major trading port. Debbi was not comfortable bartering and was given a hard time by Peter after she paid three times as much as she needed to pay for an outfit. She was happy with her buy.

We walked along the beach and in the buildings. Two weeks later, this was the site of a terrible massacre when gunmen opened fire on tourist buses like the ones we were in. That was freaky.

The town of Calvi on the island of Corsica was interesting. It is under French rule. It had cobbled streets, and the medieval citadel and cathedral on the clifftop overlooking the marina offered a picturesque sight.

We were supposed to go to Marseille, but there was a political demonstration there, so our captain decided to go to Toulon instead. The problem we had was that Bob and Vikki had travelled from London to Marseille to meet us for the day. We had to inform them of our change of plans. Fortunately, they could train it to Toulon, a journey that took two hours. We waited in a beautiful square in the middle of Toulon and had a couple of glasses of wine in a rather decadent way. We met them at the train station and had a long lunch at a restaurant in the same square. It was great to see them and to catch up with all the gossip.

In our half-inebriated state, we proceeded to walk to the waterfront, where we planned to have dinner before going back on board. On our way, a roving steel band was playing rather happy music. Debbi followed them, dancing all the way, and I captured it on video, unknown to her. It was good to see her enjoying herself despite her illness.

Our next stop was Monaco. It was good to visit a second time, and Debbi and I explored more of the city this time. We learned that it was better to book into a hotel in nearby France, which was much cheaper than Monaco. People in Monaco went over the border to shop for the same reason. It was a beautiful, clean city.

We visited the Palace of Monaco, home of the prince. The Grimaldi family had occupied this palace and ruled Monaco for over seven hundred years. We saw the Formula One street circuit of Monte Carlo and the casino.

Our cruise finished in Barcelona. There, we acted as tourist guides to Peter and Mary, as we had been there many times before. From Barcelona, Debbi and I flew to Dubai to connect to our flight home.

South Pacific on Royal Caribbean's Explorer of the Seas

Even though we had been on cruises to the Pacific Islands before, Debbi and I decided to go on one more, which took us from Sydney to Noumea, Vila, and Mystery Island. Debbi was not very well, so we did not do a lot of sightseeing. In fact, I alone went ashore for a couple of hours on Mystery Island. I couldn't leave her for long, as she became disorientated easily.

One lunchtime, I asked her to wait in the dining room after lunch while I took some water to our cabin. Because I took a little longer than expected, as I had to go to the loo, she thought I was not coming back. She left to go to our cabin.

When I returned to the dining room and could not find her, I became worried. I searched the shops, our room, and the lounges, and finally saw her coming out of one of the lifts looking confused. I rushed down the stairs and met her. We returned to Sydney having had an enjoyable ten days together.

Brisbane to Cairns via the Barrier Reef Islands on a P&O's ship

Debbi was ill and still needing chemotherapy. During one of her breaks from treatment, I decided to give her a bit of a holiday. We went on a cruise from Brisbane to Cairns and back via the Barrier Reef islands. It was our last cruise together, only months before she passed away. It was wonderful to share this time with her and was indeed very special.

Future Travel

It is my wish and hope that I will be able to continue travelling in the future, as there are many more places I would like to visit and experience.

CHAPTER 17

DEBRA JOY BHOLA—THE WIND BENEATH MY WINGS

I have already covered my life with Debbi in previous chapters, so in this section I wanted to say something about Debbi the person. We were together for thirty-eight years, and as time went on, our relationship grew stronger. The horoscopes suggested we were not a good match because of our star signs. I am an Aries, and she was a Libran. We proved them wrong. The very fact that we were so different in many respects seemed to be an attraction, giving credence to the theory that "opposites attract and likes repel." We appreciated that these differences produced a certain richness in the relationship. We learnt a lot from each other, as we had open minds and appreciated our individual strengths.

Debbi was always kind and considerate. She even had a philosophical trait. I remember her saying to me, as she left for Tasmania to reconcile her first marriage, "If you love something, set it free. If it returns, it is yours; if it doesn't, it never was." She put her own ambitions on hold to support my career and our children. She never tried to tell me what to do and respected my decisions, even if she had reservations at times. She was truly "the wind beneath my wings." I could not have achieved what I did without her support.

In high school, she wanted to become an architect, but her father told her it was a man's field and that it would be better for her to do a secretarial course, which she did. Her interest in buildings stayed with her throughout her life, however, and during our travels, she was always keen to visit buildings of architectural significance. I am positive she would have been a good architect.

She wanted to be a naturopath and later a writer. She planned to write for travel magazines and holiday brochures. She could easily have done this, considering the extensive travelling we have done and her ability to assess accommodations and services. She loved writing poetry and sent me many poems while she was in Tasmania, before she came to Port Augusta.

She was an excellent state-level-two netball coach and wanted to apply to coach the Adelaide men's team, and later the Jamaican netball team, as she saw their potential. This did not fit in with our lifestyle and my commitment to my practice, so she never applied. It would have involved a lot of travel interstate and internationally, which did not please me. I was not in support of the idea, as I felt it would destroy our marriage.

She had a thirst for knowledge and was always reading and researching. Her capacity to self-learn was demonstrated convincingly when she completed her degree in tourism and event management as an external student at the University of South Australia. She had to study and still be a mother and wife. We were not very helpful to her. It was not easy, and she wanted to quit several times, but we encouraged her to persevere once she was over halfway. I know I could not have done what she did.

She was such a good student that the university invited her to do a law degree. We were all very proud of her. Unfortunately, before she could utilise this qualification in the workforce, she became ill. She saw some suitable vacancies and was about to apply, but because of her illness and the need to start treatment, she never did. She regrettably passed away after five years of chemotherapy and radiotherapy.

Her culinary skills were impressive. She learnt to cook at an early stage from her mother, aunt, and the chefs in her parents' hotels. She told me that as a child, she could cook for twenty to thirty guests when her mother was unwell. Her repertoire was wide, and she was not afraid to tackle any dish. She made food from different nationalities, such as Indian, Chinese, Thai, Italian, French, Greek, English, and Moroccan. This ability made her an excellent hostess, and all our friends and family looked forward to being invited for dinner.

She seldom used a cookbook, and it was interesting to watch her in action, putting in a dash of this and a pinch of that, not measuring anything. I gained a lot of my cooking skills by watching her and later getting her to supervise my cooking.

She impressed my sisters by making up a curry mix of different spices from scratch. This gave her curries a better taste than theirs. On one occasion, early on in our relationship, she freaked me out by deciding to cook curries for the parents of my Indian partner, who had come for a holiday from India. It turned out well, and they could not believe that she followed instructions from a cookbook. I was a very lucky man, and my stomach certainly appreciated it.

Debbi was a generous friend and saw the good in everyone. She was supportive and always willing to offer advice, suggestions, and help to anyone who asked. She was a counsellor when the occasion demanded it, or she was just be happy to be a listener. Her wide knowledge and skills encouraged friends to seek her counsel.

I have not always listened to her opinion, and I've paid the price for it, especially in business matters. I was always too strong-willed and impetuous, backing my own judgements whether they were right or wrong. Even so-called friends who did the wrong thing by her were generously forgiven in time. She was counsellor and adviser to her children, siblings, and me. This is something we all miss very much now that she is no longer with us. I wish to sincerely thank her for her generous support of me in my work and life in general.

A better mother and wife you could not find. She made personal sacrifices for us all the time. She was always there for us. To allow me to meet the commitments of my busy job and lifestyle, she was mother and father to the kids and attended to all our needs. She ran the house and most of our business interests. She even had a large part to play in setting up the surgeries, building our house in Port Augusta, and renovating other homes and investment properties.

She ran a health food shop, a music store, and a laundromat. Her interest in naturopathy taught her a lot about vitamins, healthy eating, and alternative medicine. The surgery social functions were a success largely due to her organisation. In addition, she made all the arrangements for the many holiday trips we had. I would not buy any item of clothing without her input, as she knew more about the materials used in making them. She also had very good fashion sense.

The ability to visualise things gave her a sense of good taste. This was why she was good at interior décor. She organised the internal fittings and colour schemes of the surgeries and our houses. The draughtsman in Port Augusta was so impressed that he got her to do the same for the golf clubhouse in Port Augusta. He wanted her to work in partnership with him on other projects, but she was not interested.

Like her sister, she could feel the presence of other life forces. She could read palms and Tarot cards, which freaked her out so much at times that she did not like doing it. She could feel oncoming rain and predicted things before they occurred, even movements in the financial markets.

We bought a miner's couch for our hallway in our Dulwich house from an antique store. Every time our dog went past the couch, she would bark at it. No one was sitting on the couch. We decided it had a ghost, so Debbi did some research and tried various ways to get rid of the ghost without success. Her sister suggested that the ghost was feeling threatened and that she should have a conversation with her (assuming it was female). This she did, reassuring the ghost that we would not harm her and that we were happy to share the couch with her. To my surprise, the dog stopped barking at the vacant couch!

When I decided to stop paying her life insurance due to escalating premiums, expecting her to live to be over ninety like her mother, aunt, and grandmother, she said, "Don't be so sure. You are forgetting there is another side to my family, and they all died in their sixties and seventies." She was referring to her father's side, where cancer was prevalent.

I then asked her how long she would live. After pondering for a moment, she said, "Sixty-four." This was before she became ill; she was fine at the time. I did not take her seriously and asked how long I would live. She thought for a moment and then said eighty-four. That freaked me out. She passed away at nearly sixty-three!

Nothing fazed her. She was willing to tackle anything, from IT challenges to painting the house, and to do hard work in the gardens. Once she stacked two tons of firewood in our house at Dulwich, having to fetch them by wheelbarrow from the front drive to the backyard. The next day, she had one ton of mulch delivered, which she spread all over the garden beds after removing a heap of cannas by fork, which she did not want, as they were taking over the whole garden bed.

To try to keep up with IT, she did a course at WEA adult learning. She did another course there in Spanish for travel and pleasure, which I also did at the same time. She was much more IT savvy than I was and helped me a lot in this regard.

She entertained our grandson Ollie with children's programmes on YouTube. When he was about three and a half years old, I was looking after him while Debbi went to town. He wanted to watch Fireman Sam on the computer. I said I didn't know how to bring it up on YouTube, to which he said, "I'll show you." He proceeded to instruct me to press this button, then that one, and guess what: he successfully found his programme. I felt rather dumb to be given computer lessons by a three-year-old!

Debbi always lived up to her name as a busy bee. The characteristics of a Debbi are described on her keyring below "a learned and knowledgeable person, queenly and majestic, she flows into a room, lighting it up with her presence, slow of temper, yet quick to smile, astute, hard-working, an accomplisher who does it all with a positive attitude, a true friend when it counts, she can always be relied upon in times of need." She lived up to every single one of these qualities.

 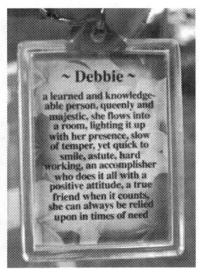

Debbi's keyring

CHAPTER 18

DEBBI'S BATTLE WITH ILLNESS AND MY RETIREMENT

For some time, Debbi complained intermittently about pain in her right lower abdomen. Nothing was obvious on examination, and the pain always settled in a few hours. She'd had multiple abdominal operations in the past, such as cholecystectomy, appendicectomy, hysterectomy, and oophorectomy, plus prolapse repair. We hence thought she had adhesions that were causing the pain. Abdominal X-rays and ultrasounds were negative, as were blood tests, except for a slight iron deficiency.

I discussed her pain with my daughter Nalini, who is a radiologist, and she advised a CT scan of her abdomen. This showed the possibility of a thickening in the wall of her caecum, and the radiologist advised a colonoscopy to check it out. We were about to embark on a six-week trip to America and Canada, and a cruise in the Caribbean with my brother and sister-in-law. After discussing it, we decided that we would pursue this investigation on our return. Debbi had no problems during the trip and felt well. We had a wonderful holiday. However, one evening during the cruise, she had some pain and couldn't join us for dinner. After a few hours, the pain had settled.

In June of 2013, on our return home, we were due to move into our new house within a week. She had further pain and, on the advice of Nalini, we had the CT scan repeated. The radiologist rang me very concerned about what he was seeing. He consulted with Nalini, who burst out in tears. They were looking at a large caecal tumour.

I got Debbi in to see a gastroenterological surgeon immediately, and he admitted her for an urgent colonoscopy and biopsy. It turned out to be a very aggressive adenocarcinoma of the bowel. She had an immediate laparoscopic right hemi-colectomy at Calvary Hospital in North Adelaide. The histology showed complete resection of the tumour, but eight of the ten lymph nodes removed were involved in tumour spread. This was a worry, as we could not be sure if the tumour had spread elsewhere.

She was referred to an oncologist, who decided she needed to commence six months of chemotherapy to mop up any stray tumour cells. She had a port put in the right side of her upper chest in the subclavian vein for easy administration of the drugs. The port became infected and required intravenous antibiotics in hospital. This caused some delay in commencing her chemotherapy.

She eventually started and received treatment every two weeks. It was a combination of several cytotoxic drugs, one of which had to be continued over forty-eight hours at home. She was given many tablets to combat the many side effects of these drugs. The doctors and staff at Calvary were marvellous and treated patients with respect and compassion. I accompanied her to every consultation and stayed with her most of the time during treatment, which went on for three to four hours. She had a blood test before each treatment could be commenced to make sure her blood count was high enough to allow treatment safely. She had some thinning of her hair and lots of bowel symptom due to the drugs.

She was relieved when the six-month course of treatment was finished and happy to say goodbye to the nursing staff. One nurse said, "See you when you return."

Debbi said, "I am not coming back."

The nurse replied, "You will come back. They all do."

That's not what Debbi wanted to hear!

This was in January of 2014. We went on a cruise from Singapore to Malaysia, Thailand, Cambodia, Vietnam, and Hong Kong to celebrate, and she had a wonderful time. We also booked a trip to India in October of that year, thinking we should get on and do the things we wanted to do while we could. Mary and Peter convinced us to join them on the cruise in the Mediterranean in the summer, which was great. At that time, Debbi felt well.

In October, a few days before we were due to fly out to India, Debbi showed signs of memory loss and was a bit unsteady. After discussing her symptoms with her GP, I organised an urgent MRI brain scan at Memorial Hospital. The radiologist called me into the viewing room to show me the large secondary brain tumour in the right side of her brain. There was much swelling around it.

I did not know how to relay this to her and our son Ramil, who came with us. I took them to a nearby restaurant and, during the meal, told them the bad news. Debbi did not seem too upset and merely asked, "What does that mean?" I said I would consult her oncologist immediately.

She was admitted to Calvary the next morning for dexamethasone treatment to shrink the swelling around the tumour. The oncologist visited her that night and seemed worried that he had missed this lesion by not scanning her head routinely. I asked why that was, and he explained that only 1 percent of secondaries from a bowel cancer went to the brain. Debbi happened to be in that 1 percent. Earlier detection would have made the operation a little easier.

Two days later, she saw the neurosurgeon, who said we had no choice but to accept surgery. He explained that it was a large tumour and that the operation would be difficult and risky. Without the operation, however, she would have passed away in a matter of days from the pressure build-up.

While she was being wheeled into theatre, I could see the fear in her eyes as she said to me, "I love you." She was so brave! I was beside myself with worry and started to imagine the worse. Would she come out alive? Would she recognise me afterwards? Would she be left with any residual disabilities? These were the thoughts that occupied my mind as I watched the theatre door close behind the barouche carrying her into the theatre at Memorial Hospital. I had such a heavy heart, and I knew I would not hear anything for several hours. As a diversion, I went shopping for garden supplies and equipment at Bunnings in Mile End.

That evening, Ahsha and I visited Debbi in the high-dependency unit. She was awake and recognised us but was distressed, as she wanted to go to the bathroom to do a wee, and the nurses would not let her off the bed. They wanted her to use a bedpan. When they were not paying attention, she tried to get off the bed—and fell onto the floor, disconnecting the drip. They were horrified and got her back on the bed.

I had to intervene and explain to her why she needed to use the bedpan. She listened to me and calmed down. She then used the pan successfully.

The neurosurgeon arrived soon after and was not happy to hear what had happened. He explained to me that he normally liked to remove these tumours as a complete whole, but he couldn't in this case, as it was too large. He had to remove it piecemeal, and that meant he could not guarantee that he got it all. This was a worry, and for several months she had repeat MRI scans to check for local recurrence.

I visited her several times a day. She slowly improved and was eventually discharged. After a few weeks, she commenced two weeks of radiotherapy to her brain as a precaution, in case there was some residual tumour locally. She was surprised that she felt nothing during treatment.

Two weeks later, her hair started to fall out in clumps until she lost the lot. We had to buy her some wigs. She was also given some beanies from Calvary. She eventually made good progress and attended her sister's wedding in Launceston, Tasmania, in February of 2015.

She was kept under regular review by the oncologist. Later that year, a CT scan showed some evidence of a deposit in one of her thoracic vertebrae which responded to more radiotherapy. It did cause her some pain.

Unfortunately, a few deposits appeared in her lungs, and she required more courses of chemotherapy. It was amazing that she had no secondaries in the liver, where most spread from bowel tumours end up. I think that was a blessing and allowed us to have her for a few more years. Luckily, she still had the port, which was kept patent by flushing it every two weeks. The oncologist changed her drug regimens several times, as was the normal custom. Apparently, those drugs are not as effective when used a second time and can have more side effects.

New drugs meant new side effects. One caused her to have very dry skin, and I had to moisturise her skin heavily after her showers. She also needed eye drops to prevent dry eyes. The lung lesions were kept under control with the drugs, and she felt well enough for us to go on another couple of trips, which was great.

She was getting weaker and weaker, and less able to do everything. By this time, I had taken over all the household chores and business commitments. It was obvious that I needed to be home to look after her. I happily gave up work and decided to retire fully to be with her and to look after her. It was a pleasure being able to do this for her.

I did all the shopping, cooking, washing, ironing, cleaning, and gardening. She felt very bad about me having to do everything and was always offering to do things, even though she could not. She even told me not to iron her clothes, as it did not matter what she looked like, to which I replied, "I can't have you looking like a hobo, so I will iron your clothes."

Sometimes I cooked a nice meal, but she was having cravings and preferred prawn dumplings from the Chinese restaurant or original chicken tenders and chips from KFC. I was only too happy to indulge her cravings.

Debbi remained brave and philosophical throughout her ordeal. She never complained and took everything in stride, accepting her fate. She even managed a smile regularly. She kept saying, "I must be here long enough for my grandchildren to remember me and to see my son Ramil get married." This determination kept her going and gave her something to look forward to. She loved having the family around for dinner and enjoyed the grandkids. Ramil's wedding date was fixed for December 22, 2018.

True to form, she had some advice and requests for me. She said, "When I am gone, don't be lonely. Find someone for companionship and to play with, but you don't have to marry her. In addition, I want you to take care of the children and grandchildren." I promised that I would do that. Her other piece of advice was not to go back to work. She said, "You don't need to. You have had a good run, and nobody has ever complained about you. Keep it that way."

In February of 2018, she was having difficulty walking and was veering to one side. I thought she was weak and tried a walking stick and a walking frame, but she had difficulty using these. I hired a wheelchair, as she was losing the use of her legs.

An MRI scan showed that she had a second brain lesion in her brainstem. This was, as we say in medical circles, in "tiger country." That meant the operation was fraught with danger. The neurosurgeon explained that an operation might end up in death on the operating table or could leave her a paraplegic or quadriplegic. She might not be able to breathe by herself and might need ventilation through a tracheostomy. She could end up having to be fed through a gastrostomy tube and might not be able to speak.

The odds were too high. Debbi at first said he had to operate, as she must be here at Christmas for the wedding. But I eventually dissuaded her from having the operation, as I could not bear the thought of her suffering any more or living like a vegetable with no quality of life. That would have broken my heart.

It was obvious that she was not going to survive too much longer. By this time, I was having to transport her around the house by wheelchair, shower her on a shower chair, and have the shower door removed to allow easier access. I even had a detachable shower head and grab rails installed. She was unable to bear weight. She wanted to stay home for as long as she possibly could, and I was very happy to look after her. The oncologist said he could make a bed available to her in the hospice whenever we needed it.

Ahsha and I decided to persuade Ramil, Olivia, and her parents to bring forward the wedding date so Debbi could be present. Her sister Vikki came from London, and my daughter Nalini came from Albury. The wedding took place in the church and with the priest they had selected. Only immediate family was allowed, as Ramil and Olivia wanted to keep it a secret, and to have a renewal of vows and the reception in December as planned. It was a beautiful wedding, and Debbi was present. We had a small reception at our house afterwards. Debbi was pleased and kept asking Vikki if Ramil would be okay now. She was reassured and was happy to stay up chatting to everyone.

The next day she was okay, but on the following day, she did not want to wake up. It became obvious that I could no longer manage her at home, so I rang the oncologist and a bed was arranged in the Mary Potter hospice. It was as though her job on earth was done, and she had decided it was time to go. The two grandsons, Oliver and Max, were brought from school to say goodbye to her at home, before she was transported by ambulance to the hospice.

Ramil and I accompanied her in the ambulance. She never said another word but opened her eyes once and looked at Ramil, who was beside her. At the hospice, she was made comfortable, and I was allowed to stay with her. She was given excellent care by the doctors and nursing staff. I too was looked after very well and provided with meals and a bed. She was heavily sedated.

We summoned her mother and brother from Tasmania. The Catholic priest who married Ramil and Olivia, and twice gave Debbi Holy Communion at home, did her Last Rights. Her mother and brother eventually arrived, but we were not sure if Debbi realised it. She stirred on hearing their voices and tried to say something when Ahsha and I were talking. I understand the last sense that goes is hearing, so she may have heard what we were saying.

The family went home, and a couple of hours later, she was breathing intermittently, so I called them back. I did say to her not to struggle but to go in peace and save a spot for me. I also promised her that I would look after the family. Two minutes later, she took her last breath. It was the evening of May 10, 2018. The family arrived after that.

The funeral took place at Berry Funeral Parlour in Adelaide on May 16. All our friends and relatives were present. Ahsha arranged the slide show and bravely did the eulogy. I had a speech read out for me, and Nalini did a reading from *The Prophet* by Khalil Jibran. Ramil chose a song called "Songbird" by Fleetwood Mac, which expressed his sentiments and message to Debbi. The same priest officiated and did a wonderful job. We were very happy that it was such a beautiful funeral service.

Her memorial card quoted a special message by Ralph Waldo Emerson, that she had framed and placed in her study. It read as follows:

Success

To laugh often and much

To win the respect of intelligent people

And the affection of children

To earn the appreciation of honest critics and endure the betrayal of false friends

To appreciate beauty

To find the best in others

To leave the world a bit better, whether by a healthy child, a garden patch, or a redeemed social condition

To know even one life has breathed easier because you have lived.

This is to have succeeded!

I believe Debbi succeeded.

At home in front of family and friends that evening, we were all blown away by the four grandchildren who, of their own volition, each gave a wonderful speech in Debbi's honour. It was very moving considering that, at their tender ages, they compiled the speeches to complement each other and delivered them so bravely. It started with Ollie's idea. He wanted to say something at the funeral service, which was so brave of him.

Debbi was later cremated, and on October 10, 2018, her ashes were scattered in the ocean at Coolangatta, in accordance with her wishes, for that was a special place where we spent many happy days. As a tribute to Debbi, I made a promise to give regular donations and support to the Mary Potter Foundation, in recognition of the wonderful work they do. To keep her memory alive, there is a gold leaf on display on the Tree of Life in the foyer of the Mary Potter Hospice. The inscription says, "In loving memory of Debra Joy Bhola, forever in the hearts and memories of your family and friends." And so she remains.

Debbi's Memorial Plaque at Mary Potter Hospice

The Tree of Life at Mary Potter Hospice in North Adelaide

CHAPTER 19

REFLECTIONS ON A RICH TAPESTRY OF LIFE AND MY LEGACY

On reflection, because of the different influences on me, the various paths I have followed, and the different countries I have lived in, my life has been a rich tapestry. Coming from a large family and spending my childhood in a small village in a virtual Third World country was character-building, giving me a sound foundation and an appreciation that nothing should be taken for granted. It also taught me values that have influenced my dealings with others.

This rich tapestry of life can be demonstrated by separating the different roles I have had in life.

My Family Roles

Ram the Son

I was not a difficult child and gave my parents no headaches or cause for concern. I always felt loved by them. They were extremely proud of me. I was always willing to help them.

Ram the Sibling

I was number eight in a family of nine and have been fortunate to have had a wonderful relationship throughout life with every one of my siblings. We may have lived on different continents for most of our lives, but the love between us has always been evident when we correspond or meet face to face. This closeness was the result of living together in the family home during childhood and being able to visit those who moved away after marriage.

Gem, Seerojnee, Rita, Ram, Betty, Jack, and Seeta at a family wedding (deceased: Dooreen and Jackula)

The excitement of my siblings whenever they heard I was planning a visit was always tangible. The special effort they all made during my visits to entertain me and my family was also evident and appreciated. This was also true of their children. I always returned home after my visits a lot heavier, as they would cook my favourite Guyanese dishes.

Unfortunately, I have already lost three sisters and one brother. My surviving siblings are Jack in Orlando, Betty and Seerojnee in Toronto, and Seeta in Adelaide.

Ram the Husband

Most men only ever look after one wife. I, however, have had two marriages and hence two wives—not at the same time, of course. The first marriage to Moira was from 1969 to 1978. It was during our student days and early professional lives. We got on very well and had a happy marriage. We still do not know why we separated. I like to think it was immaturity.

Debbi and I were married from 1982 until she passed away in 2018. We had a wonderful life together and were deeply in love with each other. A better wife and friend I could not have hoped for. She was entirely supportive of everything I did and supported my ambitions totally. I am told by her sister and mother that she loved me very much and was proud of all my achievements. She was an ideal country doctor's wife and certainly the best thing that ever happened to me. We were soul mates.

Ram the Parent

I am fortunate to have three wonderful children. Maybe I have not spent as much time with them due to my long work hours. Their mothers did a wonderful job looking after them. I always tried to spend as much time with them as I could, and we have had some wonderful times in the swimming pools and picnicking in the national parks around Port Augusta with friends. I made sure I took eight weeks of holiday each year, and we always went away as a family to some wonderful locations locally, interstate, and overseas.

Ram, David, Nalini, and Debbi

Christopher, Oliver, Ahsha, and Max

Ramil and Olivia

Ram the Grandparent

I am very proud of my four grandchildren. Nalini and Dave have Abigael and Morrison, and Ahsha and Chris have Oliver and Max. It is very interesting and pleasing to note that there has been an equal distribution of genes responsible for their outward appearance, in that Abigael looks like Nalini, Morrison like Dave, Oliver like Ahsha, and Max like Chris. Their inward characteristics and personalities are a mixture and harder to attribute to any one parent.

It has given us enormous pleasure to watch them growing up to be such beautiful children with interesting personalities and enormous abilities in all aspects of life, especially in education and sports. I wish them much happiness and success in their future lives.

Abigael and Morrison

Max and Oliver

My Other Roles

Ram the Student

Because of the encouragement given to me by my father and the ambition he had for me, I always took my studies seriously. I was so driven that I felt nothing would stop me from achieving my goal to be a doctor. It made me very competitive, and being anything other than top of the class was never an option.

This competitive spirit flowed on to other aspects of my life. I studied late into the night and had little sleep most nights. I knew it was difficult getting into medical school, so I worked hard to get the necessary grades to be accepted. I breathed a heavy sigh of relief once I got there and was a little kinder to myself from then on.

Ram the Sportsman

I was a bookworm, but not to the exclusion of sports or exercise. Apart from doing chores around home, I played cricket with friends in the village and at primary school. I also made it into my house team at high school and the medical school team. I even represented the university on one occasion when we played against Leeds University.

Once, I was encouraged by a friend to fill in for the medical school hockey team, even though I had never played hockey before. He assured me it would be a piece of cake for a cricketer like me and quickly explained the rules to me just before the game. Within the first few minutes, an opposition player whacked me on the left elbow with a hockey stick. I was not impressed. It was painful, and I ended up with a huge swelling on my left elbow, which I still have. I threw my club down and walked away there and then, muttering, "If this is what hockey is all about, I don't want any part of it." I have never held a hockey stick since.

When I was about six years old, my brother gave me a cheap beach ball. I was the only one of my peers with a ball, so I had lots of friends. We played soccer on the school cricket ground. I was so competitive that I did not allow them to get the ball from me and scored all the goals. They lost interest, and I lost my soccer mates. It was a serious message in learning to share.

Ready for bodyboarding in Surfers Paradise

I played a little tennis and did a lot of recreational swimming over the years. I discovered bodyboarding later in Australia and loved it so much that we even bodyboarded in Hawaii. I discovered squash in Port Augusta and absolutely loved it. Because of my work commitments, I did not play competitively but only socially. Debbi thought if I had discovered it earlier, I could have been a world-class player. As far as golf went, I only played socially with Ramil.

Ram the Friend

I have always been a loyal friend to those I consider good friends. I have, like most people, lots of acquaintances but only a handful of good friends. Good friendships take a long time to cultivate and need to be nurtured to keep them alive, not unlike marriages.

People have always remarked that I have an unusual collection of friends from all walks of life. This is because I take everyone as I find them and am more interested in their personalities and qualities than their colour, background, or profession. Amongst my friends are doctors, nurses, train drivers and stewards, fitter and turners, a Catholic priest, an industrial radiographer, an age-care worker, a real estate agent, secretaries, teachers, cleaners, a school support officer, a national parks and wildlife worker, and office workers. I do enjoy this cross-section of friendships, with each one having something different to offer.

Ram the Dancer

As a child, I only danced Indian-style. At university, I attended parties and learned to copy and dance disco-style. My Sierra Leonean friend Llewelyn taught me to dance to soul music, and my sister-in-law Mary Rose got me into reggae dancing. I learned ballroom dancing in London.

Now I love dancing and seem to be able to combine the lot to create moves that are unique to me. I feel the music and do whatever it tells me to do. This makes it difficult for partners to follow. I at times feel I could have been a professional dancer.

Ram the Doctor

I took my profession seriously and did it to the best of my ability. Debbi used to say she came a poor third on the podium, as medicine was my number one interest and my children number two. I don't quite agree but would admit that my patients' welfare was always paramount. I have often left Debbi at a party or restaurant to go and attend to a patient. I kept up my post graduate education to be the best GP I could possibly be.

Ram the Trainer

I set up my practice to be a teaching practice and had a regular flow of medical students and trainee doctors from Adelaide and overseas. I also recruited many overseas-trained doctors to work in my practice and orientated many of them to work in other country practices. I not only taught them what was expected of them as doctors by the Australian public but instructed them about life in Australia, and I included information on taxation issues, housing, investments etc. Consequently, many of them did better than I did, as I did not have the privilege of such support and advice on my arrival in Australia.

Ram the Businessman

As time went on, I acquired an interest in business and investments. It started when I found myself paying too much tax and sought advice on ways of minimising that. I learnt about negative gearing and started investing in real estate. That involved dealing with banks to arrange loans and mortgages. Later I found out about the share market and dabbled in that.

I became more ambitious, as I was working hard and had a good cash flow. I started taking more risks and made mistakes, from which I learnt a lot. As the saying goes, there is no such thing as a mistake if you learnt a lesson from it.

This interest became almost an obsession and gave me much pleasure. It was a welcome diversion from medicine. At first it was a hobby, but in time I showed a preference for it over medicine. I ended up owning two shopping centres, two petrol stations, some residential real estate, a pine forest, timeshare units, and two surgeries. I ran the surgeries like small businesses, providing the best possible service, and this was reflected in their success. Debbi commented that I could have done just as well as a businessman as I did as a doctor.

Ram the Business Partner

I have had business partners in the Shell Roadhouses and in the surgeries. I have always done the right thing by my partners and worked hard for their success as well as mine. So honest and upright was the relationship with Dr. Victor that our partnership lasted thirty-four years, until retirement.

Ram the Traveller

I am surprised as I write about our travels that we have visited so many places in Australia and overseas. These trips have already been described elsewhere in this book. I love travelling and fully intend to continue travelling for as long as I can.

Influence of Others

There have been many people who have influenced my life along the way to create in me an interesting mix of Indian, Guyanese (West Indian), English, and Australian. People often are confused to see this Indian-looking man who has an accent that belongs to nowhere and sounds educated and sophisticated. I often create a certain curiosity when I am in a room. I feel grateful to the people who have made me what I am and would like to make specific mention of them.

I have inherited many qualities from my father, including his looks. Like him, I tend to set impossible goals and agendas, and I'm never afraid to take risks. I was ambitious and backed myself totally. Hard work never fazed me, and I did things to the best of my ability. I was fair and upright in my dealings with others. Through dedication and organisation, I generally achieved my goals.

The downside to inheriting these qualities is that my work and goals took priority over family life. I did not spend enough time enjoying my family, and it is the one thing I would change if I could. Having said that, I thoroughly enjoyed the time spent with the family, and we have had some wonderful family holidays at home and abroad.

My brother-in-law Ivan, with whom I lived for five years, was a quiet, peaceful, religious man and a hard-working teetotal vegetarian who had an interest in politics and comparative religion. He read many books and would engage in discussions late at night with his customers and myself. I learnt a lot from him.

In London, Paul and Edna had a huge role to play in westernising me. They taught me many social and life skills. It was Edna who taught me how to look after myself and what code of behaviour was acceptable in English society. She showed me how to use the London Underground and surface trains. My appreciation of food that was different from what I was used to came from her. Paul was a very peaceful, likeable gentleman. He taught me to use a knife and fork. He also was a perfect example of how to respect and treat women. Together they encouraged me to take ballroom dancing lessons.

My first wife, Moira, and her family showed me what life was like for the upper-middle classes in Guyana. They further developed my social skills and gave me my first cocktail drinks. Moira taught me to dance and enjoy a party.

My friend Llewelyn was a lovely intelligent African from Sierra Leone. He widened my appreciation of music and showed me how to dance to soul and reggae music. He also improved my table-tennis skills.

The person who had the greatest influence on me was Debbi. Her broad interests, knowledge, and life experiences made her an excellent teacher. My fashion sense came from her, and I always valued her opinion when buying clothes. Her insatiable appetite for new information made her read many books and magazines. Later, she used the internet freely to get more information. She fostered my wide appreciation of food from different nationalities and was a great cook herself. She knew how to throw a party and be a fantastic hostess. I found myself seeking her opinion on many things constantly. Her common sense and ability to think outside the square made her opinions invaluable.

What Could Have Been

I often ponder on the different stages of my life and think of what could have been. I could have gone along many pathways and ended up a totally different person and in a different place. In a quiet way, I like the limelight and fancied myself on the stage as a singer or dancer, but alas, I don't think I possessed the talent or ability in that respect. I liked law and fancied myself as a courtroom barrister.

I ask myself: what if I did not get into medical school? Maybe I could have made it in the business world. At one point, I nearly gave up medicine to run the rice factory in Guyana. What if I had been accepted into the British army, navy or air force? How different my life would have been! I could have gone to Canada or the United States or remained in England. Maybe I should have continued specialising in obstetrics and gynaecology. I could have stayed married to Moira. Debbi might not have returned from Tasmania. I could have ended up with any of my previous girlfriends.

The possibilities are endless, but the exercise is also pointless. If I had to choose my life again, I would not make any changes. I truly have no regrets and consider myself blessed to have enjoyed the life I have lived so far. Debbi generously believed I would have made a success of whatever life dealt me. I think the same about her.

I made many poor investments decisions, and how different the result might have been without them! However, many useful lessons were learnt.

One thing I would change if I had my time over again was the decision to separate the family in 1996. That was a poor decision, and it resulted in many heartaches for Debbi and me.

My Legacy

The legacy I have left so far are my three wonderful children and four fantastic grandchildren, of whom I am very proud. The memories of wonderful times will live on for a lifetime. The doctors and staff at my surgeries still cherish the wonderful times they have had and the lasting friendships they have created. This is evidenced by our regular catch-ups, even though they may now work elsewhere. My former patients in Port Augusta still relive the good old days when they had a reliable medical service. My one disappointment is that for various reasons, both my surgeries have been ruined and are only a shell of their former selves.

CHAPTER 20

THE PRESENT AND THE FUTURE

Debbi's passing has left a great void in my life. My friends and family have provided wonderful support to help me get through this tough period. I have had counselling and have kept busy sorting everything, including selling the family home. I am now settled in a lovely apartment and finding it a little easier as time goes on.

Of course, the memories and reminders are always around, and I would not want it any other way. I believe it is part of the healing process. Thirty-eight busy years jam-packed with wonderful times are to be celebrated and treasured, not forgotten.

It has taken me some time to pluck up the courage to travel again without Debbi. I visited my relatives in Canada and America in May and June of 2019 and had a wonderful time. Since my return, I have formed a new relationship with a wonderful lady called Yvonne. We have spent a lot of time with each other and have been on several holidays, including one cruise so far. We are enjoying each other's company. She is intelligent, caring, fun-loving, a conscientious worker, and a wonderful friend. Like me she loves travelling, good food, and adventure. We share a love for dancing.

She is interested in me and my background and has accepted my family and friends with open arms. I think I challenge her and take her out of her comfort zone regularly. I get the impression she likes this challenge. I also enjoy getting to know her family and her close friends. I have a positive feeling about this relationship and feel it is the start of a new and wonderful chapter of my life.

Ram and Yvonne

At present, the world is in the grip of the Covid-19 viral pandemic, which apparently started in the Wuhan Province of China and has spread to affect most nations of the world. It has already caused thousands of deaths and has had an enormous adverse social and economic impact everywhere. The full extent of its repercussions is yet to be felt, but I think it is likely to change the way we live and do things forever. The travel industry has been greatly impacted, and all my plans to complete my bucket list are on hold.

In conclusion, I would like to say that if I have been a help to some people and have made a difference to others, then my life would have been worth it.

ABOUT THE AUTHOR

Ramdyal Bhola is a retired medical practitioner who graduated in 1971 from the University of Newcastle upon Tyne, United Kingdom, with a bachelor of medicine and bachelor of surgery (MBBS). In addition to the MBBS degree, he acquired postgraduate qualifications in obstetrics and gynaecology (DObst.RCOG), general practice (MRCGP), and rural and remote medicine (FACRRM). He was born in Guyana, South America, where he attended primary and secondary schools before going to England for college and university education.

He practised medicine for thirty-four years in rural Australia and ten years in the city of Adelaide. He was active in medical politics at a local level and provided medical education for medical students, trainees, and overseas-trained doctors.

Practice management was his passion. This passion, combined with his commitment to patient care and community, culminated in a high-quality practice at Port Augusta Medical Centre. In recognition of this, the practice was used by the Royal Australian College of General Practitioners to help set the Standards for Accreditation of General Practices.

Printed in the United States
by Baker & Taylor Publisher Services